4-25-21 ☺!

To Christine,
Thanks for your friendship & support!
Laural Harris

Secrets of the Hall

An Addie Simmond Mystery

by Laural Harris

CHAPTER 1
1569
Burnley, England

Mary froze, not breathing, listening closely. The sound of horses and soldiers. Marching up the long hill to Towneley Hall. The needle work dropped from her shaking hands into her lap. The day room was bright with sunlight, but it suddenly seemed shadowed. She steadied herself as she arose, thinking only of Father Henry. She must make haste to the chapel. There was not a minute to spare. The chapel was on the second floor of the imposing manor house, beside the courtyard portico. It would most certainly be where the soldiers were heading. Fortunately, she was not in the gardens nor in the kitchen reviewing the day's menu and chores with the staff. Mary sprinted through the long corridor and up the stairs, worn by centuries of footsteps. She ran with all her strength, as though a life were at stake. Because it was.

The dark skirt and petticoat strangled her ankles like vines, frustratingly slowing her down. Her green eyes were narrowed and darkened with worry. As she rounded the corner to the hallway leading to the chapel, her light brown hair was escaping from her day cap, sticking to her neck, wet with sweat.

Thoughts tumbled through her head, pushing each other, yelling over each other. *Listen to me. Me first. This is important. Thank God, thank God, John is not home. Let him not come hastily, early. Father Henry. Let them not take Father Henry. Slow the horses. Give me time. More time. There must be an informant. Who? How could any here do such a thing?* Queen Elizabeth's men were coming through the village of Burnley. Coming to the Hall.

She hiked her skirt and ran faster, soft shoes making slapping sounds on the wooden floors. Reaching the chapel she paused, took a deep breath to relieve the panting, and peered into the dimness for Father Henry. He had lighted no candles or incense, which would surely have given his presence away. The chapel was large, as it had for centuries served the people of the community. It was sparse, as modesty required, but the religious paintings on the walls and altar were lovingly rendered by skilled artists, adding to the reverent atmosphere. Father Henry knelt at the altar, almost invisible in his brown robe. He looked up with a questioning gaze as she entered.

She was dizzy, the competing thoughts now muffled by the sound of her own heartbeat. Her words came in gasps, "Come with me, Father. The Queen's men are only minutes away. You must hide."

Mary led the way quickly through the hallway to the quarters that she and John occupied. The wooden floors were well constructed, and no creak gave them away to any servants who might be nearby. Entering the reading room, Mary turned to Father Henry, "Father, help me move this chest. The priest hole is here."

They struggled to move the heavy chest a few feet. Mary knelt and pushed the end of a board. A small panel sprang back, revealing a room cleverly hidden between the floors. It was tall, though not quite high enough for the lanky priest to stand. It was just large enough for a person to stretch out. Dab, a mixture of clay and rushes, provided soundproofing. An inadvertent cough or gasp would not be heard. Temporary safety, needed since King Henry VIII outlawed Catholic worship.

"You cannot replace the chest alone," Father Henry whispered.

"I am stronger than you may think. Only John and I know of this hiding place, and letting others help might risk your safety. Don't make a sound, even if you think it is I or John. Open the inside latch only if you hear my voice and I use your given name, Henry Crane. They are full of tricks to find priests in hiding. You will be protected here, through God's intervention."

Father Henry lowered himself into the dark, claustrophobic space. He quickly noted a low bench where Mary had placed water and food, and a covered pan beneath it, in the event he had need of such. A small hole had been drilled through the thick rock of the back wall, to provide at least a bit of air and light. It was carefully positioned to be invisible from the outside of the building. Once the panel closed, he would be almost totally in the dark. He made the sign of the cross to Mary, and quietly latched the panel from the inside. Even if somehow the top latch was found, the panel could not be raised. Although the priest hole was cramped, and he might well have to spend an uncomfortable night there, it was a far better alternative to the prison cell, or worse, that awaited him if he were to be found.

It was more difficult than Mary remembered to maneuver the chest back into place, pulling it along by the carpet under it. Precious time was passing. She must not be here when the soldiers arrived. As the lady of the manor, it might raise suspicion if she were upstairs at this time of the day.

Finally, the chest moved into place. No tell-tale scratches were left on the clean wooden floor. She checked the room for anything that seemed out of place. In front of the window, framing a view of the great lawn, two comfortable reading chairs flanked a small table which held candles and two books. An armoire sat beside the chest she had moved back to its original spot over the priest hole. The soldiers would search the armoire and chest, but hopefully not look beneath.

She took several deep breaths, willing the deafening swish-swumk of the heartbeat in her head to clear, before walking down the main stairs to the day room. Picking up the abandoned needlework, she tried to relax. Her face was flushed, and she was trembling slightly, the needle still unsteady in her hand.

The Queen's contingent advanced up the hard-packed lane, horses to the front, foot soldiers following behind. The officers, in an unnecessary show of force, galloped to the portico, raising clouds of dust, which blew into the courtyard. Samuel, the head butler, could hear the huffing of the tired horses and the tinkling of their bridles as he reached the door. The hilt of a sword pounding on the door rudely announced their presence, instead of the usual sound of the coat-of-arms knocker. Opening the door, Samuel was roughly shoved aside by a soldier as two officers entered the foyer.

"I am Captain Farrow, under commission from Her Majesty Queen Elizabeth to search this house and property for a Catholic priest who, we have been informed, is here in violation of Her Majesty's proclamation. Tell Master John Towneley to present himself," the taller of the two demanded, not even glancing at Samuel, as he replaced the sword into its worn leather scabbard.

Samuel bowed to the captain. "Most certainly, sir, this house welcomes those who come in the name of our most beloved Majesty. Please bid your men rest their horses in the stables, and I will have refreshments brought to them. Master John is not at the Hall, but I will inform Mistress Towneley that you are here about the Queen's business."

"Have your grooms tend the horses. My men will wait in the courtyard."

Samuel nodded, turned and walked to the day room with the dignity of one accustomed to receiving and announcing important guests, anger at the rude treatment and haughty attitude of the captain carefully held in check. Samuel had been in service with the Towneley family for more than twenty years. It was an honor to be head butler, and he took the well-being of the family seriously. The staff in the Towneley household were valued, and always treated with respect. He was unused to being treated with such arrogance.

Samuel was well aware of the meaning of the soldiers' visit. Since 1260, the landed gentry at

Towneley Hall had supported the village. The family had avoided taking sides during the chaos of the Wars of the Roses, many years before. The battles raged around them, but never on their property. But now was a dangerous and uncertain time, and fortunes could disappear in an instant, along with the prosperity of the entire area.

John Towneley held a powerful position in this territory, with ties to even more powerful relatives in London, but that would not exempt him from scrutiny. Entering the day room, Samuel bowed to Lady Mary, with a smile to her two brown-haired little boys, playing by the window. Mary suggested that the nanny might take them to the nursery or out on the great lawn.

“M'lady, there is a military contingent from the Queen requesting your presence.”

“Of course, Samuel. Please bring their officers to me and make their men comfortable.” In a whisper she added, “And send quickly a message to John that he should delay homecoming until the morrow eve.”

Samuel was relieved. It was obvious from her calm demeanor that Lady Mary had the situation well in hand. He did not rush to the entry hall, nor in returning, now accompanied by the sound of heavy boot steps.

“M'lady, Captain Farrow.”

Farrow was clearly a seasoned soldier. A small, straight scar accented his left cheek, as though inflicted by a dagger. A larger, jagged scar showed on his right arm as he removed his gloves. His stern demeanor seemed to be an integral part of him.

Even should he smile the deep frown marks between his dark brown eyes would not be erased. He did not smile.

Mary laid her needlework on the table beside her chair, her hand steady and her gaze frank, if not warm. She remained seated, offering her hand to the officers as though they were welcomed guests.

"Thank you, Samuel. Have Jane bring refreshment for us. Gentlemen, please sit and rest from your ride. My husband is away, conducting a count of the sheep in the holds near the Severn. It will yet be several days before his return."

Captain Farrow made a perfunctory bow, bringing Mary's hand to his lips without actually touching it. He and his lieutenant sat, rigidly, on the proferred settee across from her. The light from the windows behind Mary emphasized the harshness of his features.

Captain Farrow's demeanor in Mary's presence walked a fine line between military curtness and respect for Lady Mary. A step too far in either direction could result in unwanted consequences. He met Mary's trivial questions regarding the weather and travel conditions on their ride from Manchester with curt answers. The officers partook of little that Jane and Samuel delivered from the kitchen. A continuous light tapping of his boot revealed his impatience.

"I apologize m'lady, for disturbing your home," he stated after only a few minutes of conversation. "Her Royal Majesty Queen Elizabeth commands that we search for a Catholic priest who, we believe, is even now here. Her Majesty is reluctant to think that her true subjects would be so traitorous. Even so, we must verify that all is as it should be at Towneley Hall. By order of the Queen," he paused, stood, and stared at Mary, "we require that you provide entry to all areas of the house, out buildings and grounds." His voice was deep and had a harshness and rasp that hinted of a cruel nature. She showed no intimidation.

"But of course, Captain Farrow," Mary replied, remaining seated. "Our humble home is, as always, at the service of our Royal Monarch, as it is truly hers to do with as she would. You will most certainly have full access to any part of our home and lands. A servant will go with you to unlock any door, and show you anything you desire. You will find that Towneley Hall has nothing to hide from our most beloved Royal Highness."

"Your hospitality is appreciated," Farrow's cold stare held no indication of appreciation. "We will start immediately. Send word to my men to join me."

Captain Farrow and the lieutenant bowed curtly. Mary nodded to Samuel, who had been standing unobtrusively at the back of the room, to lead them through the adjoining door to the much larger Great Hall. The tall ceiling and white-washed plaster walls created echoes and enhanced sounds within the room. It was an excellent setting for the parties and dinners often held there, always resonating with music and joy. The dusty soldiers who now filled it seemed out of place. Mary could hear the officers assigning groups of soldiers to each area of the main house, as well as the below-ground kitchen, cistern and storage rooms. They were to move furniture, seek out hidden stairwells and doors, even empty wardrobes of their contents.

The soldiers seemed to invade the manor. The sound of their boots echoed throughout the home, grounds and outbuildings. The search was conducted meticulously, with little consideration for those living and working there. The soldiers barked orders to the household staff. They did not bother to return any area to the condition in which they found it. The stables were particularly scrutinized, to the distress of the high-spirited horses, which could be heard whinnying their annoyance. Hours of searching revealed nothing that raised any suspicions.

The setting sun was throwing spears of pink into the sky above the darkening hills as the soldiers completed their tasks. Although this Pendle Hill area could be chilly and damp on even the mildest of evenings, Captain Farrow declined Mary's offer to make the contingent comfortable for the night, rather than camping in the hills. Mary instructed Jane to bring bread, cheese, dried fruit, and ale for the soldiers as they returned to the Great Hall, and prepare supplies for their journey. Best they think kindly of the family.

When the soldiers were fed and ready in the courtyard for their departure, Captain Farrow pulled his gloves on and strode to the door of the Hall. Mary walked with him, but stood at the door rather than descending the steps to the courtyard, as would have been polite. Captain Farrow was forced to look up to Mary as he mounted his horse and issued a warning, "Mistress Towneley, it is true that we found nothing to report to Her Majesty regarding the presence of a Catholic priest. However, it is well known that you have not renounced the most despised Catholic faith. If you continue to defy Her Royal Highness, we will be returning."

As the soldiers marched down the wide and well-worn lane from the Hall, Mary saw a stable hand slip out and unobtrusively merge into the ranks of the soldiers.

"So," she mused, "there is the informant. It is well that he is gone." With barely controlled anger, she turned to Samuel as he stood beside her. "Samuel, ask the head groom if any stable boys earlier here, are now gone."

CHAPTER 2
Fort Worth, Texas

It's hot. Sooo hot. I love these lingering Texas Indian summers. I pop another chocolate-covered cherry into my mouth, savoring the flavor. The cherries swim in a sweet bath of liqueur. Leaning back, I close my eyes and bite down slowly, so that the juice settles sensuously on my tongue.

My hair is pinned carelessly on top of my head. Tendrils escape and cling to my neck, tickling in the light breeze from the ceiling fan. The comfy rocker on the porch squeaks as I push with a bare toe, gazing absently at the lake. It is low, languid, evaporating in the heat.

My name is Addison Simmond. Addie. I love this house by the lake and my neighbors. I have great friends, an interesting job, and a loving family. I've always been content with my age. No identity crisis at thirty or forty. Thought I was immune to that type of uncertainty. Well, now at 50, I find that I'm not. Maybe it's just that divorce has forced me to look a bit harder at myself and my comfortable life.

The stillness is broken by a fish hurling itself out of the water, stalked by an egret. It misses, and with much bravado, quarrels with a heron over the fishing spot. The loser retreats with a harsh squawk and a flurry of white feathers. The oft-repeated battle makes me laugh. The victor, Henry the heron, is a permanent resident. The sturdy gray bird, exceptionally large and distinctive, is always winner of the challenge from the other herons and egrets. "Hi, Henry."

He ignores my greeting, totally unperturbed by my presence. I worry about the white goose, though. Her mate flew off with an ugly Muscovy duck last year. How could he leave such a beautiful, elegant mate all alone to go with that totally unsuitable duck? A duck, for heaven's sake! Her calls every morning and evening make me sad, but also hopeful. I'm not sure if my feelings are about her or myself.

Cicadas buzz in the elm trees, sound rising and falling in rhythm, the constant background of summer. October is a dull-edged month in Texas. There's no clean, sharp edge marking the change from summer to fall. The edge of October is not actually uncomfortable, so it doesn't provide much motivation to move toward the time of bare trees and no cicadas.

A year and a half gone now since the divorce. For awhile it felt like being on a sharp edge, like there could be a clean cut to a new life. Now it's more a dull ache. There has been no clean cut between what was and what's next, between the known and the possible. I could sit on this edge and it would become more comfortable with use. Or maybe I would just develop callouses.

There are points in life that move you into a new phase whether you're ready to go there or not. You graduate from school, and rearrange your life. You get married, and rearrange your life. You have a child, and rearrange your life. I thought I was through rearranging my life. Then he chose the girlfriend over the wife and moved out. Shock, surprise, rage, despair. Yep. Felt it all. At some point all that emotional momentum slowed down.

Life swirls around me as I sit on the edge, not really separate from it, just not fully part of it. Not exactly unhappy with where I am. Just not exactly happy either. Though the chocolate-covered cherries do help. I think I need a shove off this edge so I can splash around in the invigorating pool of life. I've splashed around in that pool before, and it was a heck of a lot of fun!

The sun is setting, slowly converting the dull brown lake into a water-color swirl of blue, orange and pink. There are benefits to living alone. One is that I can do pretty much what I want, as long as I want. That, of course, means it's very easy to lose track of time.

I've intentionally slowed down my sometimes too-busy career. It may be time to kick it back up a notch. I'm a detective. No, not that kind of detective. Not a cop. Not a private investigator. I do track evil things that kill, though. Things that kill not one or two people at a time, but hundreds, thousands, hundreds of thousands.

My field is public health. Doesn't sound that exciting? Did you know that worldwide, six times more people die from communicable diseases than violence, including murder, war and terrorism? Well, want to be truly terrified? Research the flu. Think about how many hundreds of thousands died of COVID-19. There were so many ways we could have been better prepared to recognize that threat, and respond to it. There is certainly another, just lurking, waiting to decimate humanity. Plenty of work in the public health field.

I'm working on my contract to sleuth out the source of a mumps outbreak in a Fort Worth suburb. Mumps is a serious, very painful, mostly childhood disease. It can result in deafness and cause brain swelling that can result in death. The phone's bagpipe tone breaks my concentration.

"Hey, Addie! Let's go see the new exhibit at the Kimball. It's a collection from the British Museum!" The slightly breathy voice belongs to Jeanette.

"So, what kind of art are we talking about?"

"I know what you're thinking, but this time I just know you will love it!" she says, with a laugh like running water, and a bit too much enthusiasm.

I'm pretty sure she has me set up for a day of staring at some incomprehensible modern-abstract-multimedia-digital whatsit. But the Kimball doesn't generally show modern art, so I'm probably safe. What I'm really thinking is how on earth a blank canvas with two blobs of green can be worth $500,000.

"It's an exhibit of 15th,to 18th, century paintings. Very old and very rare. Not my usual, but I thought you would enjoy it. I'll even buy lunch at the museum restaurant."

Now she has my attention. It's a great restaurant.

"OK, I'm in. I'll buy the wine, but this better not be a bait and switch, or you'll owe me a bottle of wine."

"I promise, it's really from the British Museum and not in the least modern. It's at the Kimball, for heavens sake."

I especially enjoy very old art. I love how it reflects the values of its era, and the possibly opposing values of the artist himself. Rarely a herself. Pity. Things might have been portrayed rather differently. I took some art history courses in college, though certainly don't consider myself an art expert. Jeanette is absolutely right that I would be interested in this exhibit.

We agree on two days from now. Gives me time to study the catalog. My dearest friend will not study. I can hear her now: "Knowing too much about a painting ruins the immediacy and the personal interpretation. The artist expects the viewer to invest some time in bringing it to life in her own context." Probably true of abstract art, but artists in the 1400s were attempting to convey messages about their faith, their government, historical events. It was their social media. I much prefer to understand art in its own context.

Shutting down the mumps report on the computer, I pull up the museum's website and review the paintings in the exhibit. I become ever more absorbed in the scenes before me. The sound of traffic on the street becomes the crunch of wagon wheels on dirt. The glare of the street light becomes the glow of a burning torch. Faint rock music from next door becomes a lute and a war drum. Time recedes as I drift into the world of kings and queens, mythical beings, violent wars and death, balls with haughty women in beautiful dresses, idealized depictions of Christian stories, and even the realistic representation of abject poverty. Yea! A Jan Van Eyck, my favorite. I'm going to enjoy this exhibit.

I pick Jeanette up at her condo near the University, where she is a history professor. She likes for me to drive because, well, I always have great cars. Right now, it's a Dodge Charger SRT Hellcat in black. It rumbles and growls and has to be held in check to keep it from pouncing. Hellcat is the perfect name for it. Jeanette's neighbors look out the window to see what's causing their house to vibrate.

With a tap on the gas, the Hellcat launches out of the semi-circular drive while Jeanette is still clicking the seat belt. Can a car pull 4Gs? We get our breath back by the first stop sign. Probably no need for the seat belt in this car. Centrifugal force keeps you plastered to the seat quite effectively. Love it.

At the museum I slide out of the Hellcat, stretch, and toss the keys to a startled valet. I always use valet, not because of convenience, but because it's fun to see the valets' expression when they get behind the wheel of such an amazing car. Or maybe the expression is because they don't expect to see a petite, red-head woman driving such a boss car. Ha - fooled them!

Jeanette and I make an interesting pair. She, dark-headed, brown-eyed, tall and a bit curvy. Me, red-headed, green-eyed, short and slender. Guys definitely give us second look at the coffee shop. Not that it has resulted in even one offer of a latte. I tend not to notice, but Jeanette gets a bit insulted. Especially if she considers the guy in question to be my "type." Whatever that is. I haven't figured that out, but she clearly has.

We take a table in the cafe courtyard, with a perfect view of the larger-than-life-size Maillol bronze, "L'Air." I make a mental note not to even think about comparing the perfect reclining nude before me to my own imperfect reality. Of course, since I made a note not to think about that, I most certainly do. Huh. At least I'm not made of bronze or artificially sculpted.

After a yummy shrimp salad lunch, and a couple of glasses of prosecco, we're ready for the real reason we're here. We spend hours admiring the marvelous art: Jan van Eyck, Hieronymus Bosch, Roger van der Weyden, Bouts, Campin, Massys, Stefan Lochner, even some Leonardo da Vinci, Michelangelo, Raphael. Such different choices of subjects, styles, use of color and media. On canvas, linen, wood, flax. It's amazing that such delicate works could have survived centuries. I'm invigorated. Jeanette seems just a bit tired and maybe a bit bored.

So, back to the Hellcat, delivered with reverence and screeching tires by a grinning valet.

The British exhibit got me thinking about my Towneley ancestors. I dove into family genealogy for awhile, and it made me want to know more about them. Maybe a trip to England to see where they lived is just the thing. I certainly don't lack a sense of adventure, and I have a valid passport. So, why not.

I fire off an email to the curator of Towneley Hall in Brunley, England.

Dear Curator: I have been researching my genealogy, and realize I am a descendant of several British families. I would love to come to England to visit Towneley Hall and learn more about that branch of my family. Would you be available to spend some time with me?

When I began disguising the gray in my hair years ago, I released amazing red highlights. So I surrendered to having red hair. Which definitely gets more attention than basic brown. Most people have forgotten that my hair used to be light brown. Those who remember say that the red is just right for my complexion and hazel green eyes anyway. Other women tell me they love my hair color - and is it natural? Come on, at this age your natural color is gray. I say yes. Go Braveheart. I am a Scottish lass!

I would not blame Towneley Hall if they didn't respond. I probably wouldn't either. But respond they did, and offered their assistance. Well, isn't that just great! I'll go in May. Then again, why wait. Impulsively, I book my flight. I call Jeanette.

"Are you kidding me? For real? Who's going with you?" There is silence when I say no one. I know she's teaching and can't just run off to England for a couple of weeks. I can't think of anyone else who could either. Being a consultant gives me more flexibility than most of my friends have. Have computer, will travel.

"Wow. You don't know anyone there, do you? But you know what? You're used to traveling for your job, and I think you'll have a great time. Actually, I know a curator at the British Museum. I've known Edmund since I took a graduate course at Cambridge. He was in the class. He's helped me with several projects over the years. Really attractive guy, but married when I was in England. I bet you'll find time to go to London, and maybe he could give you a tour. Shall I send him a quick email?"

"That would be wonderful. I've never been to the British Museum, and having someone who knows his way around would be ideal. Think I'll go to Burnley first, so maybe London the first week of November, if he's available."

I book a hotel, pack for a couple of weeks, grab my passport, and off I go to England.

CHAPTER 3
1570
England

Alexander Nowell, Dean of St. Paul's Cathedral in London, had been unexpectedly summoned to the Queen's presence.

A convert to Church of England many years before, Alexander fled to Germany during Queen Mary's brief reign, when the Catholic queen failed to support the Church of England. He returned to serve Queen Elizabeth, daughter of Henry VIII and Anne Boleyn, who ascended to the throne after the death of her half-sister, Mary.

He was a respected adviser, though he had offended Queen Elizabeth by, perhaps unwisely, preaching a sermon criticizing her unmarried state and with several other actions, all well-intended. She now seldom called on him for advice, and rarely received him warmly. He had little doubt why he had been called to attend her now.

Alexander had chosen to remain in the simple black robe and shawl of his office, foregoing the more formal neck ruff and fur collar he usually wore to court. He was careful to affect an attitude of meekness as he entered the receiving chamber. As the page announced him, he moved toward the queen slowly, his head down. He passed by intricate tapestries stitched with gold thread and a young musician playing lute, without even noticing them. Gentlemen and ladies of the court, dressed in embroidered taffeta and silk, were scattered around the room, quietly conversing. Some who were known to obstruct his influence offered smiles that did nothing to conceal a smirk.

Baron Burghley, now the Queen's Secretary of State, but no good friend of Dean Nowell, moved closer to the queen. Queen Elizabeth sat upon a low throne covered in gold leaf, red velvet cushions at the back, seat, and arms. As always, she was adorned in jewels. Today it was tear-drop pearls in her hair, around her neck, and stitched to the elaborate cream- colored satin gown. A ruff rose from the collar of the dress and stood tall behind her, accenting her red hair and the pearl and emerald crown she wore. Burghley placed his hand possessively on the back of the throne without even a challenging glance from her. Alexander removed his cap, bowed deeply, and calmly waited to be acknowledged.

"Dean Nowell," the queen began tersely, without offering her hand to be kissed, "I am concerned in regard to the continued defiance of your brother, John Towneley. It may be that the Towneley estates should return to the Crown. Tell me why it should not be so ordered." She had not smiled. She had not nodded a greeting. She had not asked after his health. She was deadly serious.

John and Mary were clearly in jeopardy. He had expected this conversation would come. Queen Elizabeth had a reputation for thoughtful decision making, but had become a harsh ruler to Catholics as a result of plots to overthrow her. He could not say what she would do. He quietly prayed that his intervention might prevent disaster for his brother, but he was no longer sure how much influence he wielded. Many recusants' property had been confiscated, they had been imprisoned, had even been executed.

"Your Majesty, as part of the Duchy of Lancaster, the Towneley estates report directly to you, only," Alexander carefully stated his case. "How can it benefit to confiscate properties so well managed, bringing so much revenue to Your Majesty? My half-brother John is recusant, but he has always supported your throne. Never has he been known to speak against your rule or administration of the kingdom, nor the Church of England. I beg you to be patient with him and merciful."

Elizabeth fixed Dean Nowell with a steely stare. "Do not presume to lecture me, Nowell. I well know the revenues of the kingdom. The Catholic Church has long accumulated both wealth and power, and followers cannot be allowed to retain either, to prevent opposition and outright rebellion. My father was much too lenient on those who defied his edicts, and I see only too clearly what the result of that has been. We will take the plight of your brother into consideration, but only for a short while longer. Perhaps you can reason with him."

She held out her hand to be kissed, clearly dismissing him without any additional discussion.

"Yes, Majesty. I will ride to Burnley immediately for the love of my brother, but more for the love of my Queen." Alexander took the few steps to the throne, kissed the queen's offered ring, and backed from the room, anxious to be away from the whispers and muffled laughs from the courtiers.

As Dean Nowell exited the room Queen Elizabeth turned to Baron Burghley. "Assure that more than one of Nowell's servants are in my employ," she whispered. "It is wise to be careful in whom we place our trust."

Alexander was pleased to be going home, but his thoughts turned quickly to the serious plight of his half-brother John. Many times had he begged John to accept the Church of England, if only to appease the queen. Others had done so and were not persecuted, even though they were known to covertly hold to the Catholic faith while attending Church of England services. He prayed that this time he could convince John and Mary to sign the pledge to the Church of England. There must be some way to appease Queen Elizabeth. The long trip ahead would provide time to think of a plan.

The horses could easily make the trek to Burnley in ten days, but the business of the queen and the church would take at least three weeks. It was refreshing to leave behind the crowds, noise, and smells of London, to be replaced by welcoming friends, quiet roads, and fresh country air. Extra stops, and more than one night in many places, were required in order to avoid slighting his hosts. Besides, it was always wise to remind allies of their loyalties and responsibilities to the queen. Information and gifts he brought back might well return him to her good graces.

A small group of servants and armed men accompanied Alexander. All were on edge traversing the numerous forests, due to the thieves who frequented them. Alexander huddled under his heavy leather cloak as the weather became more unpleasant the farther north they traveled. Rough roads over the Pennine Mountains and along the river valleys had been laid by the Romans centuries earlier, making the journey somewhat easier, though still challenging for the horses. No longer the young, strong man of years gone by, Alexander felt every jolt from his tired mount.

The chilly and damp weather of northern England, so unpleasant to its human inhabitants, rewarded the countryside with a carpet of vivid green grass. Forests of oak, ash, walnut, and elm crowded the rolling hills. The Pennine Mountains area, though isolated by geography and weather, provided excellent grazing for sheep and cattle.

Nearing Burnley, Alexander noted with pride the flocks of woolly sheep and herds of fat cattle in rock-fenced pastures, the major source of Towneley wealth. He smiled, absorbing the pleasure of homecoming, as they approached the small town, less than an hour's ride from Towneley Hall. Riding slowly through the picturesque River Brun valley, he recognized the homes of friends dotting the gentle hills and perched on the sides of the Pennine mountains. The first sight of the looming, barren Pendle Hill dominating the valley, sent a shiver down his spine. As usual, heavy clouds were trapped between Pendle and the Pennines, resulting in a light mist.

The ancient village church, tucked into a bend of the River Brun, conjured thoughts of a carefree childhood spent in the shadow of Towneley Hall. The small church was largely funded by the Towneley family. As a child he had imagined hearing ghosts in the graveyard as he played among the tombs of relatives and ancestors. “Elijah,” he said to one of the escorting soldiers, "ride on to Towneley Hall to announce our soon arrival. They will surely be happy of the time to prepare. We will tarry a bit here."

His mother's family had accumulated great sections of land ranging from York, to the northeast, to Lancaster, on the west coast. Some of the early acquisitions were made with little concern for the current residents. They were sometimes forced off the property or the commons were fenced, displacing the sheep and cattle and collective farms, leaving them no way to make a living. Locals said they see the ghost of an old woman who died of a broken heart after being evicted from her home by the first Towneley landowner. Successive Towneley heirs tried to make amends by supporting the town market and church, though Alexander knew that old resentments still simmered and loyalties in the village were often divided. That was especially true now that there was such a serious conflict between the Catholic faith and the Church of England.

His thoughts turned uneasily to his beloved brother, who was not tormented by ghosts, but by his divided loyalties to church and crown. Alexander stepped into the quiet church and sat in one of the hard pews. He bent his head, praying for his family's safety, and for wisdom to protect John and Mary from Queen Elizabeth's harsh edicts. If he did not succeed in his mission, John might soon rest beside his ancestors.

They arrived at Towneley Hall early in the evening. As the group rode into the courtyard, John and Mary rushed down the steps to greet Alexander with hugs and handshakes, and warm smiles. "Samuel," John directed, "have my brother's companions shown to their quarters to rest and freshen from their journey." The always efficient staff were standing by to lead the tired horses to the stable to be groomed and fed. As Mary led them into the Hall's foyer, John kept his hand on Alexander's elbow, directing him to the day room rather than to the stairs. "Alexander, sit with us for a short while for a glass of wine before you go up to your quarters. Mary and I are anxious to hear of your journey, and too long it has been since I gazed upon your pleasant visage."

Alexander was more than happy to relax with his favorite family members, tired though he was. "A glass of your fine wine will be most welcome, as well as your company. Tell me of your delightful boys. Growing quickly, so I hear." The next hour was spent in pleasant banter and conversation regarding matters of the family and the estates. Alexander tried, though failed, to push his true mission from his mind for at least this short time. Later, as he was led upstairs to his room, he passed several excellent paintings depicting religious scenes. Truly, he had barely noticed them before. Gazing at them now, an idea began to form.

The ringing of a pleasant bell announced dinner. Rested and changed, Alexander found his way to the Great Hall. He noted that Mary had prepared for his arrival, adorning the hall with greenery, new rush carpets and the finest tallow candles, and an inviting fire warmed the room. Alexander and the most senior of his group were seated at table with Mary and John. Those of lower status dined in the kitchen with the Hall staff. Towneley Hall had a reputation for the excellence of its kitchen. Alexander had been looking forward to both the food and spending this evening in pleasant company.

Having enjoyed many wonderful meals here, Alexander knew that the beef, lamb, fowl, and rabbit were from the Hall's own pastures and forests. He had enjoyed many a relaxing day fishing for trout in the streams flowing through the estate. Mary had always taken pride in the Hall gardens and orchards, and their products were abundant. Carrots, peas, cabbage, chestnuts, baked apples, and spiced pears were heaped in steaming bowls or displayed on platters. Alexander breathed in the aroma of bread, fresh from the ovens, mingled with the green smell of the rushes. Cider and ale, made at the Hall, flowed in abundance. Forcing the reason for his visit from his mind, he instead savored the excellent wines, imported from France, Germany, and Spain, which accented each course.

Talk at the table was light and cheerful. John was excited about the new foals that promised to be excellent hunting horses. Mary answered Alexander's questions about her Nocton properties and the new ice house they had dug behind the Hall. They inquired as to the health of Alexander's family, and his thoughts about issues the next Parliament might address. They touched not at all on political intrigue or religious matters. Their lives at Towneley Hall were far removed from Alexander's life in London.

Throughout dinner Alexander gauged John's mood. The affection between John and Mary was obvious to Alexander. They were dedicated to each other, to their God, to their children, and to the management of the estates they controlled. Life was busy at Towneley Hall. It seemed that they had little concern for the affairs of distant others. It saddened Alexander to be the bearer of news that could force them to face the power of their monarch.

"I bid you a most peaceful evening, dear friends," John said as he rose from the table when his guests were full and satisfied. "Retire when you so choose, but please enjoy the music and pleasant company here until that time. Timothy will tend to your needs should your cup be empty or you desire another of Jane's tasty cakes. Dear brother, and my beloved wife, come retire with me to the library. It is too rare an event, your visits. I treasure every moment we have together."

As they stepped away from the table Alexander wrapped his arm around his brother's shoulder. The time to discuss the purpose of this visit was near. Reluctant to break the congenial atmosphere of dinner, he slowed his pace. "John, who is now head caretaker of the estate when you are absent? It is obvious that all is handled with great expertise. Every field is tended, the animals are fat and content, the servants are efficient and pleasant. I see no detail that is missed."

John laughed, and glanced back at Mary, who was catching up to them, haven given the staff instructions before she left the Great Hall. "We are blessed to have managers who are expert in all aspects of running the estates, though I do handle legal matters, and see to the husbandry. But it is my dear Mary who has, in truth, taught me of running such a large estate. It is she who manages the managers."

Mary blushed slightly and, with a wry smile, replied, "Indeed, dear husband, it is my life and my joy," as John opened the gleaming oak door to the library. The warmth from the fireplace embraced them, a welcome contrast to the chilly hallway. A collection of books, befitting a family of means and education, lined the shelves on two walls of the large room. A small rectangular table of inlaid wood, in front of an embroidered settee, already contained a carafe of port and three crystal glasses, sparkling in the firelight. John offered a soft, well-worn leather chair by the fire to Alexander, and took a matching one beside him. Mary claimed the settee, across from the men. Alexander sat stiffly, hands folded in his lap, anxious, and unable to relax.

"Dear Alexander, do not be so ill at ease," John said, touching Alexander's arm. "It is lately that we were visited by Captain Farrow, with warning that he would be back. Surely your visit, being so timed, relates to this matter."

"Indeed, John," Alexander relaxed slightly, relieved that John had suspected his mission. "The queen has given me leave to visit, to persuade you to take the vow to support the Church of England."

"Ah, Alexander. We have had this conversation more than one time. We are directly descended from Spartalingus, sent by Rome to convert this island to the true God some seven hundred years past. Until King Henry chose his sin over his religion, our family was blessed by our love of Christ and the one holy church. Even so, I can understand those who bowed under the weight of Henry's demands. You have done well for yourself and your family by doing so. I offer no criticism for your decision. But Mary and I cannot break the chain that has held for so long. I cannot sign such an oath. I cannot let my soul die to save my body." John lifted his head slightly, chin out, defiant.

Alexander leaned his slender frame closer to the fire, as though he were chilled, and pulled his scarf from his shoulders to warm his neck. His long thin face, paler than usual, was solemn.

"John, mind you well what that attitude has resulted in for other good men. The fate of Sir Thomas Moore, who Elizabeth's father loved, but even so put to death for this very issue, should inform your decisions. Elizabeth has proven herself well able to eliminate those who oppose her."

John added a log to the fire. It hissed and popped and caught in a font of sparks. The orange glow lit their faces and cast their eerie, flickering shadows on the wall behind them. Alexander looked at his brother, in appearance so similar to himself, and the sweet Mary. The slight swell under her heavy dress seemed to indicate another child on the way, even though the second was less than two years old. He thought of their marriage. One of love as well as opportunity. It had taken the approval of the Vatican, as they were cousins. And it kept the estates intact, as Mary was the direct heir. A woman could not have inherited the entire estate unless she were married. He could not imagine John in prison and Mary destitute. That simply could not happen.

"The Queen will begin making demands soon. If you remain fixed in your position, then, brother, we must see what may be done to lessen Her Majesty's wrath. Have you considered what might be offered for fines?" His head was beginning to ache. He had hoped that this time it would be different. That John would finally agree. That hope was fading.

"Surely our status as part of the Duchy of Lancaster will offer protection from severe penalties. And we have been most circumspect in our religion. The Queen is well aware that we are recusant, and never have we done anything that would antagonize her. We have managed our properties well, and much to the benefit of the Royal coffers."

"True, John, but she has become increasingly concerned about Catholic plots to overthrow her rule. Her advisers are suggesting that your personal wealth and local power are a threat. I do believe that some very difficult times may be in your near future." Alexander stared at the flames building in the hearth, blue, yellow, and red springing up from the log. It would be so easy for the Queen to consume all they had, just as the flames consumed the dry logs, and they were just as powerless to stop her destruction.

"Dear Alexander," Mary spoke softly, "please tell us what recourse you may see for us."

"I have been putting much thought to your situation," Alexander continued. "Queen Elizabeth is well-known to enjoy acquiring works of art. Towneley Hall has a modest collection of art, but it is of good quality, and might prove to be a most welcome bargaining tool should things come to that. I know that parting with them would be difficult, but much less so than time in a prison."

He hesitated a moment before continuing. "You know that I spent considerable time in Germany while awaiting the time to serve Queen Elizabeth. I am well acquainted with some Flemish and French artists with rather exceptional talents. Her Majesty may send me to Antwerp soon to assess the recent insurrection there. I could make some discreet inquiries on your behalf."

"It is always well to renew old friendships," Mary replied.

John looked at them, with a slight frown. "God will guide and protect us, Alexander."

"I pray that it will be so, John."

Mary gave Alexander a brief nod when John looked away.

CHAPTER 4
England
Monday

After a long, restless night on the plane, the terminal at London Heathrow Airport seems too bright and busy, though, surprisingly, not as noisy as I would expect. I sit at a table outside a coffee bar, drinking a strong, flavorful coffee and eating a scone. I kill time watching the colorful parade of the world, until my flight to Manchester.

It seems that we are preparing for landing in Manchester almost as soon as we take off from Heathrow. The stewards speed down the aisle grabbing half-finished drinks, and checking that seatbelts are fastened.

Uncertain of my ability to drive a standard shift car, on the wrong side of the road, where I do not know the directions, groggy from jet lag and little sleep, I had splurged, and made arrangements for a driver. After I go through customs I easily spot him near the baggage carousel. He carries a sign "Welcome A. Simmond." He smiles broadly, shakes my hand vigorously, and introduces himself as Otto. The decision to get a driver seems wise, as I feel like I'm sleep-walking. Otto rescues my bag, and I follow his bobbing brown head to the exit. He laughs cheerfully when I look confused for a moment when we reach the car. "Uh, miss. Umm. This be England, ya' know. The driver be on that side, and the passenger on this 'un." He opens the door, tips his hat, and effortlessly stows my bag in the rear. Uggh. I really do need a nap.

Otto smoothly pulls away from the curb and merges onto a busy six-lane highway upon leaving the airport. I battle to keep my eyes open. "So," he says, "what brings ya' to Burnley? Not too many visitors 'ere from America. We're a bit off the tourist route."

"I'm a Towneley descendant. Thought I'd do a bit of family research."

"Oh, not one of them what thinks they might be heirs ta Towneley Hall are ya'? Thought all them gullible Yankees losing all that money in the fraud would a' put a stop to that. If y'are thinkin' that, I might as well just turn 'round now and deposit ya' back at the airport."

"Well, perhaps I could become the Lady of the manor after all. You never know," I reply with a bit of attitude, given his insult. I'm "thinkin'" that I wouldn't mind learning that I had inherited the Hall. The countryside we are passing is lush, dark green and forested. Ancient oaks and chestnuts, leaves beginning to turn red and yellow, lean over the road. As we leave the main highway, weathered stone fences mark the boundaries of fields, many now plowed, some with barley or oats, brown, heavy heads blowing in the breeze. Sheep, white and fluffy with the beginning of their winter fleece, graze peacefully on the rolling hillsides.

"Just kiddin'. That mess is long settled, I suppose." He keeps up a cheerful banter and travelogue during the half-hour drive to Burnley. I imagine my ancestors traveling through this countryside, possibly little different from today. Well, except I am on a smooth multi-lane highway in a speeding car, where they would have been on rough paths in wagons or on horseback.

Otto points out a huge, barren mountain with a flat top that dominates the landscape. "Ya' may 'av 'eard o' the Pendle witch trials in 1612? Twelve was arrested as witches, just one of 'em got off. One died in prison. Ta' others was burnt at stake. They wasn't witches, ya' know, just self-important old women and some others what knew 'em."

I feel a chill thinking about those poor, persecuted women. What passed for justice in those days was subjective and brutal. I look back at Pendle Hill as we turn into a driveway skirting a manicured lawn. The hill seems ominous, covered in mist from a layer of low gray clouds.

" 'ere ya' are. The Oaks 'otel. It's good taste ya' 'ave, as this place is nicer than the other places 'ere what ya' could a' booked." The setting sun is turning the misty sky a soft pink as Otto deposits my luggage in the foyer. We agree upon a time for him to pick me up tomorrow for my first visit to Towneley Hall. As he turns to leave, he glances up at the massive crystal chandelier in the lobby, tips his hat, winks, and says, "Mind ya' watch fer them ghosts. All our old mansions is 'aunted, ya' know."

Not sure if I hope there are ghosts or not, but the Oaks Hotel is the perfect place to steep myself in local history. The lobby smells faintly of lemon oil and rosemary. Polished dark brown trim complements the glistening chandelier, adding to the impression of wealth and comfort. Through open double doors, I glimpse a formal dining room, tables set with perfectly crisp white linens, polished silverware for multiple courses, and gleaming glasses for wine and water. An elegant grand stairway rises on the right, spliting at a landing that boasts a magnificent stained-glass window. I make a note of the pub-style room to the left. Maybe later.

Check-in is efficient and pleasant, which is fortunate since I don't think I could stay awake if it took very long. My ground-floor room presents a view of manicured lawn and impressive chestnut trees. A harlequin-colored magpie comically hops around, poking into grass and shurbs for the last elusive meal of the day. Pleasant prints of the countryside decorating the wall make me anxious to explore tomorrow.

It's late afternoon and I'm tempted to take a nap, but I won't adjust well to the six-hour time difference if I do. I take a quick, cool shower instead, which wakes me up a bit. I make a reservation for dinner in the restaurant then wind my way through a rabbit warren of musty hallways to the bar. Might have been a good idea to leave bread crumbs to find my way back. It's early yet, and I'm alone in the bar with only the bartender for company. I'm not familiar with most of the beers on the menu. His recommendation for a British beer beginner is an IPA. I order a pint. I gather several of the colorful brochures displayed in the entry. As I snuggle into a cushy leather armchair under a painting of a farmyard scene, the sunset fades into a misty purple glow. Eight hundred years pass in parade through the stories and pictures of the Lancashire historical sites.

The hostess from the restaurant comes to invite me to dinner. I can barely keep my eyes open, but I absolutely want to celebrate this first evening in England. An excellent meal is just the thing. I text pics of the hotel and me at dinner to my family and Jeanette. Fatigue catches up with me over dessert. I negotiate the rabbit warren back to my room, with just one wrong turn. I hope the bed is comfy, but doubt I'll even notice. I burrow into the layers of lavender-scented pillows, within seconds asleep.

Burnley, England
Tuesday

The morning is much the same as last evening, misty and chilly, when Otto arrives. He steps around the car with an umbrella.

" 'ello, Doctor," he greets me with a tip of his cap. "Typical Burnley weather fer 'ya. Smart o' 'ya to bring a mac, an' a brolly too. Careful now, ya' don't slip. These cobbles tends ta trip up people, 'specially in weather like this." He holds the umbrella over me as I slide into the front seat.

"This mist really does chill, doesn't it? Please, just call me Addie. So, let's go to Towneley." I lean back into the seat, enjoying the warmth.

The drive to Towneley Hall takes us through narrow, curving streets lined with row houses, some well-kept, some seemingly abandoned. The structures vary little. Most are made of stone, now turned gray. The trees overhanging the streets are dropping their leaves, and the tiny front gardens are desolate. I imagine the trees in full leaf and the gardens blooming in a rainbow of zinnias. What now seems uncared for would likely be cheerful and inviting come spring. Above, the rolling hills are still green with grass for the sheep and cattle. The low mountains are studded with larger homes. The uniform of the day is obviously umbrella and beige or black raincoat. Although the town reflects the downturn in the local economy caused by the closure of the textile mills, it is appealing, with its ancient pubs and churches and the rivers Brun and Calder running through it.

"Ya' see that river?" Otto points to what we would probably call a creek. "Used to be it was jus' a dump. Polluted so the fish even left. There's a new program to clean up the rivers in Burnley. Is making great progress, it. Even fish ladders 'ave been included to 'elp the trout come back." Fish need ladders? I don't even ask.

We pass under the Leeds-Liverpool Canal, precipitously situated along the hills above town. I just never thought about a canal being elevated like an aqueduct. Signs consistently point the way to Towneley Hall.

Otto slows and turns under an ancient archway capped by the Towneley crest in weathering stone. This is the home of my ancestors, *my family*. Suddenly history weighs in on me. I begin to see things through new eyes. Ancestors' eyes.

The road gently curves beside the shallow River Calder. "These fields what ya' sees once was forest of oak and ash trees. They was felled ta build parts o' tha Hall, but mostly ta pay fines ta the monarchs. Bein' restored now, but 'ave a ways ta go." Otto points to manicured lawns on either side of the road. "Can't see the town givin' up that golf course 'or there, nor the football pitches."

As we drive up the hill and around the curve the mist clears and the sun appears as though by magic. My first full view of the Hall almost brings tears to my eyes, though I don't tend to become emotional easily. "So, tis it. Luvly, eh? Be back in fur hours fur ya," Otto says as he drops me off in the parking area.

I gaze up the gentle hill to Towneley Hall. This place, this home, does not know me, its child. The weathered gray stone is now glowing golden in the morning sun. I feel welcomed as I walk toward the Hall.

Imposing is the term that comes to my mind. Goldilockish. Not too large, not too small, just right. No wonder this was a favored subject for the famous landscape painter J.M.W. Turner. It is a comfortable combination of architectural styles, obviously added to and remade through centuries of living. Though not exactly beautiful, it draws me in. A fountain sprays faint rainbows in a pool populated by a noisy flock of ducks. I pause to laugh as geese chase a girl, squealing as she tosses bread onto the wide expanse of lawn. Child and goose footprints show darkly on the damp, glistening grass. The three wings of the Hall form a large, sheltered courtyard, with the entrance directly in the middle of the structure. Strangely, a huge clock rests just above the entryway arch and engraved coat of arms. A dark, ancient wooden door is decorated only by a large brass knocker. I barely resist the urge to run up the steps and use the knocker to announce my presence. Solid stone buttresses at the corners of each wing support the three stories. Battlements line the roof. Windows on each floor face into the courtyard, reflecting the sun, shielding from view what may be behind them. Centuries of footsteps, laughter, conflict, sorrow, desire, joy. Marriages, births, deaths. Centuries of the lives of my own relatives.

I stroll past a picturesque cafe. A plaque identifies it as the former stable. The smell of fresh bread and herbs drifts over to me. People are laughing and talking at tables inside. Green and white awnings shelter open, floor-to-ceiling windows. A trio of elegant Afghan hounds lounge beside a table under an awning, occupied by an equally elegant woman with long blonde hair and a man holding the leash of an English Bulldog that is noisily lapping at a bowl of water.

Signs direct me up a gravel path to a new wing housing the visitor center and offices. The modern addition jars me back to the present. At the welcome desk I ask for James Norton. As the Towneley Hall and family historian, he has spent years studying this family and its impact on the Burnley area. I'm honored that he agreed to help me. The clerk nods and dials his office. Hanging up the phone, she turns to me with a look of consternation. “Mr. Norton is not expected in this morning. Did you have an appointment?”

“I thought I did but failed to confirm when I arrived yesterday. Would it be possible to call?”

“Certainly, who should I say is asking after him?”

“Oh, sorry. Addison Simmond. I'm here from Texas to do some Towneley family research.”

She dials again and provides my information to the person on the other end. “He has been detained at a meeting, I'm afraid. He hopes to be here shortly, if you wouldn't mind waiting. You are welcome to explore until he arrives.”

I'm only slightly disappointed. Accepting the invitation to wander, I follow arrows to a room labeled “The Great Hall.” Stepping into the room, I instantly feel small and insignificant. From the marble floor, white plaster columns line the walls at regular intervals, rising to a neck-craning height of three stories. Plaster reliefs adorn the corners, the brick-red spaces between the columns, and the fireplace. Glowing crystal chandeliers dangle, adding to the bright sunlight from the tall windows. I note the excellent marble busts resting on columns around the room, which stretches almost the entire length of the center wing of the house. A guide standing by the fireplace nods to me and smiles. "Welcome to Towneley Hall. This is the Great Hall. It was part of the second phase of construction, somewhere in the early 1500s. Before that only the southeast wing was built. The house used to be four wings until the enclosed courtyard style fell from favor." It's easy to envision guests, dressed in their best silks and velvets, dining and laughing around the huge table. A fire would be crackling in the fireplace, and servants coming and going from the kitchen, bringing multiple courses of the fine dinner and refilling glasses with wine. Maybe a trio playing in the corner.

It is only about twenty minutes before James comes to fetch me. He introduces himself with a polite smile and handshake, but with perhaps a bit of the famous English reserve. He is slender, wears glasses and a sweater, and his hair is thinning. He is perfectly charming.

"Thank you so very much for offering to help me with my family research. I'm so pleased to meet you and actually be here at Towneley Hall," I chatter as we shake hands.

"We actually don't have many American visitors, and it will be my pleasure to show you around. Shall we head upstairs and discuss what you want to learn?" He leads me back though the visitor entrance, punches in a code on the lift, elevator if you speak American, and it discharges us on the second floor.

The office wing is functional and simple. James introduces me to Towneley Hall and Burnley Corporation staff as we travel down the bright corridor. Some express surprise that an American has so much interest in the Towneley family. All offer their help, and make sure I know where the break room is, should I be in need of a cup o' tea. James does, in fact, stop by the break room.

“Cups, microwave, and water are here. I'll make us a cup of tea, and we will go to the archive and get started.” He fills two cups with water, inserts tea bags, and pops them into the microwave.

“How was your trip? Quite long from Texas, right? Have you found The Oaks Hotel to be satisfactory? Has Otto been helpful to you?”

As I answer his questions, the microwave beeps. We add sugar and cream to the steaming cups, and I follow him down the hallway, still answering his questions. He once again punches in a code to open the door to the archives.

James shoves books and papers away to clear a space. “So, where do you want to start?”

I turn a 360, gazing at the two-story room, packed with books, file boxes and stacks of papers.

“I want to get a feel for the family. For the area and how people lived. The challenges they faced, the stories, their impact.”

He laughs. “Well then, you can start pretty much anywhere.” He pulls a couple of tomes from a shelf, climbs the tight spiral stairs to a loft and returns with several file folders.

“The family history starts around 900, though it is a bit sketchy at that point.” He pulls a manuscript out of the stack. “Read through this first and see what is most interesting, and I'll help you find more on that.”

This is a far better way to do research than on the internet. I'm actually in Towneley Hall, drinking tea, and reading original documents. The drinking tea and holding original documents is a bit worrisome, though. I browse through the family history document James suggested. A brochure describes the history of the Hall from 1250, and one discusses the current use of the Hall. It's now an art museum but houses little that was once actually Towneley property except for a set of ornate Catholic vestments, saved by an ancient ancestor when Whalley Abbey was destroyed. They are apparently priceless. There are copies of sculptures purchased by an 1800s occupant, the originals of which have now been donated to the British Museum. There are also some very nice paintings, which I'm anxious to see. Over the centuries various family members added wings, removed the front wing, built outbuildings, remodeled portions of the exterior, designed gardens. James takes time to give me a very quick tour of the building, and a promise to give me a more thorough tour when we have a bit more time.

Disappointingly, most of the art is fairly recent, 1700s to late 1800s. I wonder why there is not more from previous centuries.

The desk calls to say that Otto is waiting for me. Four hours already?! James invites me to stop by tomorrow morning and sends me off with a stack of homework. Otto takes a different route back to the hotel. I'm quite lost until the turn into the hotel's drive.

I'm tired and feeling slightly disoriented. Jet lag, I bet. I eat a quick dinner in the bar. Fish and chips and a pint. Yes, I know, cliché, but with good reason. The reason is, it's really good. Back in my room I immerse myself in the world of the Towneleys until I doze off, brochures sliding to the floor.

Burnley, England
Wednesday

The perpetual morning mist burns off early, leaving a pleasant, sunny day. I had told Otto that I would not need him today, and I decide to take the bus to the Hall. The hotel desk clerk directs me to the bus stop across from the hotel. The bus driver almost does not stop. I hop up and down, and he stops at the very last minute. I get on with a friendly smile, but get a scolding for not waving so he knows to stop. No smile. Impatient with my lack of skill in using British coins, wants to know if I need a transfer. I don't know, so he must take several more seconds to ask where I'm going, ask for a couple more coins, give me a transfer and tell me what bus I will take to Towneley. I'm clearly holding up his schedule. The next bus driver is, fortunately, more helpful. I walk the half mile up the hill from the stop. James meets me in the entry lobby. “Would you like a behind-the-scenes tour?” he offers.

“I would! I truly would!” I exclaim with a smile. “Please point out the ghosts, in case I miss them.”

As we wander the floors, he describes the changing use of the rooms. He points out stairs that now go nowhere, doors that were once hidden and even spaces that were designed to hide people, particularly priests. The basement vaults are whitewashed but still feel dank, the result of a spring diverted centuries ago to supply a cistern below ground level. I ask about a rumor that the basement once housed a dungeon.

"No, that was never the case," he insists. "There are only a few recorded instances where anyone was held there for a day or two until the sheriff could come take him for trial. And there are indications that they were treated unusually well. The Hall was known for its excellent cooks, and they would most likely have eaten much better here than in their own homes."

Still, it's not hard to imagine locked doors, stone benches, and shackles in these rooms instead of the wine, fruit, meat, and vegetables that they were designed to hold. Now there are only random objects that for some reason have settled in to rest in the dark. Desks, mirrors, broken chairs, broken lamps, dented file cabinets. Dusty and neglected. I delay our tour a bit to peruse paintings stacked against the walls in one dim room. They are were mostly of the Hall and its former residents, though probably no older than a hundred years, and most not of very good quality. I don't recognize the artists.

"James, I don't understand why there is so little art from the earlier centuries of this family. Seems like they would have had a really good collection."

"We've wondered the same thing. The family was very prosperous, and would have certainly had access to art, both in England and the continent. No records have been found of acquisitions before the 1700s. There were some after the early 1700s, but those paintings were either sold to help with costs of the estate or donated to the British Museum. Perhaps the family simply did not have a tradition of collecting art, which many in this area of the country found to be pretentious."

As we go outside, James describes in detail the changes made by various occupants of the Hall. "You might notice the difference in the architecture between the wings," he comments. "Various occupants made significant changes. Amazingly, an entire wing was dismantled and moved stone by stone to the back and side of the house. That wing was at the front of the Hall, with a portico to the interior courtyard entryway. It housed the library and a chapel. The chapel was reconstructed in its new location, on the side of the house, almost exactly as it was."

"It looks from the battlements on the roof like it was almost a fortress. Were any conflicts fought here?" My curiosity naturally shifts from architecture to wars. I imagine archers in the turrets and behind the battlements.

He laughs. "No, those were added in the 1800s, simply for appearance. The Towneleys tended to avoid taking sides over the centuries, so few battles were fought around their properties. There were some notable exceptions to staying out of the conflicts, but still, no wars here."

By the time I catch the bus back to the hotel I feel a bit dizzy from all the information. I've taken a book about the art and collectors at Towneley Hall with me as bedtime reading. Tomorrow I'll go to Preston to visit the Lancashire County Records Office, where James says some of the original Towneley papers are archived.

Preston, England
Thursday

The trip by express bus to Preston takes less than an hour. The road winds through rolling hills, crossing canals and the River Ribble, which is much wider than I had expected. The closer we come to the west coast, the flatter the land becomes. Cultivated fields dot the countryside, in a patchwork quilt of colors. We pass the city of Blackburn and enter the flat plain between the hills that hosts Preston. More buildings are now red brick instead of the gray stone so common in the Pennine area. The bus drives past modern offices and well-kept houses and stops near the train station.

The few blocks to the Lancashire County Records Office is a quick walk. I'm surprised at the very modern two-story glass facade. The interior is brightly illuminated by florescent fixtures. I guess I was expecting an old building with incandescent lights and rows of old books. Not that I'm at all disappointed to work in the more contemporary atmosphere.

I fill out paperwork at the desk. A clerk leads me to a room, shows me where to find maps and bound historical information, and says she will be back. I sit down and just look around. Really, I have no idea where to start. I don't even know what I should be looking for. I find a section on Burnley. A book about Towneley Hall is interesting but doesn't contain much other than what I learned from the Hall archives.

The clerk returns, wheeling a cart with two banker-style boxes labeled “Towneley, Burnley, Lancashire.”

“Not sure what you may be wanting, but these boxes contain some odds and ends. Letters and lists and such. We're in the process of cataloging and digitizing such items, but have not gotten to these, so I cannot tell you what they actually contain. The contents are somewhat in chronological order, if we could tell when the document was from.”

“This should be interesting, thank you. Would I be allowed to make photocopies?” She nods and points out the copier in a back corner.

I put a box on the table and open it. The musty smell of old paper floats out along with dust particles that bounce around in the sunlight from the windows. In fact, much of the paper is yellowed with age, ink fading. Most items are in plastic sleeves, which is good, as many of the sheets seem brittle, with chips in corners and edges. Notes accompany each piece, indicating where and when it was acquired. There is very little from the earliest time of the family. James had mentioned that the original church in Burnley, founded sometime before 1100, had often been damaged and remodeled, so many records had been lost. There are some estate inventories, books of accounts, receipts for purchases, lists of Hall staff, letters. I sift through the documents, one at a time, not knowing what I will find, but intrigued. Epidemiology research has taught me patience as well as a curiosity to look into things that might matter, but just as likely might not. You never know.

An account book from 1520 catches my eye. The old English writing is scratchy and dim, but in general I can scan it. I'm excited by an entry documenting an acquisition of art by Robert Campin. There is no listing in the information from Towneley Hall about art owned by the family so long ago. I flip through the pages, looking for other art entries. Three years later another entry, a painting by Sandro Botticelli, is noted as taken in partial payment for a shipment of wool. Another five years and I see a purchase of art by Jan van Eyck. In 1530 the entry is a work by Albrecht Durer.

I'm a bit startled to find two entries in later journals for art by Hieronymus Bosch, again noted as taken in payment for a shipment of wool. It seems that the estate owners in the 1500s were patrons of their contemporary artists after all. I pull out other years' journals and quickly scan them. I reach 1560 and realize that the art purchases seem to have stopped in 1535.

I page through more entries during the late 1500s. The estates are now owned by John and Mary Towneley. Almost hidden among the entries for wine, cheese, livestock and household items, I find references starting in 1573 of payments to Willem Broecher in Antwerp, listed only as "paintings", occurring with some regularity. Strangely, the entries do not include the names of the paintings. For some reason, the previously purchased works of art gradually start disappearing from the annual inventories. I go back to 1550. The inventory for that year includes all six of the previously listed paintings.

I'm elated. This is turning out to be exciting. I may have stumbled on something that might interest James. I make photocopies of the pages I found and take the last bus back to Burnley.

CHAPTER 5
1571
Antwerp, Belgium

To my most dear and esteemed brother John and most honorable and gracious sister-in-law Mary, I send you my most warm and humble greetings. I arrived in Antwerp some two days past having stopped in Calais to recover from the rather rough sea voyage and to inquire as to the well-being of friends in the area. I am about the business of our most beloved Majesty, as she is anxious to know how deep the Reformist attitudes run in Belgium, and also how loyal to the Spanish Emperor. As I spent a number of years in Germany and this region during my exile from Queen Mary's persecution, I humbly profess some small knowledge of the area and language. Although I am sadly no longer first in Her Majesty's confidence, she trusts that I will be able to search out the political sentiments here. The Protestant Reformers are in constant conflict with the Catholics and the Crown has significant interest in the financial stability of our trading partners in Antwerp.

While in Calais I heard word that my old and dear friend Corneille de Lyon is here in Antwerp having recently spent some time at his home in The Hague. You may remember that Corneille visited me in London to paint my portrait for St. Paul's. It is a most excellent coincidence that my friend is in fact here as it is he whom I had hoped to encounter at some point during this trip and travel to Lyon would take more time than I am comfortable with. It is my understanding that Corneille has recently converted from Protestantism to Catholicism. Of course, I am personally disappointed in this, but I expect that he made this choice in order to remain in the favor of the French court whose loyalties seem to ever be changing. I will send to you a message presently of how goes it with our conversation. Your very assured and loving kinsman, Alexander.

Alexander walked the short distance from his quarters to the harbor, pausing momentarily to watch the River Scheldt as it flowed past the busy port. Smoky torches illuminated the dock and cast wavering reflections in the dark water. Laughter and drunken singing could be heard from the many seedy taverns dockside. He touched a scented cloth to his nose briefly to mitigate the unpleasant smell, which wafted from every port he had experienced. The River Scheldt was the dumping ground for all things unwanted and unpleasant. The outgoing tide handily carried away the town's refuse, twice daily. His destination, a trim schooner, was gently rocking by the dock, sailors scurrying between the ship and the shore, loading the last of the cargo. Walking up the busy gangplank, he greeted an officer who was supervising the process of readying to make way.

"Ho, Jackson," he greeted him warmly, handing over the letter. "Thought you might be heading out on the tide. A bit of correspondence I have here needing to make its way to England."

"Well come, Alexander. So we are," Jackson replied, tucking the letter inside his jacket. "A bit restless it is here. Happy to be back to England. I did not know you were about in Antwerp. What brings you abroad?"

"A mission from our esteemed monarch to ascertain the state of the difficulties here," Alexander leaned against the ship's rail. "Restless, is it? Did you encounter any problems with your trade on this trip?"

"Prices are up, and ships from some areas are being challenged, but not yet those under English flag. I expect, though, that may be coming. We took on as much cargo as this old ship would hold. Not sure when we will be able to make another run."

"I thought as much. Mayhap there will come soon some solution to this strife. God speed, then." He nodded, touched his hat, and waved to Jackson as he made his way down the gangplank, knowing that the letter would be securely delivered within the week. He strolled at an unhurried pace toward his friend's tavern, relaxing in the mild spring evening breeze. The tavern was easy to find, just down a quiet, cobbled side street from the new Cathedral of Our Lady. He stopped to check on the progress of the cathedral's construction. Though not quite complete, it was obvious that it would be grand when the scaffolds finally came down. Although he felt no need for escort, the unrest in the prosperous port city was palpable. He was glad that he had no need to negotiate the narrow, winding, confusion of Antwerp's streets and canals tonight.

Turning at a corner marked Moriaanstraat, Alexander felt the welcoming presence of his favorite Antwerp tavern. The brick first floor of the tavern building provided the base for two upper stories of colorful wood, punctuated with lead paned windows, now glowing with evening torchlight. He remembered the tavern fondly. It had been a regular meeting place for his friends. Businessmen, artists, writers and musicians all congregated here. A happy place. He noted with pleasure that the tables outside were all occupied, and the plates before the patrons indicated a plentiful repast. The proprietor, Willem, was firmly Catholic, a friend from his earlier life when he, too, followed that religion. Doffing his feathered cap, he scraped his boots free of the city mud and opened the ornate door. He felt a wash of pleasure at seeing his old friend by the bar. Turning around at the sound of the door, Willem put down the tray of beer mugs he carried and ran to greet him with his arms outstretched.

"So good to see my dear friend again, Alexander. Come, come, your table and friend are over here in a quiet corner." He picked the tray up again and delivered the over-filled mugs to a table on their way. "Though in truth, things are rather quiet as of late in any case. Difficult times. I hear that England is more stable under the reign of your Elizabeth. Would that it were the same in this town."

"Indeed, Willem. But even in England there is the undercurrent of rebellion. Ah, here we are. Corneille, it is wonderful to see that smile once again," Alexander said as Corneille stood and exchanged a kiss on each cheek, in the French fashion. "Willem, bring us a bottle of a nice white wine and some of those perfect oysters as you always have, to start." Alexander tossed his cap and cape onto a chair back and settled into the worn wooden chair beside Corneille. He noted that his friend had aged since they last met. More gray hair, a bit of a paunch. But still he had that mischievous glint in his eye and the long, artistic fingers were straight and decorated with expensive rings.

"I am most delighted to see you again, Alexander. Such a cryptic message you sent to me. I'm anxious to hear what you are about. Something fun, I hope."

"Well, that may well depend upon your viewpoint. Corneille, I realize that you have generally retired from painting, but I wonder if you would consider a commission for six paintings. It is an unusual request, but it may well save the life of a beloved relative of mine."

CHAPTER 6
Burnley, England
Friday

I sit cross-legged on my hotel bed with copies of journals and letters neatly organized around me. Between my time at Towneley Hall and the brief visit to Preston, I have a vague idea of the history of the Towneley family and their rather luxurious lifestyle. They owned an unbelievable amount of land, had huge herds of cattle and sheep, employed dozens, maybe hundreds of people to manage the properties and the Hall. They funded churches, engaged in international commerce and raised racehorses. And in general managed to avoid the frequent conflicts that plagued England.

But my mind keeps circling back to the art. Where are the works that are listed in the household expense journals? Were they sold? If so, why didn't I see a record of the sales? It seems everything else was meticulously documented, why not that? I open my laptop and type the name of the first painting into the browser. The British Museum website pops up. Well, hmm. I type in the other paintings. One after another, all noted as "on loan from a private collection" at the British Museum or the National Gallery.

I call Jeanette. It's six hours earlier in Texas, so it should be midmorning. She might be in class, but

I try anyway. I'm kinda missing hearing a familiar voice.

"Hey there, world traveler. How's it goin' over there in merry old England?"

I smile at the phone. "Hey yourself. I was afraid you would be in class."

"Well, I will be in twenty minutes, but right now I'm just having a cup of coffee at my desk."

"I'm glad I caught you. To answer your question, it's been very interesting. People have been so helpful, and I totally fell in love with Towneley Hall. I've been doing some archive research. Were you able to reach your friend at the museum?"

"I certainly did. I'll text you Edmund's phone number. He's looking forward to showing you around. So, have you met any interesting people?"

"Well, going into the pub last night for dinner a forty-something guy stopped me and asked if I was taken. Had to think a minute about what 'taken' meant."

"So, did you have a dinner companion?"

"Not actually. Something about him said 'not my type'. Maybe the cigarette? The bad teeth? The little girl, around five, with him? I stammered a bit and said 'Taken, uh yes. 'fraid so.' He said 'no 'arm in askin', and I gave him a little smile and practically ran inside."

"Chicken."

"Yep. Cluck, cluck. It seems that British men don't generally speak to strangers. Which is fine with me, so far. I'm really interested in some art purchases that I found when I was going through journals in the archives. What's strange about them is that they aren't shown in later inventories, and I couldn't find any mention of them being sold.

Maybe Edmund can give me some ideas when I go to London."

"Edmund may well give you some ideas. Just wait till you meet him. Gives me ideas just thinkin' about him."

"Come on, Jeanette, don't tell me you're trying to set me up."

"Would I do that?"

"Yes. That is definitely something you would do. You've done it before. Why would an ocean between us stop you?"

"Well, you can form your own opinions when you meet him."

"OK, this conversation is over. I'm not here to meet men. They would be British. And live in England. I am American. And live in Texas."

"I'm just sayin' I think you will enjoy his company and learn lots from him. That's all."

"Yeah, right. I know you. But I do appreciate the intro. Really. I think I I'll go to London tomorrow. Hope he's available to spend some time. As for dinner this evening, I'm going to have a pint and something in the hotel restaurant. Can't chance running into that guy at the pub again! Miss you!"

"You too, Red. Have a good time, and be careful. Neither will be a challenge for you, I know. Bye."

Jeanette is prompt in texting me Edmund's phone numbers. With a smiley face and thumbs-up emojis.

I call Edmund's work number. Darn. Voicemail. I try his cellphone, though it seems a bit forward. Voicemail again. Well, OK. "Hi, Edmund, this is Addie Simmond. I think my friend Jeanette may have mentioned me. I'm in Burnley and planning a trip to London. Hoping you might be available to help with some information. I'll look forward to hearing from you." I need a stretch. I push papers aside and close the computer. I've been sitting way too long. My leg is totally numb. Not quite numb enough, though, when I stub my big toe on the nightstand. I'm hopping around trying not to cry, muttering "damitdamitdamit" when the phone rings. I hop back to the bed and locate the ringing buried under papers. "Hello," I manage to take a deep breath and the pain subsides a bit.

"Hi, Addie, this is Edmund Petersen, at the British Museum." The toe hurts a little less now. He sounds really pleasant. "I'm glad you called. Jeanette sent me an email a few days ago saying you were in England and I might hear from you. I would be happy to meet with you when you come to London. When are you planning to be here?"

"I know it's short notice, but I expect to come in tomorrow. Would you possibly be available for a little while?"

"I may need to rearrange a couple of things but think that could be done. What time do you think you'll be here?" He has a nice voice. I try to set aside my preconceptions based on my conversation with Jeanette. I do confess, however, that I'm wondering what he looks like.

"I should be at the museum by mid-afternoon, say three? Do you think that would work?"

"I'm in the office all day, so ought to be able to shift a few things around. Just check in at the main desk and they will call for me."

"Thank you, Edmund. I'm looking forward to meeting you. See you tomorrow. Bye."

"I'm looking forward to meeting you as well. Good trip, and also goodbye."

As the fading light announces sunset, I grab a sweater and head downstairs for dinner. I take the long way so that I can stroll down the impressive staircase by the stained-glass windows. Makes me feel like a duchess, all grand and rich. I take a selfie with my phone and text it to Jeanette. I rarely have an opportunity to make her jealous. Better take advantage of it when I can.

London
Saturday

I'm moving a bit slowly and still have a slight limp from the jammed toe when Otto arrives to drive me to Manchester. He shows me where to board the train to London and carries my bag to the ticket booth. The station is busy. It's an effort to get through the crowds, and even more difficult to find a seat when the train arrives. A woman in the second car I try notices my limp and moves over to the window seat, motioning me to take the aisle. Hefting my bag into a rack, I smile and say thank you. She nods, then turns to look out the window. Seems British women aren't any more keen to converse with strangers than are British men. I find that a bit off-putting. I'm from Texas. Texans will start a conversation with anyone. The seats are surprisingly comfy and the windows afford a great view of the English countryside flying by.

As the station nears, passengers crowd the aisles. I struggle to merge into the human traffic with my too-large suitcase. Can't say I wasn't warned. Didn't make much difference when Otto was handling it. Trains in Europe halt only briefly at stations. People apologize as they bump into me in the rush. The human wave breaks around me and my cumbersome bag lumbering to the door. It seems like only seconds before the loud speaker announces departure in one minute. I move a bit faster and make it to the platform as the door closes inches behind me. Slightly out of breath, I pause a minute, look around, and find the exit to the taxi stand. I hop into one of those famous high-roofed black taxis for the trip to my new hotel.

I chose The Radisson Blu Edwardian-Kenilworth because I couldn't resist that name, oh, and it's very near the British Museum. Fortunately, it also has a superior rating on TripAdvisor. Easy to see why. The cream-colored marble floors in the lobby glisten. The decor is stylishly modern. Huge bouquets of exotic flowers provide a pleasant, light aroma. The clerks at check-in are professional and efficient. A porter in a sharp blue and gray uniform takes my bag, pointing out the bar and restaurant as he leads the way to the elevator. The upstairs hallway is thickly carpeted and quiet. He touches the room key to the lock, opens the door, places the suitcase on a bench by the window, and asks if there is anything I need. The door clicks softly as he leaves. I stretch out on the wonderfully comfortable bed and doze off. I wake in half an hour, a bit groggy, but refreshed, and head downstairs.

It's early afternoon. The weather is so pleasant, I wish the walk to the British Museum wasn't so short, especially now that my toe doesn't hurt so much. I stand for a few minutes just gazing at the beautiful Greek Revival-style facade, then climb the zillion stairs to the entrance. OK, only feels like a zillion. There is most likely another entrance that does not require climbing a small mountain. I realize that I forgot to eat lunch and could use a cup of coffee.

Umm...make that tea. I stop at the information desk in the cavernous and impressive Grand Court.

"Hi, I'm Addie Simmond. I'm here to see Edmund Petersen."

The young woman at the desk smiles and picks up the phone. "Certainly. He is expecting you. Just a moment." She picks up the phone. "Dr. Simmond is here to see Dr. Petersen." Replacing the phone, she hands me a brochure, with a fleeting look that seems to hold curiosity, or perhaps something else. "His office is on the far end of the museum, so it will be a few minutes. You might enjoy looking around the Grand Court."

I take her suggestion to look around. Literally. I turn in a circle, looking up.

The Grand Court is a huge rotunda. A translucent roof bathes the entire area in bright, but surprisingly subtle, light. Imaginative entrances to galleries circle the perimeter, each individually lit. They compete with each other for attention. "Come over here. The mysteries of Egypt are waiting to be discovered." "Start with me first. Deepest Africa beckons." Everything is white, and with that ethereal light softening the otherwise stark area, I feel almost as though I'm floating. It's a bit disconcerting and other-worldly. I suddenly feel very small and wish I had worn heels instead of flats. I gaze up a flight of stairs spiraling up a cylinder in the middle of the room, thinking I could be an angel, and that flight of stairs could be the way to heaven. I imagine myself in a white robe with a halo, climbing ever higher, right out the roof.

"Dr. Simmond?" The deep, melodious voice behind me is totally consistent with my concept of heaven, though I usually imagine a slight Texas drawl rather than smooth English intonation.

I startle out of the reverie that I had not realized I had dropped into. Unobtrusively giving myself a shake, I turn toward the Voice. Maybe I'm still in fantasy land. My halo slides to the side then drops to the floor, where my chin rests as well.

The Voice says, "So glad you were able to come. Jeanette has such nice things to say about you. All obviously true. Edmund." The Voice extends a very human hand.

I manage to retrieve my chin from the floor, the halo can just stay there, flash my very best smile, and take the proffered hand. It is attached to an imposing man that I am, for some reason, having trouble taking in. Tall. Beige turtleneck sweater. Dark pleated pants. Italian loafers. Dark hair with hints of gray. Oh, and those eyes. Green. Deep pool-in-the-forest green. I'm sure my hand in his is sweating. I'm positive I'm blushing. And I'm really wishing I had worn those heels. Absurd.

"Hi. Addie." I manage to squeak out. I take a deep breath and gather my wits, which are traipsing about the Grand Court like uncontrolled children. "You are so kind to meet with me. I'm grateful Jeanette was able to connect us. It's lucky for me that you're available today."

"It is a pleasure to play host to a friend of my friend. The restaurant is at the top of those stairs that you were so obviously entranced by. We are serving tea now. Would you like to start with that?"

I become suddenly aware of my growling stomach.

"That sounds wonderful. I was thinking about those stairs going to heaven. Right now a restaurant is definitely the preferable equivalent."

"Shall we take the elevator?"

"Well, if you don't mind, I would prefer to walk up these stairs. Have to be sure they don't go straight to heaven."

Edmund lightly supports my elbow as we ascend the curved staircase, pointing out the various gallery entrances below. I'm independent to a fault, but I truly do appreciate a gentleman.

"This court was once used for a junk storage area. The cylinder we are climbing around was called the Reading Room and housed the library. Hard to visualize this beautiful area as unappreciated and unused. Some of the space was a small corridor, and it was always crowded. The remodel made a huge difference in the traffic pattern for our visitors. Now, although there are many more visitors, the museum feels welcoming and spacious. Ah, here we are at the restaurant."

The stairs did not, in fact, go directly to heaven, but the cheerful restaurant and enticing smells are surely the next best thing. The Brits are not known for their culinary achievements, to be sure. Let's not even think about blood pudding, which is a staple of the big fieldhand-style breakfasts. But there are some dishes that are definitely best here, like fish and chips, roast beef and Yorkshire pudding, and the lovely tradition of afternoon tea. Edmund is greeted warmly by the host and shown to a table overlooking the Grand Court.

The restaurant is open concept, directly under that magical glass roof, which adds to the feeling of being anywhere but on this planet. A waitress promptly appears with a cart featuring an offering of teas. I select Earl gray, no milk. Of course, taking tea with milk is the British way, but I think it rather ruins the flavor. A small teapot is warmed with hot water, then the water is replaced with more hot water. The loose-leaf tea is scooped into a small basket and immersed into the pot. Wonderful smells waft out immediately. I don't know exactly what bergamot is, but its aroma makes me close my eyes, inhale deeply and allow myself to be transported ever so briefly to some exotic island.

I hope that Edmund has not noticed my embarrassing lapse in sanity. He is ordering an English Breakfast blend. The same teapot process, and a small pitcher of hot milk is included. Sitting across from him, I'm now able to relax and concentrate on his face without looking like a dazzled child. He is very attractive, yes, but in an unpretentious way. He leans his elbows on the table and smiles. He has a crooked tooth, and his hair could use a trim. It makes him all the more approachable.

He asks about Fort Worth and talks about his visits in America. I ask about his favorite places in England. Regular new-friend talk. Conversation with him is easy.

The sandwich cart arrives, interrupting the conversation. It must be said that the British idea of a sandwich varies a bit from what this Texas girl generally considers to be a sandwich. For one thing, a sandwich does not come on tiny, crustless triangles or squares. But this is not my first rodeo, so I know that cucumber and cream cheese on white, egg salad on rye, and chicken salad with cranberries on wheatberry are quite delicious. The chef here must be creative, because the offerings also include caviar on pumpernickel and smoked salmon with dill on brioche and at least a dozen other delicious mouthfuls. I almost resist the urge to ask for one of each, but quickly convince myself that my indulgence is a clear compliment to the chef.

As the sandwich cart rumbles away, Edmund suggests that the tea should be ready, and pours for me. Which I find unusually pleasant. I take a sip of tea and manage to stay in reality, which no sane woman would want to escape with this man sitting in front of her.

"Jeanette tells me you are in England doing a bit of family genealogy research. If you don't mind my asking, what line are you interested in?"

I stop myself from saying what I'm actually thinking, which is "any line that you throw out." Where on earth did that thought come from? I passed age fifteen quite awhile ago. Instead, I say "I've been in Burnley researching my Towneley family history. Towneley Hall is beautiful, and the family is fascinating. At this point I think I'm up to the mid 1600s."

Edmund picks up a sandwich and finishes it in two bites. It takes me a ladylike three for mine. He rests his arm on the table, hand under his chin. "Towneley. Did you know that the old British Museum had a Townley Gallery? Charles Townley, he spelled his name without the extra 'e', was a well-known collector in the late 1700s of Italian and Greek antiquities, primarily sculptures. Upon his death his collection was purchased by the British Museum. It appears that he had intended to donate it to the museum, but there was a strange condition in the will that made that somewhat unclear, so a purchase was agreed upon. He also required that the collection be displayed in a gallery devoted to it, hence the Townley Gallery. Almost all of the pieces are still here, and Towneley Hall has replicas."

"James Norton, at Towneley Hall, gave me a tour and showed me the replicas. I'm hoping to see the originals while I'm here. I'm particularly interested in Renaissance art, and there are some paintings I would love to see as well." I pull out my list gleaned from the journals in the archives at Preston, and hand it to Edmund.

"An interesting list. If my memory serves, I would say mostly 1400s. But I am not the expert on our art collection. My field is Egyptian antiquities. I can certainly show you the paintings, I believe four of them are here. We will have the docent in that gallery give us more information on them. Perhaps the other two are at the National Gallery."

I start to respond, but the dessert cart is heading our way, and my attention is diverted to tea cakes, scones, meringues, tarts, and biscuits, which have no relationship to what we call biscuits. These are what we would call cookies. Too many items to request one of each, which I want to do but I'm afraid of the impression I may be giving Edmund with my clear gluttony. Not to mention that the British tendency to use lots of butter and cream is surely going to result in heavy-duty exercise when I get back home.

Our tea pots are replenished and the conversation drifts to the special exhibition that Edmund is working on.

"The British Museum has an extraordinary collection, really too much to have on display at once. We rotate the items into the gallery, which keeps the exhibits interesting. For this special exhibit we are putting together loaned items from other museums and some private collections, worldwide. It will take about three years to contract for items to be shown and to design the gallery space. That is my primary project right now. After your gallery tour, perhaps you would like a look at how an exhibit is designed."

I brush the light dusting of powdered sugar off my blouse. Should have avoided that particular biscuit. "Thank you, Edmund. That would be such a treat. But please don't feel you have to spend the afternoon with me. I know you must have so much more to do than show an American tourist around."

The cheese and fruit cart is the next temptation rolling toward us.

"I will pretend to work while enjoying an afternoon with a beautiful and intelligent woman. A bit of a holiday for me. May I suggest a selection of Camembert, Havarti and the Cheddar. That one comes directly from the legendary Cheddar caves. The chocolate-covered cherries and blood orange slices go particularly well with those. The chocolate we use here is from Belgium. If you like a stronger cheese, our blue is amazing."

"Please, you choose, and I will enjoy," I reply with a sigh that conceals a small burp. God is good and this is heaven for sure.

Edmund does a bit of searching on his smart phone while we munch cheese and fruit, and suggests that we start in the Renaissance gallery, which is closest, then to the sculptures. "We will find paintings on your list in the Renaissance and Medieval galleries. The National Gallery is about a mile away, if you want to see the other two."

I think about licking the blue cheese crumbs off my plate, but decide that is rude, even in Texas. Edmund has been so entertaining and informative during our tea that I'm reluctant to leave the table. I realize as we rise that I've learned very little about Edmund.

The rest of the afternoon passes in a whirlwind of paintings and sculpture. Edmund is more knowledgeable than he indicated, and in the rare instances where he did not know about a particular object, a docent was available to answer questions or explain more about the artist. I notice that the docents are very deferential to Edmund, and he is respectful of their knowledge. We found the last painting on my list half an hour before closing.

"Let's go to my office," Edmund suggests. "We can review the things you wanted to see and make sure we didn't miss any. You also had a couple of questions that I couldn't answer, and we'll see if the right curator is around."

Edmund's office is comfortable and warm, with a dark brown desk, round table with barrel chairs and a simple Kelly-green sofa. A burgundy and gold handmade rug, obviously of Middle Eastern craftsmanship, rests on a highly polished parquet floor. A small collection of art and antiquities are on spotlighted display stands and shelves and hanging in nooks.

"I do a bit of collecting myself, and these are a few items from my personal collection," he comments as I wander around the office to view each exquisite piece.

"You so obviously recognize quality and value, Edmund. I'm in no way as informed as you, but even I recognize how excellent these items are. This small Madonna scene must be very old. 1400s maybe?"

"You have a good eye. It is possibly the most valuable piece in my office. You may have noticed that it is unsigned, but it is attributed to Jan van Eyck. This piece is believed to have been a study for his larger painting *Madonna of Chancellor Rolin,* which is in the Louvre."

Edmund offers me a chair of burgundy leather at the small round table, and sits in the one next to me, rather than across the table. He leans forward.

"Addie, I am interested in your list of paintings. What is special about these particular pieces?" He holds my gaze a fraction of a second too long. I look down and unconsciously lean back in my chair.

I hesitate. For some reason I'm reluctant to discuss my archive research. His question seems simple enough, but there seems to be an undertone of suspicion.

"Various reasons for each." I prevaricate. "I saw a couple of them when the British Museum exhibit was at the Kimball in Fort Worth. A couple of them I wrote papers on in a graduate class on medieval art. A couple are by artists I just find interesting."

"I'll visit with our curator for this area, Roger Jimeson, tomorrow. If you would like to come by in the morning, I might have more information for you. We can also take a look at the progress on the Egyptian exhibit, if you are interested. Will you have time to come back?"

"Certainly. I'm planning to stay several days, and another day at the British is on my list. I knew I wouldn't get through everything today. And I do appreciate your offer."

"It's settled then. Will 10:00 work?" I nod yes. "I'll walk you to the door. Museum requirement for visitors to the offices. Shall I call a taxi?"

"No need. I'm at the Radisson Kenilworth. It's only a short walk."

Edmund leads me on a route through hallways to a door at ground level and walks with me to the street. At the end of the walkway, he leans down and gives me the typical European peck on each cheek. Well. That is plenty for good dreams tonight! I'm glad he did not offer a handshake as mine are definitely sweating, again.

London
Sunday

The next morning, I arrive at the museum refreshed and ready for another interesting day. Edmund strides into the Grand Court as I come through the revolving door. The girl at the desk stares at me a bit longer than she did yesterday. She smiles at Edmund and lifts a perfectly manicured hand to tuck her chin length blonde hair behind her ear. I stifle a chuckle. OK, I recognize that look.

Edmund nods a brief acknowledgement to the receptionist. She looks disappointed. “Good morning to you, Addie. I hope you slept well. I love the hotel where you are staying and recommend it often. I have asked our curator of medieval art to join us for a cup of coffee. He was available for a bit this morning, and I thought he might have some interesting information about the paintings on your list. Ah, here he is now. Dr. Addison Simmond, may I introduce Dr. Roger Jimeson.”

I extend my hand, which Roger accepts with a brief, weak handshake. “Pleasure to meet you, Dr. Simmond. Edmund tells me that you are interested in Medieval and Renaissance art. I understand he gave you a quick tour yesterday, and you have some questions he could not answer.”

“Thank you for meeting with me, Dr. Jimeson,” I reply, trying to gauge his lackluster demeanor. “I do have a few questions, though they are likely very simple and even elementary.”

“Please, just Roger. I doubt any question you may have will be either simple or elementary,”

Roger responds. The compliment seems a bit obsequious. “Shall we go up for a cup of coffee? You will surely enjoy our lovely cafe.”

“And please, just call me Addie. Edmund treated me to tea there yesterday, and I did enjoy it. I would be delighted to repeat the experience.”

I'm a bit disappointed as Roger leads us to the elevator instead of the stairs. He walks with a slight limp. Is probably in his late sixties. Furrows on his forehead suggest that he spends the day in deep thought or looking at small print. Wire-rimmed glasses encase pale blue eyes. His tweed jacket is oh-so British. I'm struck by the contrast between the two men. Today Edmund is wearing a tailored navy blazer and crisp, blue button-down collar shirt, with perfectly pressed tan slacks. Beside Edmund, Roger seems a bit rumpled and meek. As we ascend there is no conversation, and I feel a slight tension in the small space.

I have a sense of relief as the elevator doors open and I'm enveloped by the soft light from the ceiling, settling on the white marble of the Grand Court. Edmund once again takes my elbow and leads us to the same table we were seated at yesterday. Today he pulls out my seat, then takes one beside me. Roger sits opposite me. Almost immediately the server stops by with coffee. Edmund orders a pastry basket. I get a very distinct image of how the extra pounds are going to look around my waist when I leave England. Worth it. Every ounce, worth it.

Roger looks at me with a somewhat quizzical expression. “Edmund shared your list with me, Addie. I find it quite interesting. What questions do you have?”

"I was wondering when the various paintings were acquired, and how they came to be in the museum."

"Ah, well. I can't give you a very satisfactory answer to that, I'm afraid. In looking at the history of these paintings I realized that they share something in common. They all came to the personal collection of Queen Elizabeth the First between 1573 and 1602. There is no record of how they came to be in her collection. In general, records from that period were quite detailed, but I find no trace of how or where they were acquired. That is not entirely unusual, but it is interesting that all those on your list have this same characteristic."

Roger pauses, and leans forward, brow furrows deepening. "Could you share with me where your list came from?"

I put my coffee cup down and stare at Roger. His expression has changed from mildly quizzical to mildly confrontational. The atmosphere at the table has gone from neutral to chill. His gaze does not waver from me. Edmund shifts slightly in his chair, and uncharacteristically fiddles with his cup, not looking at me. I struggle to understand this subtle but distinct shift in the conversation.

"Well, mostly they're by artists I'm interested in. I saw some of them at the exhibit recently in Fort Worth and wanted to see them in their residential setting. I'm surprised to find that they have anything in particular in common." I'm uncomfortable in giving Roger the full reason for the list. I'm not sure quite why, but it just seems like it might not be a good idea.

"Well, as you may know, these paintings are 1400 and early 1500. The artists are all well known, and the paintings are of considerable value, though it is unknown how they came to be in England." He sips his coffee and casually takes a pastry.

"Edmund mentioned you are from Texas. I curated the exhibition for Fort Worth, and I'm so pleased that it piqued your interest." He relaxes slightly and leans back in his chair, but the tension in his shoulders does not dissipate. "We also took that exhibit to Chicago, Atlanta, and Los Angeles. I was quite impressed by the Kimball Museum in Fort Worth. The lighting was perfect for these works, and the staff was most helpful."

Edmund changes the conversation topic to the architects of the Fort Worth museums and the Egyptian exhibit, on which he had served as a consultant for the Kimball some years before. After a few minutes Roger rather abruptly rises from the table.

"I'm sorry to have to be off, Addie. It was a pleasure meeting you. I am afraid I had little to add to your enjoyment of the paintings. I did not have time to really search our archives for information on all of them, but please contact me any time. I'm always happy to look up a particular painting or answer any question you may have. Enjoy your visit." He shakes hands with me, then Edmund, and limps back to the elevator.

Edmund motions for a coffee refill for both of us. He sits quietly for a few minutes, seemingly lost in thought. With Roger's exit, the tension has left the room. I lean back, more relaxed, and watch Edmund for his reaction. He frowns a little, touches a finger to his chin, then seems to consciously shift his attitude. Though still looking serious, he smiles and softly places his hand on mine, which is resting beside my now-empty coffee cup. The gesture, which should have been pleasant, instead makes me uncomfortable.

"I'm sorry that Roger was not more informative, Addie. Roger is generally excited to discuss the paintings he curates with anyone who will listen. He seemed rather distracted."

Distracted is probably not the term I would have used. More like antagonistic.

"I agree, it was a rather strange conversation. I'd like to take a second look at the paintings on my list today. If you're busy I'm sure I can find them myself." We push our chairs back, and he again takes my elbow as we walk down the stairs. The tension dissipates.

"I have a couple of meetings today that will take up most of my time. I was wondering, though, if you might be able to join me for dinner this evening?"

I make what I fear is a feeble attempt to contain my delight. "That would be excellent. What time?"

"I'll stop by the hotel at 7:30 if that works for you. I know a little Indian restaurant nearby, if you like Indian cuisine. Or would you prefer something else? Italian maybe?"

"Indian is perfect. I have an eclectic palate, and Indian is one of my favorites. I'll see you at 7:30."

I'm already inventorying the limited contents of my suitcase. Luckily, I brought along silk pants and top and a pair of double-loop gold earrings. I hope subtle and elegant is a good look for Indian food in London.

We part company with the same two-cheeked peck as before. I wander to the Medieval gallery and spend the next three hours looking more closely at the paintings on my list. They all seem to be as advertised. I don't understand Roger's attitude, though it is odd that they all seem to have come to the Queen without provenance.

There is something strange about my list. Wish I knew what.

Back in his office Roger dials a New York number on his non-listed international cell phone. When his call is answered he quietly says “Hey A.D. I have a bit of a concern. What do you make of this?....”

CHAPTER 7
1573
Burnley, England

This time there was no warning. The Queen's contingent rode hard and fast to Towneley Hall, not bothering to dismount before riding into the courtyard. Soldiers surrounded the home, watching for anyone who might try to leave. Captain Farrow pounded on the door, demanding entrance. Mary sat frozen in her chair. John stood but sat back down when his legs refused to carry him. Father Henry had been coming every few months to educate the children on their catechism and offer a private family mass. It was too late to secrete Father Henry in one of the priest hides.

As Samuel opened the door the soldiers burst into the entry, fanning out through every part of the Hall. It took only a few minutes for them to return with the priest, trembling and pale.

Captain Farrow stood, feet planted in front of John, flanked by soldiers.

"John Towneley, you are hereby under arrest by order of Her Majesty Queen Elizabeth for the crime of hiding a Catholic priest and plotting against the Crown."

In front of the wide-eyed children and sobbing servants, John and Father Henry were roughly bound, escorted out the door, and shoved into a barred wagon. The soldiers mounted their horses, and those pulling the wagon were pushed into a run, bouncing the two stunned passengers painfully with each bump and rock in the lane. The swirling dust churned up by the horses' hooves settled in a choking cloud upon the terrified group cowering in the courtyard.

Mary heard a scream as if in a fog. Someone was shouting "No, no, no," over and over. She looked around and realized it was herself. She was on her knees in the dirt, stomach knotted to the point of nausea, tears already soaking the bodice of her day dress.

Samuel regained his composure and ran to her. The nanny gathered the crying children, who had followed their mother to the steps, and led them back inside. The house and kitchen servants slowly resumed their jobs of keeping the Hall running and everyone fed, though they did so in tears.

Mary controlled her stomach and her emotions. She set her face with resolve, stood, and brushed the dirt from her skirt.

"Samuel. Send a message to Dean Nowell. We may soon have need of his intervention."

London

Alexander was called to the Queen's audience chamber. He had already heard the news of John's arrest. John would be arriving today for imprisonment in the Tower and questioning.

"Majesty," he stammered, and bowed deeply. His hands were cold, and a slight film of perspiration was forming on his forehead.

"It seems, Dean Nowell, that you had little influence on your brother. He was caught with a Catholic priest in his own home. They are both in the prison at Chester. John Towneley is being questioned about harboring a Catholic priest and possible involvement in seditious acts. The priest is to be executed tomorrow. It may be the same fate for your brother." Queen Elizabeth was clearly furious. She tapped her silk slipper on the floor as she stared at him.

Alexander rose slowly, head still bowed.

"Your Royal Majesty has reason to punish John. But I beg you to reconsider execution until he has been questioned about any acts that could be interpreted as treason. I know him well, and truly believe that the priest was for the comfort and instruction of only his wife and children. You will find that he has never been party to sedition. I would have heard of it through family channels. Servants gossip. Meetings with those who foment rebellion could not have been easily hidden. Also, he manages the estates to great profit, and if you act with mercy it could be to the financial advantage of the crown."

"It may be, Dean, that I am inclined to mercy if I find no evidence of treason. But the price will be high."

"As you wish, Majesty. I will see that whatever the price, it is paid."

John pulled his shirt closer, attempting to relieve the chill, not only from the cold stone bench, but also from the shock of his imprisonment. The tiny slit of a window let in little light but admitted a cold breeze.

A jailer opened the heavy door, keys clanking. "You must have posh friends. Someone has paid for you to have a nice cell and food."

He thumped a cup of water and a plate with a meager portion of bread and hard cheese on a table near the door. The keys clanked again as he slammed the door shut and turned the lock. There had been no time for John to gather anything to take with him. Not even a prayer book. He shut his eyes and thought of the lovely home, his devoted wife and children, and the emerald hills dotted with white sheep.

Drawing upon memory he recited verses from the well-worn prayer book, still at home.

"The Lord is my shepherd, I shall not be in want. He maketh me to lie down in green pastures, he leadeth me beside still waters, he restoreth my soul. He guideth me in paths of righteousness for his name's sake. Yea, though I walk through the valley of the shadow of death I will fear no evil for thou art with me."

He repeated the verses over and over until the cell was dark and silent, and he fell into a fitful sleep on the damp bench.

Antwerp, Belgium

A cryptic note with the seal of St. Paul's was delivered to Willem Broecher two weeks after John's arrest. A package arrived in Antwerp a few days later, hidden in a shipment of wool from the Towneley estates. Willem carefully hid the package and delivered the note to Corneille de Lyon when he came in for his usual Wednesday dinner when in residence in Antwep.

"The first shipment is needed."

The note was cryptic, but Corneille nodded to Willem. Corneille left with the package, unopened. Two weeks later two packages were delivered to Willem at the tavern, one addressed for shipment to Towneley Hall in Burnley and a second of similar size, that did not leave the tavern.

Periodically other notes arrived from London and packages were exchanged between Burnley and Antwerp.

Chapter 8
London, England
Sunday

People are gathering in small groups as I settle into a comfy chair in the warmly lit hotel bar. Quiet conversations float through the air, which smells vaguely of lavender. On the other side of the room the bartender is dispensing glasses of ruby red and pale amber wine, and pints of dark brown beer with thick heads of foam, to a group who seem to be regulars, judging by his friendly conversation with them. Several older women are relaxing around a table set with cups and pots of fragrant tea. They laugh, and one shakes her head and blushes. The concierge by the door hands a brochure to a young couple dressed for an evening out, directing them to the doorman for a taxi. As usual, I'm lost in the buzz around me, enjoying the friendly ambiance.

I'm trying not to read too much into Edmund's invitation to dinner. Failing, of course. I really, really like him. I really, really want him to like me. I really, really sound like a college kid, don't I? He's probably used to that reaction from women, and I'm probably not special to him at all. He's just being nice, right?

"Hi, Addie. Hopefully I haven't kept you waiting long." I turn toward the deep voice, as Edmund steps around the chair. In spite of my best efforts, my stomach knots and I can feel a blush rising on the back of my neck, fortunately covered by my hair, which I left loosely pulled behind my ears. "My apologies if I startled you. I came by the side door."

"It's wonderful to see you, Edmund. I appreciate the dinner invitation."

He takes my arm as I rise from the chair. I note that he has dispensed with the blazer and tie from earlier. The button-down shirt is unbuttoned at the neck. He looks casual, sophisticated and polished and, well, great.

"I'm pleased that you have the evening free. The restaurant isn't far, but it's beginning to drizzle. I walked from the museum, but I suggest a taxi to the restaurant."

I pick up my ever-present raincoat, which he is quick to hold for me to slip into. As I step back to put my arms through the sleeves, I can feel his breath on my neck. It seems that he holds the coat just a bit closer to him and a bit longer than absolutely necessary. It's a pleasant sensation. I reign in my errant wits, that seem to be continually escaping, and enjoy his hand on my back and his breath on my neck again as he bends to open the door of the waiting taxi.

The trip to Punjab is short. Drizzle has turned to rain, and I'm glad we opted for the taxi. Edmund walks around the taxi, sheltered by a large umbrella, as the driver opens the door for me. He puts his arm around my shoulder as we share the umbrella, dodging puddles to the recessed door of the restaurant.

A man in a white Nehru-style jacket and white pants quickly comes to greet us. "Doctor Petersen. Welcome. Your table is ready."

He escorts us to a quiet booth by a window, fogged from the difference between the chilly street and the warmth inside. The restaurant is typically small and intimate. It is beautifully decorated in black, red, and gray. A basket of naan bread and dips appear almost before we are seated.

"Addie, I would love to know a bit more about you," Edmund says as the waiter fills our cups with jasmine tea. "Jeanette mentioned that you and she met when you were both teaching at the university. Do you teach history as well?"

I pick up a piece of naan, but pause to reply. "No, actually my field is public health. Tracking epidemics, keeping water and air safe, making people feel guilty about smoking and eating French fries. I teach part-time and do some national and international consulting on community health issues."

"That sounds like it would be exciting."

"Well, I always hope not, because if it's exciting it's usually something really bad. It is, at least, always interesting. Sometimes it does involve a bit of detective work to find where a serious problem originated and developing a plan for how it can be stopped. That can be exciting, even lifesaving. That's my favorite part of the job."

Edmund munches on a piece of naan too. "How is it that you are so interested in art?"

"Art and history are hobbies. My international work exposes me to lots of new places. I enjoy learning about the history and culture wherever I'm assigned. Understanding the local culture can be important in crafting a plan to intervene in public health issues. It's an easy transition to be interested in the art of a region as well."

Well, "exposes" may have been a poor choice of words. I'm exposed to plenty more than local culture. I leave out the information about searching for viruses and bacteria in the field. Creeps some people out to think I handle Ebola, HIV, malaria, and various nasty viruses. I've had every immunization known to man. I've grown to hate mosquitoes, in spite of the fact that swallows probably would not exist except for their mission to search and destroy them. I love and admire swallows. They may be the answer to most of mankind's ills. When we figure out how to rid the world of mosquitoes, maybe the swallows can just switch to a diet of flies. Same for frogs. And fewer people will die.

"How did you get to be so interested in Egyptology?" I throw the question back to Edmund.

Edmund looks up for a few seconds, as though he is looking backward in time. "I think that was because of a visit to the British Museum when I was just a tyke, maybe six or seven. Went on a class outing, and they had to come find me when it was time to leave. I was in the Egypt gallery, of course. After that I was on a single-minded path. Not interested in any other course of study. I was absolutely entranced by pharaohs and pyramids, ancient religion, cities buried in the sand and lost treasure. Still am. I get to do a good bit of international travel too. The museum is always looking for acquisitions and doing remote exhibitions. I have even been on a number of archeological digs. I'm living a dream. I can't think of anything that could be more fun."

His enthusiasm and smile are infectious. No immunization needed.

"Well, Addie, your hobbies seem to have turned up an interesting mystery," he continues. "Roger has been quizzing me about you and your interest in those particular paintings, though I'm not sure why.

I have a feeling that you have more than the casual interest in them that you have expressed to us. Would I be right about that?"

I've learned over the years of field work to decide pretty quickly whether or not I can trust a person. It may be hard to believe that a mom might lie about whether a family member has Ebola symptoms, or a guy might "forget" that he has had fifteen partners, instead of the three he listed on his HIV clinic intake form, but it happens all the time. I've developed a sixth sense about when someone is obfuscating. In this case, I'm not totally sure, but this is not a life-or-death matter. Just an intriguing question. One that Edmund may be able to help answer.

"I don't know really. Several things came together for me while I was doing some family research. First, I saw a Jan Van Eyck painting in your exhibition at the Kimball. I've done several papers on him, and I loved this painting and wanted a bit more time to study it. Second, in the Towneley files in the archives at Preston I found entries in expense journals for paintings that the family had acquired over several generations. That painting was on the list. So were several others that you have at the museum." I pause to evaluate his reaction. He has a slight frown.

I wonder about the frown but continue. "What I could not find is when and how they left the possession of the Towneley family, even though the journals are very detailed for other items. It's also strange that I found records of several art purchases made later, during the John and Mary Towneley time at the Hall, in the late 1500s. No names for the artwork or the artists. Payment was made to the same person for all of them, and I can't find any record that he was an artist. Whatever paintings were purchased during that time, they never appeared on any inventory of art at Towneley Hall."

Edmund blinked and leaned toward me over the table. "Are you saying that these paintings at the museum, for which we have no provenance, were from Towneley Hall?"

"I don't know for sure, but they were purchased, then in another generation they disappeared. And they seem to have been in possession of the monarch for a very long time, with no record of how or when they arrived."

I think Edmund has been holding his breath, because it comes out in a whoosh. "Whew....do you realize how important this could be?"

"It doesn't seem so much important as just interesting."

"No. It could mean that the ownership is in question since we do not know how they came to be in the possession of the Museum. That would explain why Roger has been so interested."

My turn to be surprised. "Well, I don't think there is anyone who could claim rights at this late point. After all, it has been more than five hundred years. What I'm more interested in right now is the art that was purchased by John and Mary Towneley that also seems to have disappeared. I'm thinking about going to Antwerp, which is where the money was sent, to see if I can track down the person they made payments to for those pieces. I think I'll need a local contact, though. Do you happen to know anyone there who could help me with the research?"

"I do have a friend there, and I'll also ask around the museum for other potential contacts. When do you plan to go?"

"I thought maybe I would spend another day in London then go over for several days. I had intended to be in England for my entire vacation, but this Antwerp connection is too interesting to leave without following up on it."

The rain has stopped by the time we finish dinner. A light fog begins to settle, turning the streetlights into soft glowing balls of orange. It is damp and quiet, and colors are muted. At the hotel entry Edmund gives me a hug and, another surprise, draws me a bit closer for a soft kiss, barely touching my lips.

"Thank you for spending the evening with me, Addie. I'll call tomorrow. If you are able, perhaps we can have dinner again and sort through this art mystery a bit more."

I'm caught off guard by the kiss. I was expecting another one of those double cheek pecks. Aren't the British supposed to be very reserved? That was not reserved. That was...really nice. I'm having trouble getting my breath. I may be overreacting, or not. I do manage to say, "That would be lovely. Talk to you tomorrow." As I walk into the hotel my legs are just a tiny bit wobbly, and I'm smiling.

In my room I send a quick text to Jeanette. "Girl, you are impossible. Should have warned me that he is about as perfect as a man gets. You will have to beg for details. Maybe even bribe me with a bottle of wine."

Edmund walks slowly back to the Museum. He uses his card at the staff entrance, nodding at the security guard as the automatic door swung open. He spends an hour on his computer, then another thirty minutes in the Medieval art section. After making a phone call, he leaves by the same door he came in, crosses the park, and walks through deepening fog the two blocks to his London house.

London
Monday

My cell phone rings, showing Edmund's number. Earlier than I expected.

“Hi, Addie,” he says. “I'm sorry, but something has come up that I must tend to, and I won't be available for dinner this evening after all. I've been asked to go out of town to check on an acquisition and won't be back for several days. Josef Bruding, at the Museum Mayer van den Bergh in Antwerp, might be helpful to you. They have an excellent research department there, and the art collection focuses on the period you are interested in. He is expecting your call when you get to Antwerp.”

“Thanks so much, Edmund,” I reply. “I'm glad you called early. I think I'll go to Antwerp this afternoon if I can get train and hotel reservations. Could you recommend a hotel and maybe the best travel method to get to Antwerp?”

“You might consider the Hilton Antwerp Old Town hotel. I have stayed there, and it is quite close to the museum. Antwerp hotels tend to be a bit modernistic, even stark, but the Hilton is not quite as irritatingly so as most. There is a train route that goes directly from London to Antwerp, with a change of trains in Brussels. It takes just a bit over three hours.”

He takes a quick breath. "Sorry to rush, but my flight leaves in a couple of hours, and I am catching a cab now. Hope you have success in Antwerp."

"Thank you again for the lovely dinner last night, and the great information. I might spend the morning back at the museum before I leave."

"That would be great. Kay, at the main desk, will recognize you and can help with anything you might need."

"Hope you have a good trip too, Edmund. I'll let you know how things go." I suffer a distinct pang of disappointment when we hang up.

Miracles do happen. I'm able get a reservation at the Hilton in Antwerp as well as a train ticket for late afternoon. I check out of the Radisson Blu. Dragging my suitcase, I amble back to the museum for a last look at the paintings on my list before I leave. I stop by the front desk to ask Kay if there is some where I can leave my suitcase.

Kay greets me with a smile that does not quite make it to her eyes. "Hi, Dr. Simmond. Dr. Petersen said that you might be coming back by today. The checkroom is down that small hallway, first door on your left. So, where are you heading? Back home?"

"Actually, I'm going to make a side trip to Antwerp. I'm catching the train in a few hours, so thought I'd save some time by leaving straight from here. Thanks for your help."

I check my bag and go through the Grand Court to the Renaissance Gallery. I catch the front desk out of the corner of my eye and notice that Kay is on the phone, though I can't think why that would seem unusual to me. I spend my time viewing each painting on my list. They are of excellent quality, of course. There is not a thing that's unusual about them. Except, of course, that my ancestral family once owned them all, and I seem to be the only person who knows that.

"A.D., I am really uneasy about anyone snooping around these paintings. It is too sensitive a time in our negotiations to have any questions raised. Yes, everything on our end is still fine." Roger listens intently to the voice on the other end of the phone call. "I agree." Another pause. "Well, that may be difficult as she is going to Antwerp. What are you thinking?" A frown deepens the lines between his eyes. "Yes, I will take care of that. Talk to you later."

CHAPTER 9
1575
England

John held back, unwilling to leave the cell. This was the end. Was he to be beheaded? Burned at the stake? Two years of an almost starvation diet and little sunlight had left him emaciated and pale. Mary had been allowed only infrequent visits, to bring books and fresh clothes. They were allowed little time together on those visits and a guard listened outside the door. He had not seen any of their five children. A visit to the prison would have been traumatic for them. Now he regretted that. He would have liked to see their faces again before he died. When he thought of them playing on the lawn or by the pool, he still saw them as babies, though Richard was now nine.

He squinted his eyes as the guards led him through the Tower gate. He looked up into the faces of his half-brother Alexander and his dear Mary, who had tears running down her cheeks. So, they would be witnesses to his execution. He was unsure whether that gave him comfort or distress. The guards unlocked the chains around his legs and wrists. And stepped aside. Mary rushed forward followed closely by Alexander, both talking at once.

"At last, you are free!" "Your sentence has been commuted!" "We have missed you so!" "Our carriage is waiting." "Let us make haste to leave this evil place." "The Queen has shown mercy!" The words layered over each other. John at first did not understand. He was slow to shift his thinking from the probability that he was to be executed today, to grasping that he was free. He stumbled as Alexander and Mary almost pushed him toward the waiting carriage, impatient horses stamping their hooves at the excitement around them. He stopped and pulled Mary into his arms.

"I am free? I am going home? You are here to bring me home?" He released Mary only slightly so that he could turn to Alexander. He touched his face and looked deep into his eyes. Quietly, so that only the three of them could hear, he whispered, "I know that my life is spared because of you. However this has been arranged, know that I am forever in your debt."

Alexander kissed his cheek and helped him into the carriage. He whispered, "I will not be able to come with you, nor will I even be able to communicate directly with you, as you are still under suspicion of treason. But know that I will always be working on your behalf." He closed the carriage door and signaled to the driver. The carriage lurched forward, then the horses set into a quick trot, with John looking back at him.

At the inn on the first night, John was provided a warm bath, the first in two years, and a light but delightful meal in their room. Too heavy a supper would have caused his stomach to object, though he longed for the bountiful table at home. As he and

Mary sipped warmed ale, his head began to nod in exhaustion. Mary gently led him to the soft bed and lay down beside him, holding him in her arms, as the fire burned low and he fell into the first deep and restful sleep since his imprisonment.

The trip took seven days, each blessed with cool, sunny weather. They picnicked under spreading oaks beside tumbling streams or took meals in inns along the way. They sat close, or held hands, unable to satisfy the need for touch. The color began to come back to John's face, and he started to regain strength. The nights were full of a new moon and stars. So many stars. More than John remembered being in the sky. They made love gently, and slept skin to skin, arms and legs tangled, head on the same pillow.

Their arrival at Towneley Hall had been announced by a servant who had ridden out to watch for them. The children, close friends from nearby estates, and all forty of the Hall servants gathered in the courtyard, talking excitedly. "Is the Master with them?" "Can you see the carriage yet?" "How long will it take for them to arrive?"

One groom stood quietly at the back, watching the group through narrowed eyes, making note of who had come to celebrate the homecoming of the recusant.

The carriage came up the drive and the group grew silent and expectant. As it pulled into the courtyard John leapt out, not waiting for the horses to draw to a full stop. The waiting crowd burst into cheers, and the children rushed to hug their father, the baby, Thomas, carried by the nanny. Friends pushed forward to embrace both John and Mary. The servants stood lined up at the door to welcome the Master back to the Hall that bore his name. The homecoming was chaotic and joyful.

Mary led John into the library, where a fine wine was already decanted and glasses ready for them and their friends. He sank into a soft chair and picked each child up, one by one, for kisses and hugs. The youngest he had never seen, as Mary was pregnant with him when he was arrested. The next youngest whimpered to go to his mother, having no memory of his father. It hurt John's heart, but he knew that he would become familiar to them soon.

The table in the Great Hall was set with all of John's favorite dishes, each course more wonderful than the one before. Jane and the kitchen staff had spent days lovingly and carefully laboring over the preparations. The celebration lasted far into the night, with music and dance, and wine and ale in abundance. The guests left only after the children, then John, had gone to bed.

The next morning John came downstairs early, eager to be out in the fields. The aroma of bread, just out of the oven, drew him to the family dining room. Mary rushed to embrace him, and turned to fill his plate with sausage, eggs, bread, and squash grilled with herbs. As he and Mary took breakfast, their conversation naturally turned toward his release.

"Mary, you must have paid a very heavy fine to assure that I did not lose my head. I cannot imagine how you and Alexander managed to arrange my release. I fear that the estate must be missing a great deal of funds and a significant parcel of land."

"Alexander was skilled in negotiating your release, my dear. Yes, the fine was heavy, but we sold no property. The estate is intact and, though somewhat poorer, still fully able to bear its expenses."

John savored each bite, almost feeling the pounds lost while in prison resettle on his thin arms, his vitality coming back. His heart swelled with gratefulness for this amazing woman, his wife, and their close partnership, the way they balanced each other. Gazing fondly at Mary, John thought that this marriage might have been one of convenience. Dear Mary had made it so much more.

Although Mary had inherited the estates at a young age, she had quickly become fully competent in overseeing the management and finances of the extensive holdings. His branch of the family was not poor but did not hold the large amounts of land such as were now owned by his wife as heir to the Towneley Hall and lands. Trained as an attorney, he was able to handle any legal issues and learned to oversee the planting and husbandry, leaving Mary to run the home and deal with the sale of the estate's products. She was skilled at negotiating prices both for purchases and sales. She had a keen sense of timing for their exports of wool and had developed contacts abroad to extend their markets. Although she had an unusual amount of involvement for a woman, their partnership worked well. They respected and trusted each other. They were able to discuss business matters and work out problems together, much to the benefit of the family and those who relied upon them. Rising from the table, he met Mary's eyes, and with a feeling of surprise, realized how very much he, also, relied upon her. Although reluctant to leave Mary's presence, John was anxious to go about the estate and to ride his favorite horse again.

He had been home several weeks before he noticed the bare place on the chapel wall, where the Jan van Eyck painting once hung. When questioned, Mary explained that it had been sent for some minor restoration.

Chapter 10
London and Antwerp, Belgium
Monday

I had asked Kay to order a taxi to pick me up at 1:00 at the Museum. It was more than fifteen minutes late. I was just able to make the train. Unfortunately, I had no time at all to enjoy the beautiful Victorian-era St. Pancras station. I muscle my bag into the area between the seats only minutes before the doors on the modern bullet-style Eurostar train close. The countryside is quickly a blur as the train ramps up to its cruising speed of around 180 mph. A slight decrease in speed marks the entry into the awe-inspiring engineering feat called the Chunnel, and the twenty-minute trip under the English Channel to France. In just over two hours I arrive at the bustling Brussels station.

I'm getting used to maneuvering my traveling companion, now named Wheeler, on and off various transportation modes and through crowds. We rarely bump into things and have not yet tripped anyone. I still wish, however, that I had enough forethought to pack more conservatively. After a bit of consternation about which platform we need for our Antwerp connecting train, Wheeler thump thumps behind me like an obedient small child, and sits politely on the second train.

Sunset colors are fading to purple when I arrive in Antwerp. The station is an intriguing mixture of architectural styles, a jumble of towers and archways, delicate lattice work, steel and glass. It lives up to its reputation as one of the most beautiful train stations in the world. I stand in the vast hall as other travelers flow around me. I easily imagine myself in the early 1900s, long skirt, large plumed hat, modest bodice of Belgium lace and perhaps a parasol. Elegant and rich.

Outside the image lingers. Lights are coming on, and the buildings around the station are lit in multiple colors. The temperature is surprisingly mild for a fall evening. The map on my phone tells me that it is less than two miles to the hotel. I think about walking but decide against it. It's getting darker, and Wheeler is becoming a bit more of a burden. I step into the taxi "queue." I'm grateful when my driver hefts Wheeler into the "boot" of the taxi. I'm quite proud of how much English I am picking up. Even if I am in Belgium.

In only a few minutes the taxi arrives at an attractive, historic building housing the Hilton, next to the even more historic and graceful Cathedral of Our Lady, in Old Town Square. Both are washed in white light. The feeling of being in a different century stays with me. The historic part of the hotel does not extend past the exterior. I step into a recently renovated, modern lobby area. I find that my room is very comfortable and modern and overlooks Old Town Square. I'm a lucky girl. Also a hungry one. I noticed several restaurants in the square, all potentially delicious. Think I'll take a quick shower, change clothes and find dinner.

The porter has hefted Wheeler onto a suitcase stand. I unzip the suitcase and feel uneasy. Although I did make the mistake of bringing a too-large suitcase on this trip, I've traveled extensively and am compulsive about organizing my suitcase.

I'm sure this is not how I packed it. It is not exactly jumbled, but items are not where they should be, and the clothing is not as neatly folded. My notebook computer is on top of the clothes strap rather than in the zipper compartment. Nothing seems to be missing, though. If I had taken a flight I would say that the bag had been inspected. But I took the train and had it with me every minute of the trip. I mentally retrace my steps from hotel to the museum, the London station, the Antwerp station, and to the room. Yes, I had it in my possession the entire time. Except at the museum.

Did Kay rifle through my bag? If she did, what was she looking for? I'm reminded of her subtle but obvious curiosity. Hmm...maybe she has a thing for Edmund and was looking for confirmation that we are having a personal relationship? Well, whoever did this, no harm done. But I certainly feel that my privacy has been violated.

An evening at a nice restaurant and exploring Old Town Square can't quite erase my uneasiness. I sit on the bed and place a call to Jeanette. It goes to voicemail. Darn. I leave a message, "You won't believe where I am! Antwerp, of all places. Tracking down an art mystery. I'll call you tomorrow. I'm exhausted and going to sleep now. Nite."

Antwerp
Tuesday

The sun rises late here this time of year, so I did as well. I call Josef Bruding at the Museum Mayer van den Bergh and arrange to meet him this afternoon. That leaves me with plenty of time. I choose a small cafe with outdoor tables on the square where I can enjoy the sun. The air smells of saltwater and I can hear sounds from the busy port, close by. Tourists begin to wander the square, checking out the diamond and antique merchants, and souvenir shops.

A couple settles into a table just behind me. From their conversation I can tell they are American. As I turn slightly to say good morning, I notice a man sitting several tables behind me. He is unremarkable, but vaguely familiar. He wears a blue long-sleeve shirt, and dark slacks. His sandy blonde hair is perfectly cut, and he wears stylish glasses. It's the glasses that I recognize first. I think we were on the same trains from London all the way to Antwerp. Yep, sure of it. Clothes style, hair, glasses. Same guy. He looks up from his laptop and quickly back down with no sign of recognition on his part. I shrug and go back to watching the tourists.

The first part of the day is spent wandering around Old Town. The gothic cathedral is first on my list. I stop at a plaque by the entrance which offers a brief history, fortunately in English. Started in 1351, and mostly completed by 1521, the interior was tragically destroyed by fire in 1533. Rebuilding took more time. The repairs and subsequent renovations left the original exterior, but the interior reflects the various reconstruction periods. It is a masterpiece of architecture and art. A soaring tower of intricate stonework is embellished with large clocks on the sides. A dark, onion-shaped dome looks a bit out of place. Stepping into the visitor vestibule, I pay admission and pick up a booklet about the construction and art. I'm especially interested in the art. The Peter Paul Rubens altar pieces and other works from the early 1600s are worth the price of admission. Napoleon stole the altar pieces, but they were eventually returned to their original settings. Rubens was a resident of Antwerp and his house is now a museum. I will definitely visit it before I leave. I could spend lots more time here, but I have an appointment with Josef, at the Museum Mayer van den Bergh, thanks to Edmund.

The walk to Museum Mayer van den Bergh is a short one. I pass antique shops that might sell actual antiques. Armoires, paintings, and chairs are artfully crammed into small display windows. In Texas an "antique" is anything older than twenty-five years. I leave the Old Town area for a more modern street. The Museum is in a house that was built especially for the private art collection of its namesake. When the desk attendant rings Josef, it takes him only a couple of minutes to appear.

"Mr. Bruding, it is so kind of you to take the time to visit with me," I offer my hand.

"Josef, please," he says, pumping my arm enthusiastically. Welcome to our cozy little museum, Addie. Edmund told me that you need some historical information." Josef leads the way to what appears to be a library just off the entryway. The armchairs seem too old and fragile to hold weight, but he motions me to sit, and takes the one beside mine. They both creak impressively, but, thankfully, don't collapse. "I'm more than happy to be of assistance," he says, as he folds his tall, thin frame into the antique chair and runs his hand through a mop of unruly dark hair. What a great smile he has. And he has a relaxed way of looking very directly at you that makes me feel that he has nothing better to do than spend a pleasant afternoon in my company.

"He did not have time to go into detail about your project, except that it seems to be related to art transactions in the late 1500s. The mid-1500s was really part of a golden age for Antwerp, but later the city was unfortunately chaotic, with conflicts between the Reformation movement here and the Spanish emperor, who was determined to rule this area. Much of the city was destroyed, and many of the more progressive residents left, including many of the artists. It took generations for the city to recover, and it was never the same as before. A pity, because it must have been a truly lovely place. So," he leans back and folds his hands in his lap, "please explain to me what you are hoping to learn here and how I can help."

"Well, I'm looking for a specific person who may have lived here around 1575, give or take a few years. It seems he was involved in some art transactions with the Towneley family of Burnley, England. I'm hoping to learn who he was, and maybe find out what art was involved. There's no list of the pieces in question, just of art purchases, with no descriptions. I don't speak Dutch, and I doubt that the local records are written in English. I really need help in finding the records, and in translating them if I do find something."

"Yes, I see why you might need some help," he nods. "Glad Edmund thought to send you to me. Might be a bit of good fun. Of course, records that old will likely be in Flemish, which, fortunately, I can translate reasonably well. I think we need to start with the Antwerp City Archives. It has records dating as far back as 1221. Fortunately, when the city was in conflict in the late 1500s, the files were in the very new, generally fireproof, City Hall, and were spared destruction. Bit of a miracle, that. The archive has moved to a remodeled warehouse on the old harbor. Tomorrow is a half-day for me, and I can be free for the afternoon. If that works for you, I can pick you up at your hotel at 12:30."

"Oh, that would be perfect! I would be so grateful. I'm staying at the Hilton Old Town." I'm so delighted to find someone who can help that I am almost bouncing in my chair. "Of course, I'll be happy to cover your fee."

At that his eyebrows shoot up, and he looks vaguely insulted. "Fee? No, absolutely no, no fee. It will be my pleasure. I expect to learn something more about my history as well, and I never turn down a reason to do research in the archives. I thank you for providing the opportunity." He smiles as we rise. "The archive is very close to the Hilton. It will take us no time at all to get there. Would you like to see our collection before you leave? I have some time before a meeting if you would enjoy a quick tour."

"Now, I thank you for the opportunity." Who could help but return that broad smile with an equal one, and I am surely not one to decline a tour of a treasured art collection. "I would love a tour."

We spend a quick hour viewing the collection, made all the more enjoyable by Josef's remarkable knowledge of the history of the paintings and artists. He walks me back to the entrance, pumps my arm, and waves as I walk down the stairs.

"I will see you tomorrow. It will be an interesting afternoon," he calls as I reach the sidewalk.

"I hope so. Thank you again," I smile and wave back. I decide to take a short detour on my back to the hotel, to stroll along the harbor. Although it's no longer the busiest port in the world, as it once was, it's still one of the top twenty. I watch the tugs guide cargo ships toward the ocean on the outgoing tide, trying to guess what they are carrying and where they are going. The breeze has picked up a slight chill, though I barely notice.

Coming from the dock area, I cut through the square, dominated by Antwerp City Hall. I pause to admire the surprisingly large and well-preserved building. Its four floors are decorated with multi-color flags fluttering in the breeze, towers and chimneys rise toward the sunset. The clock is showing just past five, and workers drift out to the street, flowing around the towering statue of the mythical hero Silvius Brado flinging the tyrant giant Antigoon's hand into the river. Some head toward one of the cafes lining the square. I can only imagine what it's like to work in a place that was built in 1565. I bet the electricity is unreliable and the plumbing leaks, but the ghosts might be pretty cool. The lights are coming on, illuminating city hall in golden glow, reflected in the dark cobbles. I button my sweater and pick up my pace across the square. As I turn to look at city hall, now decorated in sunset colors as well as flags, a man quickly turns his back. He has sandy blond hair, blue shirt and dark pants.

CHAPTER 11
1582
Burnley, England

"This could not be happening again." Mary sat in paralyzed silence. Her gray morning dress, covered by a crisp white apron, fell softly at her ankles as she slowly stood and looked toward the courtyard. The sound of the soldiers coming up the hill was all too familiar. The sounds from the busy kitchen were going quiet as the servants paused to listen as well. It was disturbing, as though a hive of bees had suddenly stopped buzzing.

John had now been detained for sedition four times. After Chester and the Tower, he was imprisoned at the Marshalsea near London, then York Castle, then the Blockhouses in Hull. Hull was especially vile, having no light and no ventilation, and the tides flooded the floors. Each time he was gone at least a year, sometimes two. The period between arrests often only months. It was only due to their wealth that John survived his stints in prison, as Mary was able to bribe jailers to provide a reasonably healthy diet, warm bedding and medical care. Mary suspected that Alexander had also often intervened to lighten his burden in those foul places. Each time he came home thinner and more despondent.

The first informant had been identified. He had not come back to his stable-hand position at the Hall. Someone must have taken his place, though they had been unable to discover who. They had never again sheltered a priest at the Hall. They now attended Catholic services rarely, and in secret, at the home of another recusant. After his third arrest, John had pressed Mary regarding the missing paintings. She refused to provide details of how she had accomplished the trade of his freedom for paintings. Torture was a common method of getting information in the prisons, and it was best that he not know. There were others to protect. Though she resented, even temporarily, the loss of the paintings that their ancestors had been so fond of, it was preferable to losing the estate bit by bit. It was unlikely that could ever have been recovered.

John had missed so much while in prison. Five of their children had been born before his first arrest, and Mary was even then pregnant with the sixth. Four more had now arrived. Ten. All healthy and fair of countenance. And almost strangers to him. They grew up so quickly. The oldest, Richard, was only seven when John first went to prison. He was now fifteen, and they had last year sent him to study in Belgium. She missed him terribly, but the Catholic country was safer, and better able to provide for his education.

Mary stood stoically at the desk near the hearth, her pen frozen in her hand, a sole tear glistening on her cheek. John took a deep breath. He rose slowly, held Mary and kissed her. They walked with dignity, hand in-hand, to the entryway. Samuel opened the heavy door, bowing deeply. Lathered horses, soldiers with drawn swords, children and servants weeping, and the prison wagon. Before the soldiers could strike or bind him, John stepped into the wagon, whereupon the Sheriff read the charges against him and announced that he would be transported to prison in Manchester. Mary had a fleeting thought that at least this time he would be close enough to visit if it could be arranged.

Two years passed, another parole. Two more children born. Mary released some of the house and stable servants. The dusting and sweeping could just wait. She helped more with the planting and gathering of the crops from the garden. She sold many of the prized horses and let fields lie fallow, but kept the sheep and cattle producing wool and meat for export. Another imprisonment, in Broughton this time. With each arrest she seethed inside, more determined than ever to show Queen Elizabeth that she could not defeat them. Managing the estate and caring for twelve children, soon to be thirteen, left her exhausted, but she met each day with the certainty that John would come home before sunset. And slept restlessly without him beside her.

1586
Antwerp

Alexander sat, brooding, at the corner table away from the windows, back to the door, with the tavern's owner, Willem. His cloak and cap hung on a peg in the corner. He would have preferred to leave them on, but the evening mist was heavy and cold, and they were uncomfortably damp. The dark wood and dim light from the smokey torches around the wall matched his mood, as did the plaintive music played by a guitarist near the bar. He stared into the tankard of excellent ale Willem had set before him, watching the foamy head settle. He had not decided whether he was in the mood to down it quickly and order another, or drink it slowly. He chose to sip slowly and savor the tart flavor. Willem lifted his tankard rarely, his eyes flitting nervously to the door each time someone entered or left.

It was dangerous for Alexander to be here at all. The country had been at war for years, with control passing between Catholic and Protestant factions. Last year control reverted to the Catholic Duke Alessandro Farnese. Protestants had been given two years to leave the city. Queen Elizabeth had sent Alexander once again to seek out information on the level of support for her and the status of those loyal to her. He was to arrange passage to England for those high-placed Protestants who wished to vacate the city. He would also arrange the return of Richard, John and Mary's oldest son. He had completed his education, and it was time for him to learn the management of the Towneley estates. This would be done only through intermediaries, as he could not risk direct contact regarding his Catholic relatives.

"Willem, it is time to trade out the last of the paintings," Alexander spoke in hushed tones. "Corneille's death was a blow to the art world and was especially so to me. He was a faithful friend, as you have been. No one would have suspected from his other works that he had such abilities. Although John's future is far from secure, I cannot risk your safety, nor mine, any longer. There are spies everywhere, and it is impossible to tell friend from foe. I am sure that you, as well will be glad to be done with this undertaking."

Chapter 12
Antwerp
Wednesday

Josef was good to his word, picking me up at the Hotel right on time. At the Archive the desk clerk obviously knew him. "Good afternoon, Mr. Bruding. How can we help you today?" The greeting and question were in Dutch, but easy to understand. It's surprising how many words in other languages sound like their English counterparts.

Josef switched to English for my benefit. "Good morning, Gretel. My friend from America, Addie Simmond, is wanting to do some research. Addie, please explain to Gretel what you are looking for."

"It's a pleasure to meet you, Gretel," I shake Gretel's hand, with a smile. "I'm hoping to find information on a Willem Broecher who lived in Antwerp around 1575. I was doing some research in England on the Towneley family, who are my ancestors. I found some expense entries in the family ledgers that indicated transactions for art, over several years. The payments were made to Willem Broecher, of Antwerp. These entries intrigued me, as none of them indicated what art was purchased. This was also during a period that the owner of Towneley Hall was incarcerated multiple times, so it seems strange that they would be buying art when they were clearly paying major fines. I'm hoping you can help me with this."

"Ve can for sure take a look. De census vas not yet done here in dose years, so ve must look elsewhere." Her English was spoken with a heavy Dutch accent, with "th" changing to "d" and "w" changing to "v", but was easy to follow, and pleasant to hear. "Ve vill start in de 1500s section, vit our church records. Perhaps ve find him dere. Also de land ownership records. After dat it is more difficult. So, come vit me and I start you vit de books and some computer searches." She escorts us to a room with work tables sections for the appropriate epoch.

Josef peruses the shelves. "We could start with the church records, maybe. It's easier to spot names than to try to read through ancient books. Do you happen to know his religion?"

"I'm not really sure. All I know is his name, but since the Towneleys were Catholic, I might guess that anyone they were doing business with here would be Catholic as well."

"Well, that would be fortunate, as the Catholic church maintained very detailed records. These old registers are difficult to read in original form, but they have been transcribed. It's the transcriptions that are shelved. The originals are too fragile to be on display. The entries are by year, and a name index is at the back of each year's listings. Shall I start with 1560 and you take 1580? We can probably cover at least those twenty years rather quickly."

Even though the documents have been transcribed, the going is slow and tedious. After two hours I have a bit of a headache, and cramp in my neck. "Ah," exclaims Josef, looking up from his tome. "Here is a Willem Broecher, tavern owner in Antwerp, as father to a male infant who is baptized in 1576 at what is now Cathedral of Our Lady. "

"Hmm. Name seems right, but a tavern owner seems unlikely. I haven't found any Broecher in the 1580 records. Let's at least finish out these volumes."

We spend another hour thumbing through the Cathedral registers with no further results. Gretel comes in and pulls up a chair to sit at the table with us. She has a printout with Willem Broecher 1570-1600 as the search topic. Surprisingly there are several entries, including owner of a tavern, several possible children, and some mentions in notes by a couple of writers from Antwerp as having set a fine board or providing a fine and true ale.

"Thanks, Gretel." Josef rises to stretch. "Seems that we need to check the taxation and property roles to see if we can find the name and location of his tavern." He looks at the clock on the far wall and gazes briefly out the window. "Addie, it's getting late to begin that search. Can you come back tomorrow? I have appointments, but Gretel can show you where to look and help with translation if you need it."

"Of course. I don't mind a bit coming back. I'm ready to quit for the day anyway." Gretel takes the registers we have been using and re-shelves them as I tuck the folder with my notes and the printouts into my bag. "I think I'll walk back to the hotel. You were right that it's close, and I really need some exercise and air. You've been so kind and helpful, and I'm grateful."

"I certainly understand wanting a walk. This area is perfectly safe, and it promises to be a lovely evening. My wife expresses her hope that you will join us for dinner tomorrow evening. She works for the City of Antwerp and will be off by 5:30. We will choose a quiet place with local offerings and will pick you up at the hotel if you are able to go."

"I don't have plans for dinner tomorrow, and I'd love to meet your wife. Thank you for the invitation."

My hair flutters in the cool breeze coming from the river. I take a deep breath and stretch, relieving the stiffness from sitting too long. The path by the docks beckons. I spend a leisurely hour watching the huge cargo ships slowly lumbering along. Tiny fishing boats dodge across their bows in the channel, seemingly in imminent danger of collision. The wake from the ships splashes against the seawall, mist pluming up, casting faint rainbows in the fading sunlight. As the lights begin to come on, I turn toward the hotel for a light dinner and some reading before I sleep.

A blonde man with glasses slips away from the dock, and walks quickly in the opposite direction, merging unobtrusively with the other pedestrians.

New York, USA
Wednesday

It is turning into a late night. Fortunately, he held his liquor well and the somewhat shady art dealer did not. It was not the first time they had met, but he did not particularly like dealing with the Saudi. This art dealer was as well connected to the underground as he was to the above-board activities. Some of the items they discussed, though, were of interest, and might turn out to be excellent acquisitions for the Museum. He also tended to boast when he was drunk, revealing bits of tantalizing information. Tonight had been no exception.

“I hear your museum may be divesting itself of some paintings,” the Saudi says, raising his thick eyebrows in question. He was not in traditional Saudi attire. He preferred western-style suits, mostly Italian silk, and heavy gold rings. His sharp nose and tan complexion hinted of his heritage.

“Oh?” Edmund's response is noncommittal. “And you hear this where?”

“I have good friends in private collector market, you know.”

“Indeed, you have good friends everywhere.”

“True. I hear a very rich person, don't know, maybe oil, maybe drug money, looking. Dealer here is friend of mine. He will not say who. Maybe you in town for the negotiations?” The Saudi is finishing off his fifth vodka and tonic.

The Saudi should know he wouldn't get any information from him. Edmund turns the conversation to a statue purported to be from a Babylonian temple. It is well past midnight, and Edmund declines the Saudi's offer of another round. Edmund is glad when his contact pushes away from the bar, steadies himself, and asks for his car to be called. Edmund also declines the offer of a ride, and walks the few blocks to the apartment to clear his head.

The British Museum leases an apartment on Museum Mile in Manhattan, and he is a frequent occupant. He stretches out on the sofa and turns on the TV. The news was full of the blatant plunder and destruction of Syrian and Iraqi antiquities by Muslim radicals. The museum had sent him to New York to sniff around for anything that might be legitimately, or not so legitimately, secreted out of the Middle East. For legitimate items the museum might be in the market if the price was right. For illegal items they would arrange purchase at a very discounted price. Those, and items that had been rescued and needed a safe temporary home, would go into storage or on exhibit until they could be repatriated. There were also plenty of fakes. He was expert at recognizing those, and the museum had saved millions by avoiding problematic purchases.

The evening's conversation worries him. He dozes off, still stretched out on the couch, thinking about the rumors.

Antwerp
Thursday

The new day promises to be pleasant. I don a light jacket and grab the umbrella, just in case, and enjoy a brisk walk to the archive, stopping to grab a coffee to go at a small koffiehuis. Boats passing each other on the river create waves that collide and glint cheerfully in the bright morning sun. Young mothers push baby carriages, laughing at the antics of squirrels, and greeting each other. Ravens lurk by the fishing docks, hoping for a handout or opportunity for a furtive theft.

I almost skip up the stairs at the archive. “Goedemorgen, Addie,” Gretel greets me as I breeze in. “I haf pulled some property records for you, but haf not had time to look through dem.” I settle in at the table we used yesterday and methodically start through the records. They are written in Dutch or Flemish, but frankly, I can't tell the difference. However, the words are pretty simple to translate with some minor assistance from Gretel. It takes several hours, but I finally spot something promising. Willem Broecher, 1565, purchased a building on Moriaanstraat for purposes of a tavern.

"Gretel, could you look up this address for me? It seems that the property was once owned by the person I'm looking for."

Gretel does a brief search on her computer and looks up with a smile.

"Vit is de address of De Quinten Matsijs. Vit is still here and is still a tavern. Oldest in Antwerpen. And close by here efen. Is a big find for you, ja?"

I don't even try to contain my glee. I do a little dance right there in the lobby, to applause from a couple of bystanders. Well yes, childish. But sometimes you just have to celebrate.

"Yes, absolutely, Gretel. It's a big, big find! Thank you, thank you, thank you! Is it close enough for me to walk? Can you give me directions?"

"Ja, close by enough. Take you, oh, maybe twenty minutes."

I confirm her brief directions with the map on my smart phone. I don't trust someone's directions, especially in Europe. I like to get the input of a real person because they often add detail that a map will not provide. But I cannot tell you how many times a crucial turn or landmark is omitted and I end up with a long detour. Sometimes, I suspect, because the direction-giver can't come up with the exact words in English and simply skips over that part. A detour is often interesting, but sometimes into a neighborhood that I would not choose to walk alone. I make a mental note to drop back by the archives and bring Gretel a gift.

I have plenty of time before dinner with Josef and his wife, so I spend an enjoyable hour wandering and looking into store windows, sometimes venturing inside to admire antiques. My stomach is beginning to growl. The logical choice for lunch is De Quinten Matsijs. I'm heading there anyway, why not stop for lunch. And it's just off the square from the hotel.

De Quinten Matsijs is easy to spot. The two-story building resides on a corner. The exterior is white, with black wood trim. In Texas it would be stucco. Here, maybe plaster? The banner over the door bears the name and the date 1565. The menu and beer list are posted on large sandwich boards by the door.

Stepping in, I feel transported in time. Dark beams support the ceiling, and the stone walls are mellowed from centuries of use. Colorful leaded glass windows cast interesting patterns on the walls and floors. The lighting is soft and subdued, adding to the feeling of being in another century. I inhale the complex scent of old wood, ancient stone, smoke, beer, and food. It's not overly crowded, and there is a mix of mostly locals and a few tourists. I choose a table just vacated near a window, but away from the door. It is prime real estate, near the fireplace, which is radiating warmth.

As I walk by, a sever smiles, and says “Welkom.” No translation needed. Seems that she is the only one serving, so it takes her awhile to come by my table. She greets me in Dutch. I'm understanding quite a few words now, but speaking is more of a challenge. She recognizes from my pitiful attempt to say “Good afternoon” in Dutch that I am probably an English speaker. She answers my questions and takes my order in passable English. Which is a very good thing, because I'm not at all sure what I would be having for lunch if I had to order in Dutch. I choose a Gezodenworst, which she tells me is a traditional Antwerpen sausage, served with salad and fries. I order hot tea to warm my hands and trust the fireplace to deal with the rest of my slightly chilled body.

When my tea arrives, I ask about the history of the tavern. The waitress is chatty and well-informed. She tells me that it is named for a famous artist, and has been a gathering spot for artists, authors, and musicians for centuries. The original name was Huize 't Gulick. The translation may have been "House of Happiness." I would love to spend more time visiting with her, but she has other customers, and excuses herself to tend to them.

The meal is simple and satisfying. The mustard served with the sausage is pungent enough to bring tears and a slight coughing fit. I use much less on subsequent bites. The chewy, dark bread helps to cut the burn. Why, I wonder, don't we get bread this good with restaurant meals in the States? I eat slowly, absorbing the atmosphere and imagining what it would have been like in the 1570s. It's not too hard to imagine the ghosts of patrons past, stopping by for a beer and conversation. Horses tied outside, perhaps the street was even then cobbled. Merchants doing business over a meal, artists laughing at a comment from a sassy serving girl, musicians in the courtyard giving an impromptu performance. Smoky torches lining the walls for evening lighting. The proprietor, Willem, then maybe in his forties, a bit round and red-cheeked from tasting a few too many of his own wares, directing from his post behind the bar. A happy, warm and inviting place. "House of Happiness" makes sense to me. I'm certainly perfectly content here. I'm not really sure what information this tavern has to give me, but I'll definitely be back.

The day is moving toward evening as I stroll back to the hotel. The white walls of the Cathedral of our Lady are softly illuminated as I pass by. It's still a couple of hours before Josef and his wife are scheduled to pick me up. In my room I hang up my jacket, toss my notebook computer on the bed and opt for a warm shower before I dress for dinner. After the shower I move the computer and the photocopies Gretel made to the desk. I stand there for a minute, confused. The copies that Gretel made for me yesterday are not there. I know I left them neatly stacked on the right, beside the phone. But maybe I put them in a drawer, and just don't remember. Or perhaps the maid put them away. I search the desk drawers. Not there. I have a sinking feeling in my stomach. I dress for dinner, but my thoughts are distracted. Something is definitely wrong here. When I go down to meet Josef, I'll let the desk clerk know that it seems someone has been in my room, and that documents are missing. And get my room key changed.

London, England
Thursday

Roger stands gazing out his office window at the rain. He listens to the caller from Antwerp and nods. "Thanks. Keep watching. Call anytime."

He hangs up, takes a deep breath, and dials New York.

"My guy has reported back, A.D. I definitely think we have a problem." It is raining harder now, creating a steady background noise on the window. "No, I don't think she has learned much that could damage us, but any questions raised could be at least a nuisance and could possibly cause delays." His frown deepens. "I understand what you're saying. Yes, I'll keep you posted."

The call ends abruptly. No pleasant chatter. No talk about the weather or colleagues, or art. He turns to sit at his desk, eyes closed, the frown still on his face. He rubs his temples to relieve the headache.

CHAPTER 13
1587
Antwerp, Belgium

Willem penned a hasty note to Alexander. "The last two paintings have been shipped. I am hoping to keep the tavern open, but it has become difficult, as the English blockade of the port is causing grain shipments to be greatly reduced, and it is difficult to purchase enough for bread. It is only one of the problems, the greatest being that the merchants and artists who have supported the tavern have generally left for Amsterdam, many of them being Protestants, and many others simply not being able to make a living. We will manage, though many are suffering. Those items which are yet here have been secured, should I need to leave quickly. May you be blessed in your endeavors to help those you love."

It had been difficult to smuggle the paintings out around the blockade, and he was relieved that this was over. Those still here, having served their immediate purpose, must wait until the situation was less hazardous for their transport. The hiding place was far from ideal, but he was anticipating the need to keep them would be only temporary.

1591
Burnley, England

John's incarceration in Broughton had been unexpectedly short. He sat quietly by the pond, gazing at the rolling hills, thick with a carpet of emerald green grass. Fewer sheep were grazing there than in years past, but still enough to support their wool exports. His favorite horse, Redwine, grazed near a fence. The beautiful sorrel was long past his ability to carry him around the estates. For years he had balked at the fences in steeplechase.

"Ah well, never you mind, old boy. I am past being able to ride that hard as well," he murmured. He was glad that Redwine had not been sold with most of the other prized horses that once populated the stables. He had won every race that they had entered, and sired other champions to take his place in the steeplechase. The elegant horse looked up and twitched his ears, as though he could hear his master's thoughts.

John stood, stretched, and limped over to the fence to rub the horse's nose. "I am tired, old boy. I am not so old, but prison does not keep one young and healthy. But I should not complain. So many of my friends have not lived to complain of getting old."

He leaned against the fence as he stroked the horse's face and thought how blessed he was. *God has given me a wife who is lovely and indomitable. And children. Ah, those children. Mary has given me seven sons and seven daughters. They are a delight. It is a cheerful house.*

John did regret having sent Richard to Belgium for school. He feared that Richard was leaning toward Protestantism. They sometimes quarreled. Richard made it clear he felt his father and mother had been foolish to cling to the Catholic faith when all about were falling in line with Queen Elizabeth, or falling to her retribution.

John stared off into the bright blue sky, absent of clouds. "I would never challenge her right to rule, nor plot against her, but the queen sees treason everywhere, even where it is not. I understand Richard's attitude. He is young, and young men challenge many things."

"Life for all of us would be much easier, Redwine, if I renounced Rome. But what then of my soul? Is it not more valuable than my life, for what is my life without my soul?" John leaned against the horse. The big red nuzzled his ear.

1592
London, England

Dean Alexander Nowell paced his spacious office in St. Paul's Cathedral. He was furious. A messenger had come from a friend in Court, bearing a copy of a map. It was a revision of Lord Burghley's map of Lancashire, being reviewed by Queen Elizabeth. The map itself was not new. It may originally have been produced around 1570. Estates held by Catholics were marked with a cross. These landowners and their families were to be wiped out by fines and imprisonment. He saw immediately why his friend wanted him to see the map. Towneley Hall was still marked on this new map.

Alexander threw on his cloak and cap and hurriedly left St. Paul's. He and Burghley were not close friends, but they dealt with each other frequently, given their positions in the church and Court. Burghley had risen steadily in the Queen's service and was considered by many to be the most powerful man in England. Alexander held Burghley in little regard, as he swayed this way or that with each changing wind. You never knew where Burghley stood on any issue, as he would present arguments pro and con, attempting to discern who leaned toward his own views without revealing himself. But Queen Elizabeth listened to him above all others.

On the way, Alexander reminded himself to resist the temptation to confrontation. It would not benefit John and Mary for him to seem to be overly invested in the outcome of this conversation. It took an unnecessarily long time for Alexander to be admitted into Burghley's office. Burghley rose briefly as the Dean of St. Paul's approached his desk. Alexander bowed as befitted Burghley's status. Both knew the other's show of respect was insincere.

"Lord Burghley, I wish you a good day."

"And I you as well Dean Nowell. What business do you have with me today?" Burghley sat back into his well-padded chair. He was a large man, with a full gray beard and air of assurance, or arrogance, depending on your viewpoint. He motioned for Alexander to take a seat across from him.

"My Lord, I have recently been reminded of a map of Lancashire, drawn by you, that marks certain Catholic estates for bankruptcy and their owners for imprisonment. The map is not news to me, having been used to persecute recusants in Lancashire for many years. However, a new map is circulating, with notes written in your hand. Surely you are done with persecution of John Towneley. I had your assurances that his imprisonment in Manchester would be the last. Yet, to my surprise, he was once again arrested and sent to Broughton. He was but a short time there, so I thought that surely a mistake had been made."

"Oh, I think not, Dean."

"Then I am most surprised. The Queen is better served with Towneley managing the estates. He has paid faithfully in fines and other levys and continues to provide revenue from the estates into the Crown's coffers, and other pockets as well. You can find not one act of true sedition against him. His only fault has been in remaining a Catholic. I fully understand the concern of Her Majesty that any who refuse to accept our faith may be traitors. However, you well know that he is not. You have tried to ferret out any possible crime he or his family has committed and have been able to find none." Alexander barely contained his shock and anger.

Lord Burghley stared at Dean Nowell with the steady expression he was known for, revealing nothing of his feelings.

"Come, Burghley, you and I are old. Need we any longer play these games?"

Alexander was tempted to mention Burghley's own support of the Catholic Queen Mary, which he had managed to somehow turn to his benefit when Elizabeth took the throne. But he refrained. Best not to antagonize someone who is a formidable opponent.

Burghley spread his arms and shook his head. "Alexander, I am unwell. As you know, I recently suffered an episode from which I have not fully recovered. I find that I must allow others to assume some of the burdens I have borne. I can only say that I will continue to try to moderate the attitude of those who are more enthusiastic to prosecute the recusants in our realm." He stood once more. The interview was over.

Alexander returned to St. Paul's, little satisfied with Burghley's answer.

Chapter 14
Antwerp, Belgium
Thursday

Josef and his wife, Frida, pick me up at 5:45, as expected. Unlike Latin countries I have visited, where 5:45 may mean 6:45 or later, Belgium seems to run on real time. I had come down a bit early to inform the desk of my room being disturbed and get a new key card. I recognize Josef's blue BMW swinging into the hotel drive and meet them at the curb. Josef, being the perfect gentleman, as usual, comes around the car to open the door for me. As he shuts the door, Frida turns to introduce herself. Frida is one of those people that everyone instantly likes. Her smile fills the lightly freckled face and creates smile lines around her blue eyes. Her light red hair is cropped short. She wears aquamarine studs in her ear lobes, perfectly accenting her eyes.

"Hi, Addie. Josef has told me so much about you and the research you are doing. I can't wait to hear more. You certainly found the right person to help. Josef is an expert both on art and on Antwerp." She smiles at her husband, who returns the smile. "I am delighted that you had time for dinner with us. I hope you like the restaurant we chose. It is by the waterfront and specializes in fresh seafood."

"That sounds wonderful. Frida, your English has such a slight accent. Are you originally from Belgium?"

“Yes, I am Belgian, but my father was a diplomat, and we were frequently stationed in the United Kingdom, and even spent a few years in New York. I probably have English, Scottish, Irish and east-coast US influences in my speech. It's a miracle anyone can understand me,” she says with a laugh. Her laugh fits her perfectly. It is bright and light and makes me want to laugh too.

Our trip to Dock's Cafe is short, just around the corner from City Hall. The exterior is distinctive, and the interior more so. The light, polished woods are carved in waves and swirls, which makes me think of the river and ocean and ships. The hostess leads us up a blue-green staircase, through a circular balcony area with an impressive fresh oyster bar, to a table by the window. It is almost dark, and the lights are coming on in the cargo ships tied up at the docks across the street.

Josef suggests a bottle of white wine and a platter of oysters on the half-shell and crab, which both Frida and I agree sounds perfect. I'm clueless about many of the dishes on the menu, but Josef and Frida are great at translating and making suggestions. When the waitress returns with the wine and iced platter piled with oysters and crab, Frida picks up her wine glass and makes a toast to new friends.

“Josef says that you are looking for a person who lived in Antwerp in the mid to late 1500s. How has your research progressed?”

“I'm really excited,” I reply. “Today I found a reference to the person I'm looking for. It appears that he owned a tavern. Yesterday, Josef also found him listed in a Catholic church record as the father of an infant who was baptized. So, it looks like Willem Broecher was a tavern owner and a Catholic.

I'm not sure how that all fits with art purchases made by the Towneleys. I haven't been able to find anything that indicates he was an artist."

"Was there any indication of where his tavern was?" Frida asks.

"Addie, I don't think I told you, but Frida is an expert on ancient architecture and as well is an expert on the street system of Antwerp. Her job with the city is Director of the historical research and preservation department. I wanted you to meet her not only because I thought you would get on, but I also think she may be helpful in your research." Josef is steadily downing raw oysters, creating an impressive stack of empty shells.

I crack a crab leg and nod. "Actually, I did find out where the tavern was. Remarkably it's still a tavern. You may easily guess which one, Frida."

"Only one place fits that time frame. It must be the Quentin Matsijs. Am I right?"

"Exactly. I stopped by there for lunch. The waitress says it isn't much changed from when it was first opened, as far as they know. It really takes you back to the 1500s. I'm going back to the archives tomorrow. Gretel said that she would see if there are any documents from the tavern or Willem Broecher, like expense registers or letters. Who knows, I've been lucky so far, maybe we'll find that elusive link to the Towneleys."

The three of us have a lively discussion about art, architecture, and commerce in 1500s Antwerp. Dessert and coffee are leisurely and pleasant. I could not have had more interesting dinner partners.

Frida leans back in her chair, sipping her coffee. "Addie, I know this Old Town area well. Every business, every restaurant, every street, almost every brick. It's very interesting, and I seem to learn something new about our history every day. There are certainly things that a casual visitor might not find. Has anyone mentioned the underground Antwerp?"

"I've seen a brochure in the hotel but haven't taken the time to find out about it."

"Well," Frida continues, "it is called the Ruien. It's a network of canals that date from the 1200s. Generally, they were used for defense and moving goods around town and to and from the port. Eventually, the canals became polluted from the disposal of all types of waste, and in the late 1500s there was a push to cover the canals to control odor and disease. The sewers now run through pipes, but the canals still exist beneath the streets. There are public tours, but I'd be happy to give you a behind-the-scenes tour if you would like."

"What fun! I would love that. Thank you for the offer. When would you be available?" I'm remembering the pictures on the brochure at the hotel. Old stone and brick tunnels with arches and designs, with low water still running through them.

"How about Saturday? I'm free all day. The public tour takes about four hours, but depending on your interest, you and I can make it shorter or longer. I have city credentials that allow me to be in the Ruien, so we don't need to take a scheduled tour."

"Perfect. I'll work in the archive all day tomorrow, which will leave me plenty of time on Saturday." We agree on a time for Frida to pick me up, as Josef needs to be at the museum that day.

After our most excellent dinner, my new friends drop me off at the hotel. In my room I try a call to Jeanette again.

"Hi there, you seductress," she laughs. "Got your message about being in Antwerp. What's with that?"

It's always a joy to hear Jeanette's voice. I realize I've missed hearing that slow Texas drawl. I imagine her leaning back in her swivel chair behind her always chaotic desk at the University.

"Well, number one, no seduction, though I admit to some disappointment in that area. Edmund had to go out of town, and I decided to head to Antwerp to do research on some transactions done by my family in the 1500s. And things have actually gotten a bit strange." I spend the next half hour catching Jeanette up on my exploits.

New York, USA
Thursday

The Saudi sits at his desk in a residential tower overlooking New York Harbor. He looks out at the tourist boats circling the Statue of Liberty, small from this height, like toys. He is not really focusing on the sight, so familiar to him. He holds a phone in his right hand, his left taps the dark mahogany desk.

"No, Katia. I need for you to go now. This cannot wait until next week." He pauses to listen to his contact in Europe. Their conversation is in English, as neither spoke the primary language of the other. His voice rises, and he speaks slowly, barely containing his growing anger.

"You must understand. The timing is now critical. Nothing must interfere. It is your job to make sure there are no problems from Antwerp. Do I make myself clear?" He listens with growing irritation to the former Czech intelligence officer.

"With you it is always about money. Of course. But you must be in Antwerp no later than tomorrow. That fool the Brit sent is not capable of handling even this simple job."

New York
Friday

Edmund called a cab for his 6:30 AM meeting with a Sotheby's Auction representative. They were long-time friends, both early birds, and often met for breakfast when he was in town. Lewis is American. He is young-faced and favors blazers and khakis without a tie. He is seated by the window, an assortment of pastries and carafe of coffee at hand. He stands and waves. Edmund weaves his way through the other diners to their table. Lewis is full of questions about his trip and upcoming exhibits. Lewis had been instrumental in locating some important pieces for the Egypt exhibit, and negotiations were still pending on several more. They discuss potential purchases and loans, and provenance issues for some time.

"I have a question, Lewis." Edmund looks up from the agreement he was reviewing for purchase of an ancient vase. "It is something the Saudi we both deal with said last night. I know I can trust you, but please, this must stay between the two of us." Lewis nodded. He had sometimes dealt with the Saudi and trusted him no more than Edmund did. "Have you heard any rumors about a big deal between the British Museum and a wealthy collector?"

"Maybe." Lewis pauses. "Nothing firm, but about a month ago the Saudi called, supposedly on behalf of a collector who wanted to add to his collection of medieval art. Wanted to know if we had access to any potential sellers. We didn't have any, and I suggested that he contact the British Museum, Roger Jimeson, since he's curator for that period and might know if anything was on the market. The Saudi was vague about who the collector was and whether there was anything specific he was looking for. What are you thinking?"

"Oh, nothing really. It's just that I usually hear if the Museum is anticipating any changes in the collections. As you know, we do not put any works up for sale. The exception might be assisting in the sale of works on loan to us. But if negotiations are sensitive, I might not be in the loop. With the Saudi involved I'm a bit concerned. His dealings are not always straight forward."

"Right. Well, I'll let you know if I hear anything more. Got to get moving. We have a big auction later this week, and we're still adding things to the catalog. Good to see you, as always." At the street they say goodbye, and hail cabs heading in opposite directions.

Edmund spends the morning in the Museum District, much of it talking with the Met's antiquities curator about the Egypt exhibition. Plans were being discussed to display it at the Met in a couple of years, and the details of such a major undertaking were tedious. He also discreetly visits the office of the curator of the Met's medieval collection, one of the premier collections in the world. Interestingly, she had heard the same vague rumors of a very large sale of British Museum works.

By mid-morning Edmund is pretty sure he knows what is going on. He places a call to a close colleague at the British Museum.

"Andrew, hey friend, I'm in New York, and keep hearing rumors that we are negotiating a big sale of medieval art. What do you hear?"

"Well, I can confirm that there is something being negotiated, I just don't know what exactly. It is being kept under wraps, but I'm hearing the same rumors. I've heard Roger's name mentioned a couple of times in connection with a big sale. When are you heading home?"

"Probably not for a few days. Still have some business here to finish up. Let me know if you learn anything about that, please. See you next week." They hang up, and Edmund places a call, using an agreed-upon assumed name, to the Director of the British Museum.

"The plans for the Egyptian exhibition and the purchases are coming along well. Your instincts on the other matter seem to be right on. Everything may be just as presented to you, but I'm concerned that the players are not being transparent. I think I know why. With your permission, I want to spend a few days more on this." He flips through his notes while the director gives him instructions.

When the call ends, he brings up the list of the paintings Addie had shown him, which he had rather furtively taken a photo of. He looks at his watch and decides it is too early to call Addie if he wants her to be at the hotel. He spends a few more hours in the Met's archive room perusing items in their collection that are not generally on display and might come up for purchase. Always good to anticipate an offer if something of interest comes on the market.

Edmund stops into the cafe at the Met, and spends some time deciding how to handle the conversation with Addie. At three, New York time, he calls Addie's cell phone.

Addie answers the phone on the third ring. "Hey there, Edmund. How is your trip? I never got a chance to ask where you were going."

Edmund warms at her cheerful greeting. She had a voice like fine wine–mature and deep with bright top notes and a smooth finish. Made him think of something entirely different from musty Egyptian vases.

"I'm in New York. Sorry I didn't say so. It's certainly not a secret. I'm working on purchases for the Egypt exhibit. Boring trip, but we are going to purchase an interesting vase. Just thought I would see how your research is coming."

"I'm so excited! Thank you for introducing me to Josef Bruding. I took your suggestion to stay at the Hilton. You were right on again. Also about the train. Amazingly, Josef helped me find the Antwerp contact that was mentioned in the Towneley ledger. He was a tavern owner. Catholic. It's still a mystery why he would be selling art to them. Oh, and the tavern is still here, and still a tavern. Imagine that. Josef's wife is taking me to tour the underground tunnels on Saturday."

Edmund notes that she barely took a breath. Her excitement is contagious and lifts his mood somewhat.

"Did you manage to find out anything about the paintings on your list?" Edmund is casual in his question.

"Nope. But I'm going back to the archives tomorrow and Gretel, the assistant there, is going to help me try to find some documents related to

Willem Broecher, the tavern owner. I gotta tell ya', this is more fun than chasing down flu bugs, any day. And not nearly as risky."

"Sounds like things are going well on all fronts there. Glad to hear it. Any issues, problems, questions, anything I can help with?" Surely there was no need to alarm her. "Seems like everything is fine."

There is a slight pause before she responds. "Well, mostly. A couple of strange things have happened, though. I could swear that someone searched my suitcase when I left it in the check room at the Museum. And some notes I left on the desk in my room here were gone when I came back one afternoon. I'm pretty sure someone has been following me. I keep seeing a man with blond hair, light coloring, and designer glasses. Of course that could just be coincidence but it's a bit weird, right? Why would anyone be interested in what I'm doing?"

Edmund's hands turn cold and his stomach knots. Everything is not fine. He takes a deep breath.

"Addie, I confess, I'm worried. Something is going on. I'm hearing rumors of a big art deal, and like I said at the Museum, if the provenance of the pieces is in question, it could put the negotiations off the track. Addie, your work could challenge the provenance. Someone is obviously worried about what you may find. Look, would you please be extra careful?"

"Really, Edmund? You think I could be in danger? I can't imagine that I'll find anything that will matter to anyone except myself, but there's no denying that strange things have been happening. Nothing awful has happened, and I don't feel like

I'm being physically threatened, just watched. But that's creepy itself. And having someone in my room, stealing my notes, is certainly alarming. Thanks for the heads-up. I'll be careful."

"Call me if anything at all unusual happens. And if you think you are in danger, call the police. Be safe. Lock the door if you haven't already."

"I always lock the door. Experienced world traveler, remember? I notified the hotel about the missing papers, and had my key card changed. I'll fix the door, so I'll know if anyone opens it when I'm out. Good night, Edmund. And don't worry. Really, I'm fine and having a great time."

CHAPTER 15
Antwerp, Belgium
Saturday

Frida picks me up for the trip of a few blocks to the entrance of the Ruien, just behind City Hall. It is just past nine, and the Ruien, the underground canal system, does not open to the public until ten. Her staff pass opens a door near the public entrance.

"I notified the Ruien office that I would be coming in early and have a guest with me. The canals can be a bit treacherous, so the office tracks anyone who is entering. I have unlimited access, but do have to get clearance to enter so that we don't interfere with any work crews."

We descend a short distance into an antechamber that contains disposable blue jumpsuits and rubber boots. We don the gear and pick up flashlights.

I hear running water. I was not expecting that. "Why do I hear running water if the sewers are now in pipes?"

"Oh, the canals are still fed from the river. At high tide or during storms they can flood severely. We check the tide tables and rain forecasts before taking tours in. The light rain we have today won't be a problem, and high tide is not until late afternoon. Right now it is going out, which is why you are hearing the water flow."

"Relieved to hear that," I reply as we walk to the arch marking the entry while she explains what we will see.

"This canal system dates from the 1200s. It was used for commerce and navigation, similar to Venice's canals. Homes and businesses had their own areas on the canals. Eventually Antwerp became crowded and the canals became polluted. They became a health hazard, perhaps contributing to an outbreak of a mysterious plague in 1678, referred to as the "Rapid Disease." Thousands died, though we are still not sure exactly what it was."

I stop for a few moments to let my eyes adjust to the dim interior. "That's so interesting, Frida. We studied the Antwerp outbreak in one of my epidemiology classes. We analyzed records from that time and developed a hypothesis on what the disease was. The consensus was that it was a particularly virulent form of typhoid, as typhoid was pretty common in that period, and could kill quickly."

We have been walking on a slightly raised concrete path, which deteriorates into a narrow, slippery, brick walk. My foot slips, and Frieda turns quickly to prevent a fall. "Oh man! That water looks none too inviting. I'll be more careful."

Frieda laughs. "I really don't suggest taking a dip. It would not be refreshing. You may be right about the cause of the disease, but no one could explain why it struck only in Antwerp and did not spread to other communities, or why it disappeared as quickly as it came. Antwerp was such a hub for commerce you would think that it would even spread to other countries, but there are no records of that happening."

"We could possibly do a DNA analysis of grave sites if they could be found, but I understand that the bodies were generally cremated to prevent additional infections. So, still a mystery, right?"

Frida nods in agreement. "It is still a mystery, and hopefully we will never have occasion to see it again. The canals were eventually enclosed."

"That was a reasonable solution," I stop to pull my boot out of about an inch of slime. "Fortunately, we have the technology now to understand where a disease originates and pretty good tools to treat victims and prevent contagion. It's just incredibly difficult to stay ahead of viruses, like Ebola, which mutate. It came from a monkey. COVID 19 jumped from a bat to a person. It's challenging to see what's coming at us next."

As we slog along the path, Frida points out arches in the stone walls that once led to various buildings, and bridges labeled with street names. "Each property owner was responsible for building the street over the adjacent canal. Some did a great job, some not. Some areas have needed extensive repair, and some are exactly as they were built centuries ago."

It is dank and slightly malodorous. Rats scurry away into the shadows. I imagine many more beyond the dim light. Being in their proximity doesn't really bother me, but I can't say I'm fond of them, either. We wade single-file through water sometimes a couple of inches deep. My boots are a bit too big, and often slip on the mossy bricks. They make a faint slurping sound when I take each step. Frida walks with confidence. Me, not so much.

"Did you find anything interesting at the archive yesterday?" Frida inquires.

I'd been so intent on Frida's tour narrative, and avoiding a swim, that I wasn't even thinking of the Towneley paintings research.

"I did. Gretel is a tremendous help. She found some boxes with records from the late 1600s written by Willem Broecher. It was a treasure trove as far as I'm concerned. There was a small register that documented payments to Corneille de Lyon, who was an artist."

"Oh really? Did you know that he was often in Antwerp at that time? He even maintained a residence here."

"I didn't know that. It makes a bit more sense that he may have known Willem Broecher."

I pause to listen to the water, which has been receding. It has now gone still. "Frida, is the tide turning?" I ask, with more than a bit of anxiety.

"I believe so, but you don't need to be concerned. The next high tide will not be for several hours. So, did you find anything else?"

I'm still concerned about having to swim out. Her answer didn't really mitigate my anxiety. I think for a moment and touch her back. She stops and turns around. I look at her intently before I reveal my findings. "There were also a number of entries in Willem's register for shipping expenses for art going to England. The fact that they were in the same register makes me think they must be related."

Her eyebrows arch in surprise. "Do the dates line up?"

"Well, the payments to Corneille de Lyon were dated over a five-year period, but the shipping expenses were over more than fifteen years. That seems to be the link that I was looking for between Willem Broecher and the Towneleys. But I saw no indication of what pieces of art were shipped, or where. I had the dates from the Towneley journals for their payments to Willem Broecher, but my notes have disappeared. I'm going to have to call the Archives in Preston to get another copy. I think the dates for their payments to Broecher are pretty close to those he made to de Lyon, though my memory might not be that accurate. Do you think I may be on the right track?"

"Quite possibly, though hard to tell unless there is some record of the artworks themselves." She looks surprised. "Do you suspect that the names were deliberately concealed?"

"It's a very confusing trail, but that seems pretty obvious. The other records I've seen from both the Towneleys and Broecher are quite detailed. I just can't think why it would be necessary. And it still doesn't explain the missing art, though I'm thinking there must be a connection."

We continue our slow slog, turning into a side tunnel that Frida says is not part of the regular tour. There are so many side canals that it has become a total maze for me.

Frida is quiet for a few minutes. She flips on lights as we progress. "Do you have a theory about those missing paintings?"

"I thought maybe they sold the paintings for John's bail, but I haven't seen any record of sales. They certainly paid some hefty fines. And there's the fact that the paintings are now displayed at museums in London. There's still something I'm not finding."

We halt at another side tunnel. The name "Moriaanstraat" is on the wall by the next bridge.

"This is the corner of De Quinten Matsijs. I thought you might be interested. Pretty much all Old Town streets are built over canals." Frida points out broad steps leading to an arch. "That doorway leads to the tavern. Most likely they would have gotten supplies delivered here."

"Is there a door in the restaurant that leads to the canal?" I wonder.

"There is, though I don't think it's used much. When Rachel and Stephen bought the tavern, it had been sealed up, probably in the late 1600s, as far as we can tell. At that point Antwerp shipping was in decline, as well as the population, and the canals were more of a problem than an asset for most of the property owners. Stephen wanted to be able to check on the structural integrity of the staircase and canal wall, so he had it unsealed."

The walls seem to close in on me. I can't wait to get out of this place. I suggest that we leave, trying not to reveal to Frida my sudden feeling of dread. As we backtrack to the main entrance, Frida cheerfully points out the location of other places of interest above ground, such as the Cathedral and City Hall.

A tour group is heading in as we are heading out. They are clad in the same blue jumpsuits and rubber boots. Frida greets the guide by name. I'm glad to be above ground again when we finally shed our damp and somewhat smelly gear. Frida checks out at the staff desk and we emerge, blinking at the light. The mist has stopped, but it is still overcast and chilly. We stop in at a nearby coffee shop to warm up.

"The Ruien is so unique. It would be interesting, though, if the canals could be put back into use. I expect that it would be a major undertaking."

"Definitely," Frida responds. "We're still looking for ways to use at least a portion of the canals. The problems are so complex that I doubt it will ever happen. We're still conducting archeological research in the Ruien. Every time a repair is made, we find some ancient artifact."

"I expect doing construction in Antwerp is like trying to build something new in London or Rome." The feeling of dread is receding. I'm enjoying the coffee, but conscious of the odor lingering on my clothes.

"Developers get frustrated at how slowly their construction moves along here because they have to report any finds and we have to be sure that the artifacts are preserved. Antwerp was likely first settled around 200 to 300 A.D., so there are plenty of pieces of history everywhere. Tedious work for everyone, but truly important." She laughs. "And my job security."

We chat for some time and order a light lunch. The sun is breaking out between the clouds when we are ready to leave. I'm going to take a shower as soon as I get back to the hotel. Maybe stop by for some lavender body mist.

"Thanks for the interesting morning, Frida. You are an absolutely marvelous tour guide. It was great to get a personal tour, and especially from someone who knows so much about the subject."

"You are welcome, of course. I enjoyed it also. Would you like me to drop you somewhere?"

"Thanks, but no. I think I'd like to just spend some time walking around Old Town. Maybe go back to Quentin Matsijs later." I walk with her to her car. We hug and do the European cheek-kiss thing.

"Call me or Josef anytime if you need help, Addie. It was fun getting to know you. Be sure to check in with us before you leave. I hope you find that missing link you are looking for." She hops in her Citroen, waves, and zips down the street.

I think I've exhausted the archive's information on Willem Broecher. Gretel has promised to call me if she finds anything else of interest. Seems I have an afternoon free to visit a couple of art museums. I pause on my walk toward De Quinten Matsijs to look up art museums on my smart phone. I'd like to find some works by Corneille de Lyon, as his name appeared in Willem's records. I find a couple of prospects and tuck the phone back into my purse. I look both directions and step off the curb to cross the street.

A motorcycle rounds the corner, accelerating quickly. I don't have time to respond. It skids as though trying to avoid me, but the skid on the damp pavement puts it right toward me. The back tire hits my leg, knocking me down. I land in a muddy puddle by the curb as the motorcycle races away. People nearby come running. A man helps me up, but I cannot put weight on my leg. Both my dignity and my leg are injured.

"I think it's OK," I say as I try again to stand on both legs. I'm wrong. I continue to lean on the man who has lifted me out of the puddle.

"Ah, American?" he asks. "You need to go to emergency, no?"

He speaks English. Yea!

"Yes, I think that's a good idea."

A small crowd is gathering. Someone must have called the police. I hear a siren, see a flashing light, and a small car that says "Politie" stops near me. My new friend tells the officer that I speak English. My head is swimming a bit, and I do not really get a good focus on my helper. Blonde, glasses, nice.

"Good afternoon, madam." The officer looks concerned. "I see you haf been injured. Please to tell me how. Please to come sit in car. I see you difficult to stand."

"Thanks. I do think I need to sit." My new friend helps me hobble over to the Politie car and gently eases me toward the seat. My butt is still wet, but this is a police car, after all. I'm sure it has seen worse. The officer asks my friend a few questions in Dutch and takes notes.

The officer asks me about the motorcycle. Did I see the driver?

"No, it happened too fast. The motorcycle was so quiet. It never even slowed down. A BMW maybe? Black. I just got an impression that the driver was wearing black pants and jacket and a helmet. And, well, I think it was a woman."

My helper turns to me and says, "You are in good hands. This officer will take care of you."

"Thank you. You are kind. I'll be fine."

I hold out my hand, which he shakes with a small bow and leaves me with the officer. My head is clearing a bit since I'm sitting. I look again at the man who helped me. Blonde, glasses, slender. My head is swimming a bit again, but not from pain. I recognize the man who is quickly disappearing down the street.

London, England
Saturday

Roger sits down in his desk chair, hard. "No. That is not possible. Just not possible," he says. The person on the other end of the phone call is adamant. His headache is coming back.

"I don't know. I just don't know. Keep watching. Any diversion from her search you can provide would be good. We only need to delay her another week, maybe less. Then everything will be done. But by diversion I do not mean harm. You might need to get closer to her to assure that. I'm worried about this accident. I'll make some calls. If you see the motorcycle driver again, let me know immediately."

He thinks for a few minutes and places another call.

"A.D., what the hell are you doing? I told you my agent can handle this. There is absolutely no need to jeopardize Dr. Simmond. At this point she has found nothing that will be a problem."

He listens.

"I disagree," he states emphatically. "That course will only raise suspicions. Things are going smoothly. No need for such alarm."

"Damn," he mutters, as the call is disconnected from the other end.

Antwerp, Belgium
Saturday

The ambulance the police officer called deposited me at the sparkling and well-equipped emergency center. Belgium is known for its high-quality health care. Less than an hour later my leg had been x-rayed, iced, then wrapped. I'm fitted with crutches. My leg is badly sprained and bruised, but thankfully, not broken. The doctor urges me to use the crutches for at least a week.

Well, my plans for the day have changed. I think about taking a cab back to the hotel but thought maybe Frida wouldn't mind coming for me. I dial her number and am relieved when she answers instead of the call going to voicemail.

"Hi, Frida. This is Addie. Sorry to be a bother, but I could use a bit of help." I explain what happened, and where I am.

"Oh dear! I'm so sorry about your accident. Luckily, I'm still in the area. It will take me only about fifteen minutes to get to you. I'll be right there."

What a blessing she is turning out to be. I guess the moral of this story is to always expect the unexpected. But being run over by a motorcycle was pretty far from my expectations.

She arrives in less than the promised fifteen minutes, almost running into the waiting room. I'm relieved to see her. There's something about being injured in a foreign country that makes you feel very isolated and vulnerable. It's good to see a familiar face. Even if I have known her for only a couple of days. The waiting room nurse insists on wheeling me out. Not that I really mind. They had given me a pill for pain, and I'm pretty relaxed. She helps me into the seat and puts the crutches in the back.

"To the hotel?" Frida asks.

"Yes, I think so. I think it would be best to put my leg up and just read. They gave me some pain pills, so I should be happy for the rest of the day."

At the hotel Frida insists on escorting me to my room. I appreciate that, as this is the first time I have been on crutches and I'm none too expert at it yet. We slowly make our way through the lobby, up the elevator and to my room. Frida finds a robe and pjs in my suitcase. I thump-thump to the bathroom to change. She leaves with the ice bucket and returns with it filled. After I'm all clean and relaxed, she settles me on the bed with a pillow under my leg. She fills the icepack the emergency room sent with me, putting it gently on my leg.

"That should help the pain. Call room service when you need anything and please, call me anytime. I'll check on you in the morning and I'll be happy to take you wherever you want to go. That is, if you feel like going anywhere tomorrow. Hope you do!"

"Me too. I was on my way to De Quinten Matsijs earlier. If you have time maybe we could have lunch there tomorrow? I wanted to look around now that I know about the canals. Right now, I'm pretty sure I'm going to sleep the rest of the day."

"I'd love to go with you to Matsijs. It will be fun. I can come for you around 11, unless you change your plans." She adjusts the curtains so the room is not so bright, then makes sure the crutches, a glass of water, the hotel phone, and my cell phone are all within easy reach. "The room key is on the desk. See you tomorrow."

I tuck a pillow under my injured leg and turn the TV on to an English channel. They are talking about British politics. Within minutes I am sound asleep.

Something wakes me. It's dark. The clock says 8 PM. Wow, I slept the afternoon away. I realize my cell phone is ringing. I roll toward the nightstand and my leg reminds me why I was sleeping. Oww. I reach for the phone.

"Hello?" I say, only slightly slurring the word.

"Addie, this is Edmund. Josef called me about your accident. Are you OK? He said a motorcycle hit you. What happened?"

"Uh, just a minute, Edmund."

I blink in the dim light. The TV is still on. I turn on the light on the bed table, reach for the remote, and turn the TV off. My leg throbs. The ice in the pack has melted. I should have refilled it and taken a pill a couple of hours ago, but then, I was asleep.

"Umm, am I OK? Mostly. My leg hurts like hell. I'm on crutches. That is if I can get up. My arms hurt. I think that's from the crutches. Oh god, I'm whining. I'll take another pain pill, and everything will be OK. The doc says no serious injury, just sprain and bruises. Oh, bless Frida. She put the pills and water right here by the bed." I pop a pill and wash it down with the water.

"Addie, you don't sound like everything is OK. Tell me what happened."

I'm beginning to wake up. Being more alert is not necessarily a good thing. My leg hurts more. "Well, I had just left Frida after a tour of the Ruien. You ever see the Ruien? It's a system of canals under the streets of Old Town Antwerp. Amazing. And kinda creepy. Anyway, I decided to walk over to this old cafe that I think has some significance in my ancestor's story, and a motorcycle turned a corner too fast, and I didn't see it and it didn't see me until almost too late and it slid, and the wheel hit my leg, but it didn't fall, and the driver didn't stop, and I fell in a puddle." I'm not usually prone to run-on sentences. I take a breath.

"Did you get a look at the driver? The motorcycle? Any witnesses?" Edmund sounds concerned. Sweet.

"Nope. Some. A few."

"Again?" Edmund now sounds confused.

"I mean, I did not really see the driver because she was wearing a full helmet and full gear. Nothing showing. The bike was black, and I think maybe a

BMW because it was very quiet. Definitely not a Harley. You can hear those things coming for blocks, maybe miles. There were a few witnesses. As a matter of fact, the first person to help me was the man who I keep seeing. Think I mentioned him to you. He was very nice and helpful but just disappeared after the police arrived. So, are you still in New York?"

"Yes, I am. I've picked up a vase for the Egypt exhibit. An exceptionally nice piece. I should be going home tomorrow after I see to its shipping. It's too valuable to risk taking it on the plane. Sorry about the inquisition. I was worried about you. You said 'she'. It was a woman driving the cycle?"

"Yeah. I think most people would have stopped to be sure I was OK, especially a woman, right? But yes, I'm pretty sure it was a woman. I could be wrong, but I don't think so. Even wearing motorcycle gear the impression was of a female."

"The guy who helped you, was he there when you were hit?"

"I don't know. I hadn't seen him if he was, but he got to me quickly. If he had been following me, though, surely he wouldn't have jumped right in when I was hurt. There were others that could have helped."

"Addie, too many things are happening. Why don't you just come back to England and do some more research here, or maybe go back home until your leg heals? If you give this some time, maybe whatever is going on will get resolved."

"That's probably good advice, Edmund. I can't deny that I'm worried. Really though, it was probably just a simple accident and the motorcycle driver may have had reasons of her own not to stop. I appreciate your concern about me, but I still can't see how what I'm doing would cause anyone to want to hurt me. I think I'll stick around here for at least a few more days. Antwerp is so interesting and I'm learning lots. And I'm not going to be wandering the streets on crutches. Taxis for me the rest of the time, and Frida has offered to chauffeur."

"Well, Addie, you've traveled enough to know how to take care of yourself. I apologize if I seem to be implying that you can't. I'll be back in England in a few days. Let me know if I can help you in any way. And at the risk of sounding patronizing, please be careful."

"I will. I don't think I took your first warning seriously enough, but I do now. I'll be careful. Have a good trip back home. I'm not sure of my plans, but I hope that our paths cross again. I really have appreciated your help."

When we hang up I'm left with an uneasy feeling again. I tuck the crutches under my arm and hobble into the bathroom, the useless ice pack dangling from my hand. The upside of this is that I should have dramatically improved upper body strength in a couple of weeks. I dump the water from the ice pack and look at all sides of my leg in the mirror. Swollen and turning various tones of blue and green where the bandage is not covering it. There is also a bruise on my arm and a big one on my hip where I hit the ground. I splash my face and slowly make my way back to the chair. I refill the icepack with the last of the ice that Frida left. I call room service to bring up dinner and a full bucket of ice. When room service arrives thirty minutes later the pill and the icepack have reduced the pain level to no more than an eight out of ten. I eat in the chair with my leg propped up on the handy footstool.

I think Edmund's cautions are a bit overly dramatic, but before I conk out, I remember to double lock the door.

CHAPTER 16
1595
Burnley, England

The arrest this time was not at Towneley Hall. Several Catholic families had meet for a meal and prayer at a home in Burnley. Their offense had simply been in being together. The sheriff said that it was a meeting to plot against the Queen, and that a witness swore that the talk had been of raising a rebellious force and arming them. It was a lie, but in this time a lie paid well. The sheriff's men ransacked the home and claimed to find arms. Those had most certainly been planted by a spy in the employ of the Sheriff.

All four of the men were arrested and one of the women. The other three women were placed in their carriages and sent home, without even the opportunity to say goodbye to their husbands. Mary was terrified. There was but little left with which to appease their monarch. She had used the sixth painting, the last, for bail two arrests ago. Only a minimal fine was paid for his release from Broughton. The estate could not support a huge fine. Perhaps Queen Elizabeth had grown tired of this game when no more paintings were forthcoming.

When she arrived home, Mary sent the Hall staff to gather all of the children in the day room. As she sat beside the fireplace waiting for her children, she remembered vividly the first time Captain Farrow had come here, and again experienced the sense of helplessness and cold fear.

"My Dears," she started when the last of the fourteen children came into the room. As she looked at their worried faces, she had to take another moment to compose herself.

"Dearest children. Your father has again been imprisoned."

One of the girls began to sob, setting off a cacophony of wails from others as well. Only the four oldest of the fourteen children before her remained stoic. But even they struggled to not cry. She paused until the wails subsided into sniffles.

"We must be brave, my dear ones. There is much to be done here to keep the estates running. Each of you has your own job. We must work hard so that we can provide your father with good food and drink to ease his suffering while he is in prison. I am sorry to be the bearer of such news. I know that you will each do your part, as you do always." She pulled the youngest to her for a hug, as much to comfort herself as comfort the little girl.

"Now, go back to your studies and chores. I hope to have more information soon."

Mary asked the four oldest boys to stay as the others slowly left the room for their interrupted activities.

She continued when the younger children were out of earshot.

"Never has your father plotted against our most revered Queen Elizabeth, but that matters little. This time we do not know what the outcome will be. It may be that he will not be coming home again, ever. We must be prepared for the worst but hope for the best. As long as he lives there is hope that Her Majesty will relent and release him."

The boys, now in fact all young men, sat in stunned silence. It was Richard who spoke first.

"Mother, what do you hear from Uncle Alexander? I will ride to London immediately to plead with him to intervene. Perhaps he can arrange an audience with Queen Elizabeth so that I may place our case before her. John, Christopher, and Thomas are well able to carry out my responsibilities here until my return."

John had written his will long ago and revised it each time a child was born. Richard, now thirty and the eldest of the children, would inherit the estate. He was a fine young man, still following the Catholic faith although several of his siblings were openly challenging their parents to convert. His schooling in Belgium had prepared him for running the estate, and he had taken over many of his father's responsibilities in the past ten years. He had visited his uncle in London frequently and was familiar with the political intrigue of Queen Elizabeth's court. Although Alexander was not a favorite in Elizabeth's court, he was still respected. It was possible that they could receive permission to address Elizabeth on John's behalf.

"Richard, you are brave to so offer your services. It does give me some hope. We will prepare for you to leave within the next day. Time is of the essence." She rarely hugged this grown son, respecting his dignity, but did so now, and held him close, leaving a damp spot on his shoulder from her tears.

The five prisoners were first taken to Manchester for trial. Within only three days all were found guilty of sedition. Each was sent to a different prison. John was sent to Ely, some two hundred miles from Burnley, and well known as a prison commonly used for those who were to be executed.

Although Richard had already ridden out to London, Mary had little hope. She knew there was a very real possibility that she had seen the love of her life for the last time.

CHAPTER 17
New York, USA
Saturday

Edmund sits on the balcony at the British Museum's apartment. His call with the director is anything but casual. They are both on edge.

After discussing a few Egypt exhibit items Edmund says, "I've heard a name. Tell me if your are hearing the same one. Roger Jimeson."

The director takes a deep breath. "I was hoping it was not someone in the museum's employ, but it was looking likely. Yes, I have heard his name associated with the Saudi. That made me uncomfortable."

"Yeah, me too. I'm not sure if it is coincidence or not, but remember the American I mentioned who is researching some art? She had an accident yesterday. Hit and run by a motorcycle. No major injuries, but it sounds like she will be on crutches for awhile. The temperature seems to be going up around this transaction. I'm not sure what to do about that, but with the Saudi involved I'm concerned for her safety. I'm finished with my work here. The vase should be shipped later this week. If you don't mind, I'd like to make a stop in Antwerp before coming back to London."

"I don't mind. In fact, I think that may be a good idea. If you see our friend Josef Bruding, give him my regards."

"Definitely. It's early here. I can probably catch an overnight and get to Antwerp in the morning. I'll keep you informed."

"Do that, Edmund. With the name you provided I think I can better target my efforts here. Have a safe trip."

Edmund's next call is to his friend Lewis, at Sotheby's.

"Hi, Lewis. Just wanted to let you know that I'm catching a flight this afternoon. If you hear anything else about that Medieval art deal would you give me a call, please?"

"Well, I was hoping to see you at least one more time before you leave. Guess I'll just have to take a rain check. I'll call, for sure, if I hear anything else. Hope your flight's good. See you next time."

Edmund places a third call to another contact in New York, although it is unusual for him to be available before lunch. It takes several rings before there is an answer.

"Who is? Give a guy a break. Barely light outside."

"Yeah, well, I've already put in a full day, and catching a plane in a few hours. I need some straight information from you. We had better not be working at cross purposes. So talk to me."

"Oh, is you, Edmund, my good friend," the person on the other end of the line seems less grumpy than at first. "Cross purposes? What you mean? Same purposes, not cross. You got your vase? Need another?"

"Got my vase. Do not need another. What I do need is to know what is going on with that art deal. Someone has been talking. Too many people are involved, and there are rumors everywhere."

"Oh, no no no, my friend. Not to worry. Everything fine."

"Maybe. If I keep hearing rumors everything might not be fine, it might be off."

"I understand. No problem. I hear some rumors, too."

"Names."

"Maybe your friend Roger. Maybe not so friendly Arab friend. Maybe you got too many friends who not friends? You Edmund, me, we friends. Not work cross purpose."

"I hope not, I really do. I need for you to let me know if you hear of any efforts to interfere with the sale."

"Yes, of course. It is pleasure to work with you. I got to go. Need coffee."

Edmund takes a few minutes to pack, then calls a town car for the trip to the airport. He would catch some sleep on the trip to Belgium, but it might be restless. This trip to New York had raised lots of questions.

Antwerp, Belgium
Sunday

I'm sore in more places than I expected, but able to get around. The leg doesn't hurt as much, and I can do with a couple of Tylenols instead of the pain pills. I'm beginning to get into the swing of the crutches, literally. But my arms ache, so I decide on the cafe at the hotel for coffee and maybe some breakfast. I take the first table. The waitress appears instantly and offers sympathy and coffee. I gratefully accept both.

As my coffee appears so does that blond guy with the designer glasses. He starts toward another table, spots me, nods hello, and comes over.

"It seems our paths are crossing again. I am glad to see you are getting around. I was concerned that your leg might be seriously injured. Oh, so rude of me. May I introduce myself? I believe I neglected to do that when I helped you up. I'm Mikiel Asken. May I join you? Sorry, very forward of me, I know. If you are uncomfortable, I understand."

I hesitate a moment, but I'm grateful for his help, and have been wondering why I see him so much. Maybe a cup of coffee with him can resolve some of the questions I have about that.

"That would be fine. Please, do join me."

Mikiel pulls out a chair across from me. The waitress brings another cup of coffee and menu without needing to be asked.

"I have a flat on the square and start my day with coffee here most mornings. I am sorry that I had to leave so quickly yesterday. I had to be at the university to present a lecture and was running late. It seemed that you were being well cared for, or I would not have left you alone. How badly is your leg hurt? Do you have any other injuries?"

"I ache about everywhere, and even my pride is bruised. But nothing broken. Just sprains and bumps. I appreciated your help. I really was shaken up, and it was great to have someone there who knew just what to do. I never got a chance to thank you, so this is an unexpected opportunity to do so. Thank you for helping me. As I landed in a puddle, your slacks and shirt were probably in poor shape for your lecture. Sorry. So, tell me about the lecture you were going to."

"Oh, pretty boring stuff. I came to Antwerp a few days ago to give a seminar course at the University of Antwerp on new developments in biochemistry. The university provides me with a flat, as the course is four weeks long. I come here a couple of times a year. I enjoy Antwerp, and it is a short hop from Oxford. I am from a small village near here but moved to Oxford to teach. And you? Sounds as though you may be American. Tourist or business here?"

Mikiel seems quite nice. My suspicion that he has been following me has been slightly relieved. At least his explanation for our being in the same area seems plausible.

"American, yes, and tourist," I respond. "My hobby is medieval and Renaissance art. I'm checking out some of the wonderful paintings here in Antwerp."

"I have so little knowledge of art. A shame with so much around. Are there artists who you are especially interested in, or is it the general period itself?"

"I do like the period. So full of intrigue and innuendo and interesting characters. Such a time of change in Europe, all of which is reflected in the art. And the transition between the middle ages and the Renaissance is especially interesting. Jan Van Eyck is probably my favorite artist. That's why I'm in Antwerp. He worked in this area, and some of his paintings are exhibited here." So I lied a bit by omission. I'm still uneasy discussing the research I'm doing, what with my notes disappearing and Edmund's warnings.

The waitress stops by to refill our coffees, mine American style, Mikiel's espresso. We are steadily munching our way through a basket of delicious pastries that Mikiel ordered.

"I had no idea, though I have heard of him," he says, staring into his coffee as the steam rose in swirls. "I understand the cathedral has an excellent collection of art. I've walked through a couple of times just because it is so peaceful and lovely. I imagine you have seen the collection there?"

"I have. It has some beautiful Rubens works. And, as you said, is peaceful and lovely. Hard to imagine that it has had such a difficult history. It's truly a treasure for Antwerp. Since you're familiar with Antwerp, perhaps you could recommend some places that I shouldn't miss."

"When it comes to art, I am afraid that I will not be of much help to you. I know that there are some excellent art museums here, though I expect that you know more about them than I do. Have you been to any of them yet?"

"I stopped in at the Mayer van den Bergh. Small collection, but excellent quality. I've only been here a few days, so haven't gotten to very many yet. And now there is the hurt leg, which is going to slow me down some."

Mikiel nods. "The university is closed on Sunday and I have very little preparation to do for the coming week. I would be more than happy to help with your explorations. I confess that I get a bit bored on these trips. My colleagues at the university all have their own lives and I seem to have plenty of free time. I mostly use the time to explore, so I know Antwerp rather well."

"Thank you for the offer, but I have a friend here who has offered to take me wherever I need to go." The basket of goodies has disappeared, replaced by a check, which Mikiel quickly picks up. I reach for my bag to get cash, but he puts his credit card with the check and waves for the waitress.

"Mikiel, please, I can't let you pay for me. I at least owe you breakfast for your help yesterday."

He smiles and says, "Perhaps we could have lunch today then?"

I shake my head no, though with a bit of reluctance. I rather enjoyed visiting with him over coffee and croissants. "I already have plans for the day, including lunch I'm afraid."

"Ah, too bad for me. I must be at the university tomorrow, but if you would meet me for coffee tomorrow morning I would be delighted. And I will even let you treat me. Would that be possible? You are not leaving Antwerp so soon, are you?"

"I think I will be in Antwerp for the week. I really don't want to travel until my leg heals a bit. Coffee same time, same place would be great. I need to head back to my room and put my leg up for a bit before my friend arrives. I'll see you tomorrow."

Mikiel rises quickly to help with my crutches and chair. "Eight again tomorrow is perfect. I do not need to be at university until eleven, and then have an afternoon lecture."

He walks me through the hotel lobby and to the elevators. He bows slightly when the elevator arrives and I crutch-hop inside.

"I look forward to tomorrow," he says and waves as the door closes.

I reload the ice pack with the now slushy ice and prop my leg up on the footrest. The Tylenol taken before breakfast has relieved most of the pain and left me a bit drowsy even with the several cups of coffee. I doze off. Again the ringing of my phone wakes me. Frida is calling to let me know she is on her way to pick me up for lunch at De Quinten Matsijs. I reach for my crutches and one falls over, bopping my injured leg. I let the stars clear before I pick it up and tuck both crutches under my arms. As I begin to leverage myself up, I realize that the Tylenol is wearing off. I put the crutches down, carefully, and read the pain pill container label. One every four hours. The heck with Tylenol. I take the stronger pill with a sip of the water left on the nightstand. My armpits feel like they are on fire and my arms tremble when I finally get up and slowly hop to the bathroom to comb my hair. Everything gets easier with practice, right? Hope so, because I'm seriously thinking that a wheelchair may be a better option. A power chair. Not one that I have to use my arms for. It is possible that my arms hurt worse than my leg. I look into the mirror and decide to stuff my hopelessly unruly hair into a barrette so I don't have to deal with it. The dark circles under my eyes are not covered by even three layers of makeup.

I slowly make my way to the elevator and prop myself up in the corner for the few seconds it takes to reach the lobby. Frida is waiting in the lobby, her car idling at the door.

"Addie, are you sure you want to go today? Forgive me for being impolite, but you look like you are in pain. We could have lunch tomorrow."

"No way. I have your afternoon booked today and you have work tomorrow. I just took a pill, so I'll be feeling much better in a bit. More than anything I think the issue is with my arms. I had no idea that crutches were so much work, or that my biceps were so neglected. Bit of a learning curve. So, let's get a move on!"

I smile, but Frida does not look convinced and hovers as I thump across the lobby to the car. I reach for the door handle, but realize it is going to be difficult to open the door, balance on the crutches, then sit down. Frida has anticipated this. She reaches around me, opens the door, takes my crutches, and gently helps me lower into the seat.

"How is your leg looking today?" she asks as she pulls out of the hotel portico.

I'm glad that I was wise enough to bring several pair of casual, loose-fitting pants. The black pair I opted for this morning are plenty roomy enough for the bandaged leg and fit loosely enough to feel OK on the bruised hip too. I added a long-sleeve blue blouse, hoping it would add a bit of color to my face, but it may be that it just accentuates the circles under my eyes.

"It's very colorful," I respond. "A wide variety of yellow, green, blue and black with a bit of red. Looks even worse than it feels, which is not great. The ice pack helped a lot last night and today. Thank you for setting that up for me. Oh, Edmund called last night and said to say hello from him. I'm so grateful that he suggested I call Josef. I don't know what I would have done without the two of you. Being injured in a country where you don't speak the language is really disorienting. Thank you again for rescuing me yesterday."

"I'm glad I was around to help. I'm just sorry that you were hurt while visiting our lovely city. Things like this happen so rarely here. Generally, drivers are quite considerate. I cannot even imagine someone taking off after causing an accident. So, to De Quinten Matsijs! I know the owners well. They are very informed about the history of the tavern. It must be difficult to preserve the original architecture and ambiance while making customers feel comfortable and welcome. I called ahead to be sure they would be there this afternoon. They are excited to meet you and are curious about your quest."

"That's wonderful, Frida. I had lunch there last week and loved it. I was heading back to look around when I collided with the motorcycle. Maybe they can help me put the pieces of this puzzle together."

"I expect we will learn some interesting things from them. They have already said we can have access to the entire property if we want to look around. Not all the owners of historical properties are as open to the municipal staff, but they have been great to work with. I think we will have fun this afternoon."

The little green Citroen zips through the few blocks to De Quinten Matsijs. Frida pulls up in front of the door and comes around to help me out of the car. I painfully hop to the door of the tavern, which she opens for me. The waitress who served me previously hurries over to help and Frida leaves to park around the corner.

"Oh dear. You have been injured. So sorry. Come to a close table so you do not walk so far. You have a fall?"

"Well, kind of. A motorcycle knocked me over and I hurt my leg. Not too bad, though. Nothing broken."

"Ah, good. I remember you came here last week. You are back with our friend Frida. She knows much about Antwerp."

"She certainly does. She took me to the Ruien yesterday. Interesting and creepy."

"Yes, I think you say 'spooky'. Ghosts and everything down there." She shows me to a comfy leather booth where I can put my leg up and tucks my crutches under the table.

"I will bring menus. A beer perhaps?"

"No beer today, unfortunately. Pain pills. I can barely walk on these crutches as it is. Can't imagine trying to use them after a pain pill and a beer, but at least the fall, which would be a certainty, would be less painful. Just a hot tea for me today, thanks." She laughs, greets Frida as she arrives at the table, and asks for her drink choice.

"A tea as well, Helene. And would you let Stephen and Rachel know that we are here, please?"

I once again absorb the atmosphere in the cafe. It's easy to imagine the spirits of patrons-past at the neighboring tables. I can almost smell the tallow torches, beer, and roasting meats, merging with the smell of damp wool capes drying on pegs near the fire. Rubens, with his distinctive goatee sits nearby. His studio assistant, Anthony van Dyke, is drawing a diagram on a napkin for Quentin Matsijs, for whom the cafe is now named. They are discussing the triptychs Rubens will be painting for the cathedral. Musicians are in a corner playing the lute and guitar. Spanish, French, and Flemish blend with English, spoken at a table in the back. There is laughter as well as serious conversation. The sensation of sitting with history lingers as Helene returns and takes our orders.

"Stephen, I am delighted to see you!" exclaims Frida. "Please join us. This is my friend Addie, who I mentioned."

An attractive man stands at the table, bows slightly to me and offers a handshake. "A pleasure, Doctor Simmond. It is our honor to be your hosts today." Stephen is very slender, but muscular. His dark blond hair brushes his neck, almost touching the black T-shirt he wears. The shirt is complemented by black slacks and a black apron.

Frida moves over to make room for Stephen. We are shortly joined by a youthful-looking woman, possibly of Asian descent, who pulls a chair to the end of the booth.

"Doctor Simmond, may I introduce my wife, Rachel. She is the inspiration for so much of what we serve here, and in fact for the cafe itself."

Stephen and Rachel are younger than I had imagined them to be. I think I must still be lingering in the sixteenth century. "Addie, please. What a wonderful place you have made here. So full of history, yet so twenty-first century comfortable. It must be a great challenge to maintain the original atmosphere and architecture with the needs of a busy, modern cafe. I admire what you've accomplished."

Rachel leans over to give a cheek kiss to Frida and one to me. "You are kind to say so. Stephen has worked with the city to assure that everything we do with the building is as authentic as possible. You are right that it is a bit of a challenge, as even painting a wall requires city approval. But we have come to love this place. So much of ourselves in it. And Frida has been so very helpful."

"It has been a wonderful opportunity for me to work with Stephen and Rachel. Having a business in an historic building such as this is full of bureaucratic requirements. Part of my job is to help owners muddle through the paperwork and preserve the history of the site. They must know every inch of this building as well as the original builder. Would one of you have time to give us a tour after lunch?"

"Of course," replies Rachel. "Sunday can be a bit busy, but the staff can take care of everything even without us. And we enjoy getting to show off the tavern. Addie, Frida said that you have a special interest in this building. What are you hoping to learn?"

"I'm interested in its original architecture and owner. There seems to be a link to some ancestors of mine in England, but I'm having trouble finding out what that link was. Both the original owner, Willem Broecher, and the Towneley family made mention of some art. Mary Towneley paid Broecher for art, but with no mention of which pieces. Broecher's journals included payments to Corneille de Lyon, a Dutch artist, but also without mention of which art works."

"I have heard of these people, except for Towneley, of course," Rachel says, as she takes a sip of her tea, "but why do you think they are of interest?"

"Well, the dates seem to coincide, which makes me think that the three people are closely connected. I'm beginning to think that Broecher may have been an intermediary in the sale of art by de Lyon to the Towneleys."

"I suppose that could be possible. Many artists frequented this cafe. It would not be unreasonable that the owner also served as a broker for his customers."

"Yes," I reply, "but does it seem strange to you that none of the art, perhaps as many as six or seven pieces, was named in either Broecher or Towneley records?"

"I would have to agree that it would be expected of Willem Broecher. I have seen a few of the oldest journals, and they are quite detailed.

"Exactly. It's also strange that the Towneley possessions do not seem to have included any works by Corneille de Lyon. So, you may see why I am intrigued."

Stephen nods. “How interesting. I rather doubt that we will provide much information for your search. Of course, the historical records are at the archive, and any objects that have been found here are at the Museum aan de Stroom. But we will gladly show you through the entire building and explain the renovation history.”

“Thank you. I would be so grateful,” I reply.

Our meal arrives and the conversation turns to the new menu items Rachel is considering, the recent excavations at the port that Frida is supervising, and my injury. Stephen relaxes with a beer from his tap, and Rachel sips a Perrier as Helene refills our teapots. We spend more than an hour enjoying the food and company as customers come and go.

When the food has disappeared, I stretch my leg and tentatively stand. Not too bad. “I think I'm ready for the grand tour if you are.”

“I think I must leave you in the care of Stephen,” Rachel says, and excuses herself to check on the kitchen.

“Addie, I would suggest that we start with the ground floor, as stairs may be difficult for you and there is no elevator,” Frida comments.

“That sounds like a good idea. I don't think I'm quite ready to tackle stairs. So, Stephen we'll follow you.”

The ground floor is comprised of the two dining rooms, the bar area, the kitchen, and a storage room with the freezer and refrigerators.

“The flooring is not original, of course, though most of it is at least one hundred years old. It would have started out as wood plank, which has likely been replaced many times. Being so near the river and the Ruien, the building can be quite damp, and wood deteriorates rather quickly. One of our major issues has been keeping down the humidity. The walls are the original stone. Some of the ceiling beams in the building are original. They have been replaced only when they are not serviceable."

Stephen leads us through the rooms, with a running commentary on what has been replaced, what renovated, and what is original. The building has a unique smell typical of very old places. The beams are dark with age and smoke. Undoubtedly, the ground under the wood floor is permeated with spilled beer and the odor of food cooking on the hearth. The walls are whitewashed over centuries of paint.

In the storeroom Stephen points out a door.

"That goes to the Ruien. It had not been used for several centuries. Now I use it when I check on the building's foundation occasionally. Before the Ruien was covered over, it is possible that deliveries were made to the tavern by the waterway, as it led into Old Town from the port. During high tide, access would have been easier by boat than by the street, which in many places would have been muddy and rutted."

"So, the door up here does open."

Stephen nods, "It does, though honestly we open it only rarely. The stairs are slippery and worn, and there is, of course, little light. And I am quite sure that it is a haven for our famous black and tan spiders. Hopefully not much else. The stairway has little use now and really nothing that makes it interesting."

"Is there still a door at the water level?" I ask. "Frida said that you have one but don't use it."

"Yes. It was bricked up when the Ruien became mostly a sewer, but we reopened it so we could inspect the canal side of the building," Stephen replies. "The stairwell is particularly well-constructed, so we have done little there except occasionally replace grout that is deteriorating. The tide and rain still make the water level vary dramatically, and most of the places have permanently sealed their Ruien-level entrances to prevent flooding and odors. Our door is well sealed to avoid leaks when the tide is especially high."

Our ground-floor tour concludes back at our table. Helene brings us coffee and pastries for dessert.

"I should get back to work," Stephen says as he finishes his coffee. "Rachel will be wondering if I escaped down the Ruien. Addie, you are welcome here. If you have questions or would like to see more of the building just stop in."

"Thank you so much for the wonderful tour. This has been a treat. I truly enjoyed learning more about the tavern, though I'm still mystified about how it fits into my family's history. I may indeed come back by before I leave, at least to say goodbye."

Frida slips on her coat and leaves to bring the car around. Stephen walks with me to the door, and Rachel pops out of the kitchen for a hug as Frida pulls up. I place the crutches firmly, careful not to slip on the pavement, which has a sheen from the light mist. Stephen puts a hand under my arm, just in case, as he opens the car door for me. They wave as Frida pulls away.

"Anywhere else you would like to go this afternoon?" Frida asks.

"I think the hotel would be best. I'm beginning to feel really tired and probably need to rest my arms and leg." My arms are tired, but not as painful as they were earlier. My leg is beginning to throb a bit. “I might go down for a late dinner, but don't intend to go out the rest of the day. “

“Hotel it is, then. Remember that most places are closed on Monday, so you may want to use tomorrow as an opportunity to rest.”

“I had not thought about that, but you're right. Would you do me a favor, though? If you have time tomorrow, would you do a bit of research for me on the use of the old canals for transportation and especially anything about the tavern's history that I may not have found.”

“Surely. I have a rather busy couple of days ahead, but not so busy that I can't do some quick research. I will check in with you tomorrow. Call if you need anything at all.” Frida stops at the hotel's portico and a porter opens the car door for me. I manage the distance to the elevator and down the hall to my room almost expertly.

London, England
Sunday

Roger answers his cell phone on the first ring. “Hello, Mikiel. What information do you have for me today?”

“Hello, Roger. I managed to meet Dr. Simmond this morning and shared breakfast with her. She seemed to accept my cover. Everything on the internet should check out if she does get suspicious. These short-term identities tend to be rather easy to support. She was picked up for lunch by Frida Bruding. They went to the Cafe De Quentin Matsijs. Stayed there almost three hours. She is back in the hotel now. She seems to be in a bit of pain but managing. I made a date with her for coffee in the morning. I expect that she will stay at the hotel the rest of the day, but I will keep watch to be sure."

"No more visits to art museums?"

"No, not at this point. Today seemed to just be lunch with a friend. Nothing to be alarmed about."

"Good to know, Mikiel. Anyone else following her?"

"I do not believe so. As she is a bit handicapped, she has someone at her side almost constantly, so it would be difficult for anyone to attempt to harm her. I did not see anyone suspicious."

"All right, then. Stay close. Let me know what you learn tomorrow."

CHAPTER 18
1595
Ely Prison, England

The ride to Ely was long and arduous. John felt the weather more keenly now that arthritis had begun to swell fingers and knees. Mercifully, he was transported in a carriage, though not of good quality, and with locks and bars. But at least it had a seat with a thin cushion. The horses were old, so travel was slow, and the bumps and ruts did not bounce the carriage too badly. When they stopped at an inn for the night, he and the other prisoner traveling with him were allowed to sit at table with the guards and were afforded decent food and ale. They slept in the carriage, which was usually pulled into a barn, more for security of the prisoners than for their comfort.

They approached Ely slowly, the carriage frequently slogging through water up to the horses' fetlocks. They soon had need to transfer from the carriage to a small boat, as Ely was on an island, the high point in the fens the area was known for. The rivers Witham, Welland, Nene, and Great Ouse formed freshwater marshes around the island and drained into the ocean just east of the area.

The prisoners were deposited at the Ely Porta. The building was relatively new, so not as vile as some of the other prisons John had seen. They bent to pass through the small door with a barred window. Ominously, a figure of a body dangling from a gallows was carved into the door. The room was small, with rushes on the floor. Three wooden benches served as cots. Only one other prisoner was there, though there may have been other such rooms. The surroundings enhanced John's suspicion that he would indeed not be going home this time.

He knelt beside one of the benches, head in his hands. “Father in heaven, give me comfort. If I am not to see the family I love and the green pastures of my beautiful home ever again, I pray that you will provide succor to my beloved Mary and our children. They are brave and strong, and I doubt not that they will serve you well. For myself I only ask that you keep the vision of the green pastures of both the Hall and heaven before me during my travail.”

As the sun set, a meager meal of bread, cheese and water was passed through the window to John and his cellmates. Long after the moon rose John fell into restless sleep, unsure of what tomorrow would bring.

London, England

Richard set out immediately for London to ask for the help of his uncle, Dean Nowell. He took only two armed men with him and the three most fleet and strong horses. They traveled hard and fast, stopping only when darkness made the roads too dangerous for travel. Normally, the trip from Burnley to London would take at least ten days. They arrived in London in seven.

Richard was exhausted and sore from the hard ride, but he immediately went to St. Paul's to find Alexander. He stopped briefly at the stables to hand over the tired horses, and order food and drink for his escort. He quickly changed into a fresh cloak and cap, dusted off his boots, and rushed to find Alexander.

Alexander was at a table in his office, reviewing requests from the caretakers for repairs to the cathedral. The beautiful, centuries-old Gothic building was primarily wooden. Since the spire was toppled by lightning several decades ago, the roof leaked during storms. Repairs were a constant necessity, and Queen Elizabeth showed little interest in using the wealth of the Crown for this purpose. A secretary knocked and announced Richard's arrival.

Alexander stood and, with an expression of surprise on his lean face, embraced Richard.

"My dear nephew. What brings you to London, and so short of breath? You have clearly hurried here." He turned to his secretary. "Jeremiah, bring wine and some refreshment for our beloved Richard. Richard, rest here with me and tell me what emergency brings you with such haste to my side."

Richard collapsed into the offered chair, but relaxation was impossible. He took a deep breath, closed his eyes for a moment to focus on his mission, and looked into Alexander's concerned eyes.

"Uncle Alexander, Father has again been arrested. We thought this persecution was over. He is aging and suffers from various maladies. He is no danger at all to Her Majesty, nor has he ever been."

Richard hit the table with his fist, more out of frustration than anger. "We are most troubled, as we heard that he is to be taken to Ely. We well know the reputation of that place and are fearful that he will now be executed. I come to beg you to intervene on his behalf. We do not know how much time may be left to him, and haste is imperative."

"I confess to surprise at this unexpected imprisonment." Alexander moved his chair closer to Richard, placing his hand reassuringly on his arm. "I was assured by Burghley that your father would be exempt from further persecution. I can only speculate that some overly zealous and overly ambitious sheriff has taken this action."

He paused for a moment to gather his thoughts. "I expect that Burghley is in his office. Though he has given over many of his responsibilities to his son, he still attends to the Queen's business daily. We will send a page ahead to let him know we are on our way so that he is assured to be there."

"Uncle, would it be possible to petition directly to Her Majesty? What if Burghley does not act quickly or even worse, if he cares not whether Father dies?"

Alexander shook his head. "I think, Richard, that requesting an audience with Queen Elizabeth could make matters worse, rather than better. She has become very suspicious of Catholic plots, and with much justification. However, Burghley and I have reconciled to some extent. Though he may in truth not care whether another Catholic is executed, he may be inclined to assure that my brother is protected. Best we rely upon him."

Richard's disappointment in this course of action was evident, but he had come to rely on his uncle's intuition and knowledge of the Court. The page was sent with a note requesting that Lord Burghley allow Dean Nowell the honor of an audience this afternoon.

Alexander had his personal bath prepared for Richard's use and sent a groom to bring his bag with fresh clothes from the stable. When Richard had washed and changed, they set out to meet with Cecil, Lord Burghley.

CHAPTER 19
Antwerp, Belgium
Sunday

After Frida dropped me off, I realized that I was more tired and sore than I thought. The doctor said that I could use heat on my leg starting today, so I decide on a long warm bath instead of the showers I have been taking in the separate stall. I unwrap the compression bandages on my leg and lower myself slowly into the soothing water. I close my eyes and try to concentrate on nothing other than the warmth and relaxing my tired muscles. The heat makes the bruises throb a bit, but it is not actually painful. I wiggle my injured foot and calf. Surprisingly, they don't hurt.

I soak until the water begins to cool. I hadn't really thought about how I would get out of the deep tub. Gymnastics was never really my sport. Maybe I can leverage myself up to sit on the edge. Not such an easy task to accomplish without putting weight on the injured leg. I swing first the good leg over the side, then gently do the same with the other leg. Thank goodness I had the forethought to stash a towel within easy reach. I dry off while still sitting precariously on the edge. The crutches lean in the corner by the tub. Tucking them under my now less-sore arms I swing slowly to the bedroom. Pjs, dinner brought to the room, sans wine, one more pain pill, and I fall asleep early.

Monday

The sun filtering through the curtains wakes me. I wrap my leg again and take a bit more time than usual to get dressed. Carrying things when on crutches is no easy task. By eight I'm dressed and head to the cafe for breakfast.

Mikiel is already seated by a window. He waves and comes over to walk with me to the table, greeting me with a "Good morning, Addie," and a very pleasant smile. "You seem to be handling those crutches quite well. I hope you are not in too much pain today."

I'm pleased he kept our appointment for breakfast. Or maybe it was a date. Not sure. In any case, it's nice to see a familiar face.

"Hey, Mikiel. I'm getting to be a pro with these crutches. Still sore, but not as bad as yesterday. You've ordered coffee already. Wonderful. I could use a bit of energy."

The menus are on the table along with the coffee and a pastry basket. I order scrambled eggs and a fresh fruit bowl, and Mikiel orders an omelet. He's wearing a beautifully tailored dark blue suit, which sets off his blue eyes. There is a leather binder on the table near him.

"Did you have a pleasant lunch yesterday?" he asks.

"I did. A friend picked me up. She works for the city and knows pretty much everything about Antwerp."

"That is so fortunate for you. Did you go somewhere interesting?"

"We went to De Quinten Matsijs. Do you know it?"

"I have heard of it. Have never been there. It is historic, if I remember correctly."

"So I understand," I reply between sips of coffee and bites of cheese danish.

"Does it have particular interest for you, old art or great architecture, or just a good place for lunch?"

For some reason a tiny red flag is waving in my head. I have to say, I'm a bit tired of that darned flag. I pay attention to it, though. Mikiel is carrying on a perfectly normal conversation. No need for paranoia, but maybe caution is a good idea.

"No art there that I am aware of. But it's the oldest tavern in Antwerp and is from the period I'm interested in. So yes, architecture, though it is rather more on the sturdy functional side than an example of great architecture."

"It must be difficult to maintain a building that old and historic. Is it in Old Town?"

"Just a few blocks away really. It's interesting, and the food's quite good too."

"It must be very frustrating to be on crutches when you want to be out exploring. Have you plans to visit more art museums?" Mikiel moves his coffee cup to the side as the waitress arrives with our breakfast order.

"I hope to visit several." I turn to conversation to why he is here. "Tell me about the class you're teaching."

"It is an invitation-only graduate seminar, so it does not appear in the catalog. The students must be quite advanced to participate. Only fifteen are accepted into the seminar. They choose a group research project, and each must produce a paper each week on their topic."

"I imagine it's very different teaching graduate students from undergrads. Do you find it to be more, or less, interesting?"

Mikiel thinks for a moment, finger to his mouth. "Hmm, good question. I think they are equally interesting but in different ways. With undergraduates the object is to pour in lots basic information, which may be new to many. It can be most enjoyable to see them develop an interest in, and mastery of, the subject. Graduates can be more of a challenge, as they must be taught to work with ideas and concepts rather than just information. They have a true interest in the subject and are often highly motivated. But I would have some trouble saying which I prefer to teach."

We spend time in a somewhat rambling conversation, discussing teaching challenges, a bit more about museums I'm interested in visiting, and how my leg is progressing. Mikiel looks at his watch as we are finishing the last of the meal. "I hope that I have not prevented you from getting on with your day. It has been most pleasant to visit with you. I'm afraid that now I must be on my way to the university."

I nod. "Of course. I enjoyed your company, too. And thank you again for your help on Saturday. I believe I will stay here and have a bit more coffee. I hope your day is enjoyable."

I extend my hand across the table as Mikiel pushes his chair back. We shake hands. He holds mine a bit longer than seems usual. He smiles and says, "You are most charming. Perhaps our paths will cross again while you are here. I hope your day is enjoyable as well."

I sit at the table and read the *USA Today* I brought down with me. An article on marriage and divorce rates makes me think of my own. Both marriage and divorce. I have really tried not to dwell on that subject, but it sometimes appears in my thoughts, unbidden. The thing that I admired most about him was his integrity. The thing that attracted me to him was seeing how he commanded a room whenever he entered. Well, that and he was tall, ripped, and oh so cute. It took several years to discover that the integrity was superficial. He lied easily. He not only commanded a room, he single-mindedly pursued what he wanted. That would be other women. Lots of women found him to be oh so cute. And he found them to be oh so cute too. Between my job and my ex, I'm pretty wary of men. I've dated, mind you. But generally, few guys last past date number two. And I've learned to never, ever, tell a man that you have a PhD.

I stretch my leg and wiggle my foot a bit. Not so sore today, but I think going back to the room and putting my leg up would be a good idea. Which is exactly what I do. I spend the afternoon on my laptop researching the Ruien, De Quinten Matsijs and Corneille de Lyon. I don't learn much more about the Ruien or De Quinten Matsijs, probably because I have been given the tour by the experts. I do learn a bit about Corneille de Lyon. Some of his works are on exhibit in Antwerp, and I make plans to see as many as possible.

I call Jeanette late in the evening, mid-afternoon her time.

“Hi there,” I start the conversation casually. “How are things in Texas?”

“Well, Texas is still Texas. I'm pretty sure it's more interesting in Antwerp. So, what's going on there? Any other toothless gentlemen offering to buy you dinner?”

I laugh. Jeanette can always be counted on to cheer me up, no matter what.

"Yes, as a matter of fact. I shared breakfast with a very attractive, blond professor. Seems to have all his teeth. So there."

"Tell me more. Details, please! How did you meet him? Where is he from? What does he teach? Is he really cute or more of a geek type?"

"Aren't you the nosey one? No big deal. I met him when he picked me up and called the ambulance when the motorcycle hit me. He's from Belgium, teaches biochem here and in England. He is a nice combination of cute and slightly geek."

"Wait. Back up to the motorcycle and ambulance part. What the heck?"

I spend the next half hour giving Jeanette an update on my activities of the past few days: Josef and Frida; the archives findings; the Ruien; De Quentin Matsijs. I include the several rather strange things that have happened. She echoes Edmund's concern. Not that I need any additional warnings at this point. I realize that I've stumbled into something that someone does not want me to be poking around in.

London, England
Monday

Roger is worried about his conversation with A.D. If A.D. is too aggressive he could raise suspicions. That could jeopardize their deal. He is expecting Mikiel's call when the phone rings.

"Hello, Mikiel. How have things in Antwerp been today?"

"Not so very busy. She has stayed at the hotel. We did have breakfast. You are quite right about her research being a possible problem. She is very interested in Corneille de Lyon for some reason, as well as the cafe Quentin Matsijs."

"None of the paintings we are negotiating are by Corneille de Lyon. They are all well before his time, and not at all his style. That is very curious. No sign of the motorcycle rider?"

"No, though I might not recognize her without the motorcycle and gear. Slender, blond. That's about it."

"Any hint that Dr. Simmond is suspicious of you?"

"She questioned me some about teaching. I think she found what I said to be plausible."

"Thank you for the report. Hopefully, she will be a bit out of commission until things here are resolved. Call me tomorrow evening."

"Yes, I will do that. Goodbye."

Antwerp, Belgium
Monday

Edmund arrived in Antwerp Sunday evening and checked into a boutique hotel near the Hilton. He rents a car and spends some time on Monday looking in the area around Old Town for a black motorcycle and a blond agent. He would recognize her on sight. It is not the first time she had been sent to interfere with a major deal, but he is unsure of why the Saudi thought Addie important enough to go to such lengths. He checks in with Josef. Sounds like Addie is going to take today off from her search.

Good. That would give him a bit more time to determine what is going on here.

CHAPTER 20
Antwerp, Belgium
Tuesday

I call a taxi to take me to the hospital for my follow-up appointment. The nurse who checks me seems pleased with my progress. The doctor agrees and fits me with a walking boot. He cautions me to continue to use the crutches for a few days. I'm cleared to put slight pressure on the leg and foot.

I celebrate by taking a taxi straight to De Quinten Matsijs. Rachel is outside, setting tables to take advantage of the pleasant weather.

"It is nice to see you walking better, Addie," she comments.

"Thanks. I'm cleared to hobble around a bit. And my leg doesn't hurt much today. Would it be OK if I sit here for awhile?"

"Certainly. Can I bring something to drink?" She pulls out a chair in a sunny spot for me.

"I'd love a hot tea. It's still a bit chill this morning, but too nice to be inside."

"I will bring it out." She starts to leave, then turns back to me. "Would you like to see rest of building?"

"I would love that, but I don't want to interfere with your time."

"Tuesday slow day. I have time to show you. If you like, relax and enjoy morning, I come for you after everything ready for customers." She finishes setting out the tables and chairs and seats a rather overly affectionate couple before going inside.

I people watch and sip tea until she comes back.

"Addie, there is no elevator in building. You can handle stairs?"

"I think so. The walking boot really helps, and I probably only need one crutch for support. I'm really not in any pain. I'll let you know if I reach my limit." I push back from the table as she hands me the crutches.

"OK. We start tour at top so you go up while leg is rested?"

"That would probably be a good idea, as up may be more challenging than down." I leave one crutch leaning against the wall at the bottom, using the stairway wall for extra support.

As we slowly ascend the stairs, Rachel provides a continuing commentary on the changes that have been made since the 1560s. The basic building is unchanged. The stairs remain narrow, but the treads have been replaced, probably many times. Of course, none of the flooring is original.

The third floor is devoted to the family home. The windows upstairs are new and energy efficient, made to look as though they are the originals. In the living spaces, the paint is in soothing contemporary colors. Intricately patterned rugs rest on distressed wood floors. I recognize the clean, simple lines of furnishings from the Swedish company, IKEA. A matter of practicality, what with IKEA being shipped in easily handled cartons, and the need to navigate two flights of narrow stairs.

Down the hallway, doors are open to three bright, cheerful bedrooms. The single bath is surprisingly opulent. A jetted tub, in a corner, looks so inviting, and lush towels are draped over a towel heater.

"You may notice, plumbing been updated, also electrical system. Not so comfortable when we move in. Renovations take time."

The second floor provides space for the tavern office and some storage. An interior wall has been opened to provide shelves. Original paintings in a unique style, accent the walls.

"Rachel, these paintings are marvelous. Who's the artist?"

She blushes slightly and bows her head. "I am honored you find them agreeable. I am the artist, though not so very good."

"You are, indeed. Are you showing anywhere?"

"Oh, no, Addie. I paint only for myself. Cafe keep me busy, so only few finished works. Of course, the children my first responsibility, and most of these painted before they arrive. I miss them. At university in France. Perhaps I paint now I have more time."

A small oil painting is propped on an easel tucked into a corner. It seems to be unfinished, done with broad strokes in shades of black and gray. The viewpoint is from the street, with the door open, framing the interior. Even in this impressionist style, it is obviously the tavern. But the interior walls are fewer. Crates are stacked along the wall behind the bar, and there is an arched doorway at the back. The only color is a subtle stroke of yellow on the arch. It looks old, but that could certainly be faux.

"Did you paint this, Rachel?"

"No. Gift from customer. Found in antiques shop in London. Remind her of Quentin Matsijs. We had it evaluated before framing. Is quite old, perhaps 1500s. Not unusual to find old paintings when family attic cleaned out. Painting popular hobby in Renaissance.

I stare at the painting a little harder. A small, almost imperceptible, *HG-WB* is inscribed on the exterior arch. "When it was evaluated, did they have any idea who the artist was?"

"No," Rachel replies. "Is unsigned, maybe unfinished, and not match style of known artist. Interesting, but little value."

"Do you think that far doorway is the one to the Ruien?" I inquire.

"Maybe. We stand at outside door and imagine tavern with no wall behind bar. It lines up."

"I thought all of the walls were original."

"Exterior walls, but most interior been replaced. Rotten wood or moved as needs change."

Back downstairs, she leads me to the courtyard. Vine-covered walls protect an ancient tree which casts dappled shade on the weathered flagstone. A small stage is nestled into a corner.

"When weather pleasant, music and readings are in courtyard. Sometimes musicians compose and play together. In past, many artists and musicians visit tavern, even Rubens. Antwerp trade and culture center, and tavern is in perfect spot, near port, cathedral, business center. Much religious and political turmoil, so maybe time when tavern close, or barely stay open. Miracle it survive so long."

I lean against the wall for a moment, and Rachel puts her hand on my shoulder. "Addie, you tired. Come sit. Have lunch."

She's right. My leg is beginning to ache. I'm happy to sit with her at one of the bistro tables in the courtyard. I prop my leg up on a chair, relax, and breathe in the scent of fragrant yellow blossoms on a vine that is still braving the cooler weather.

"You maybe like sandwiches? Or maybe something more?" she asks.

"Sandwiches sound about perfect. That would be wonderful. And a sparkling water for me." Rachel calls to a passing server, who stops to take our order.

"You like more information about anything, Addie?"

"I still don't understand how Willaim Broecher fits into the Towneley artworks. I'm curious about the passage to the Ruien. It rather seemed that the painting you were given emphasizes the Ruien doorway." Rachel nods, and we pause for a bit to concentrate on the recently arrived sandwiches.

"You want to go down there?" She says, with a look of concern.

"Would that be possible? Frida showed me the door on the Ruien side, and I would love to see it from the building side."

She frowns slightly. "We not go there much. Just few times to be sure building strong and walls holding up. Sometimes check bottom door not leak when river flood canals. If you want to go down, I have steps checked, and cobwebs swept after most lunch customers gone."

"That would be fantastic!" My voice reveals my excitement. "I'll be happy to rest here for awhile longer."

As Rachel goes to check on the kitchen, the image of the unfinished painting haunts me. Why would it turn up in London? It could have been painted there and never finished. It could have been a present to someone in London, but why would it have been unfinished? It looks like it was done in a rush. Perhaps someone was anxious to send it. And what are those crates? Supplies, maybe. Or are they closing up the tavern? It is almost certainly this tavern, with the *HG* drawn over the doorway. How many old taverns were named *Huize 't Gulick?*

Oh. Oh, oh, oh! Investigator mode smacks me on the head. Rushed painting. After all, they didn't have cellphones. Cryptic reference to the tavern, *HG*, which very few would understand. Initials over entranceway. *WB*, Willem Broecher? Crates. Paintings, maybe? The only swath of color over the Ruien doorway. A clue there? The puzzle is still missing pieces, but is coming together.

"Jason sweep stairway for us," Rachel says returning to the courtyard. "He say be careful. Steps damp and uneven."

I pick up one crutch and place a bit of pressure on the walking boot. The rest has had a positive result on the leg, and I'm ready to explore.

The door to the stairway from the storage room is rather new. It opens smoothly, with only a slight creak of the hinges. Stephen joins us, and turns on a switch at the top of the stairs. The light is dim, but enough to see our way down.

"It has been months since I came down here," Stephen comments. "I was planning to do an inspection soon, so this is the perfect opportunity."

"Rachel says most of the tavern's interior walls have been replaced. I imagine the Ruien stairway walls have too."

"No," Stephen replies. "They are the foundation for the building. They are constructed of stone. We have only needed to repair a bit of mortar here and there."

Investigator mode on alert. As I step over the threshold I stop. "This may sound really silly, but Stephen, would you mind tapping on the walls as we go down?"

"OK, Addie," Rachel replies. "But why?" She turns to look at me, understanding dawning on her face. "If Ruien walls are only ones not been replaced, you think painting in office is clue to something?"

"Well, the chance of that is really slim, but maybe."

Stephen looks a bit quizzical, but nods and pulls a small hammer from his pocket. "OK, Addie. Think this will work? Is every few stones enough? I'm not sure what we are doing."

"I'm not really sure either. A different sound, maybe? Areas that have different mortar?"

We slowly descend, placing each foot carefully on the slick and uneven stairs. The boot is a bit of a hindrance, as it's larger than my shoe, and thicker. It also doesn't allow me to bend my ankle. These are more uneven and more difficult for me than the steps leading to the upper floors. I go slowly and lean on the crutch for extra balance.

Stephen sweeps a flashlight along the top and bottom of the walls. "I am looking for cracks or loose stones, or signs that rodents have been in the passage," he explains. "We try to keep the stairs sealed well to avoid problems upstairs from moisture, shifting, or the creatures of the Ruien. We would not want spiders and rats to make themselves at home here. I use the hammer to test the grout, but it might be useful for a bit more than that, ja?"

With Stephen tap, tapping the walls, we make our way to the bottom of the stairs without incident or locating anything other than solid wall. "The tide is out now, and the water level in the Ruien is low. We can open the door, and maybe step out onto the landing," he says, taking a key from his pocket. He turns it in the lock, which releases with a clunk. He pushes the heavy door open with some effort.

He points to a lentil above the door as we follow him out. The carving is too faint for me to make out. “It reads Huize 't Gulick,” he says. Just above it is a metal plaque that reads “De Quinten Matsijs.” Brown Ruien water reflects the flashlight beam. It is chilly and damp, and rather uncomfortable without the overalls I wore a few days ago.

Stephen inspects the door and walls from the Ruien side, declaring them to be in fit condition for now. The flashlight continues to sweep the walls as we go back up, Stephen slightly behind, tapping on the stone. I'm climbing slowly – good leg, crutch, injured leg up a step, repeat. About halfway up I pause. As I step, the crutch catches on a rough, uneven place on the stair. It swings out from under my arm and hits the wall with a thud. Fortunately, I don't do the same. Rachel is only a step behind. Instantly her arms reach out to steady me.

“Do that again, Addie,” she says.

“What, be clumsy again? I might very well knock us both down to the bottom of the stairs!” I exclaim, a bit out of breath.

“No, I mean hit the wall with your crutch.” It seems a strange request, but I comply.

“Stephen,” she calls to him, a few steps behind, methodically tapping grout seams and solid rocks. “Come here, please.”

“Does Addie need an extra hand up?” he asks.

“No, is not that. Come listen.”

“Addie, hit wall again, in same place,” she says. I hit the wall with the crutch.

Their faces look surprised. Stephen starts wildly tapping on the stone.

“The sound is not same as other stones. You caught crutch on old piece of mortar,” she says. They speak excitedly in Dutch. I hear Frida's name mentioned.

"Rachel and I think your idea of these walls maybe not being entirely solid, could have something to it. If we had not been checking, we would not have even thought about the sound your crutch made. This old building is full of surprises, but this is the first time we have thought to check for a hollow spot down here. I think we must have Frida come over."

Stephen uses a red florescent marker to put a prominent X on the spot my crutch hit. We finish our climb, and he locks the door behind us. Rachel directs us to the side dining area, which is now free of customers, being between the lunch and supper crowds. Stephen dials a number on his cell phone.

"Good afternoon, Frida. This is Stephen. I am at the tavern with Rachel and your friend Addie. We have just had a rather remarkable thing happen." He pauses for Frida's comment. "No, Addie is fine, though I think we have made her rather tired. The remarkable thing is that I think Addie discovered a hollow space in the tavern's passageway to the Ruien." He puts the phone on speaker.

"That would be most unusual." Frida comments. "How large is it? Are you there now so I can get more detail?"

"I am unsure how large it is. We came straight up to call you. We would have called from there, but there is no service below the tavern."

"Well, this is exciting. I am just finishing up things at the office for the day. I could come over when I'm done, if that would be convenient. I will bring some equipment, if it is available, that would be able to tell if there is a hollow area and how large it is. Could be that there are just a few loose stones or a large chink behind them."

"Yes, do come as soon as you can, please. We are most anxious to know if there is something there. We will be waiting for you." The three of us sit at the table looking across at each other.

"I think I would like a beer. Anyone else?" he asks. Rachel and I both reply in the affirmative, though I suggest a small glass for me. He brings back three mugs and sets the smallest in front of me, foam spilling over the sides. I watch the bubbles expand, travel slowly down the mug and explode in a creamy puddle on the dark wood.

Stephen picks up his mug and holds it out. "To mysteries," he says, and we clink the mugs together in celebration. "To mysteries!"

We have plenty of time to finish our beer and the Belgian fries that Rachel brings out. Frida arrives, pulling a case on wheels. She parks it by the table.

"Now, tell me exactly what has been happening. How is it that you were in the passage to the Ruien? Addie, surely you are not up to that yet."

"Honestly, my leg is pounding. I guess it was a bit of a stretch to think I would be just fine. As a matter of fact, I wasn't any too surefooted on the way back up. But that's part of the reason we found that hollow-sounding spot. I slipped."

As we explain the afternoon's adventures in some detail to Frida, Josef arrives. "I called Josef, as we were going to meet for drinks and dinner this evening," Frida explains. "I thought he might be interested in Addie's adventures. So, shall we haul this equipment down the stairs?"

"I think we're all ready to know if we've discovered anything." I'm back on my feet. Well, on one foot, a walking boot and a crutch. "What's that thing you brought, Frida?"

"It is a light-use GPR, a ground-penetrating radar system. It is used for just such investigations as we will do here. If there is a void in the wall, it will show it, how large it is, and if there is anything in it, though it is a low power unit and will not be able to tell us specifically what is there. Josef, would you help in getting it down the stairs? It is a bit heavy."

Stephen and Rachel lead our small procession, Josef and Frida next, with the GPR unit. I slowly thunk thunk down last, being more careful of my footing this time. I'm visualizing a slow topple down the stairs, taking down each of my companions like dominoes. A giggle escapes at the thought, and Frida turns with a quick questioning look. "Spider web," I say. "Tickled."

Frida stops when Stephen points out the mark he made. She sets up the unit on the step and turns it on.

"The equipment emits some electromagnetic energy, so put several steps between it and yourselves."

Stephen, Rachel, and Josef go down several steps. I go back up several. Frida moves a wand along the wall, starting at the bottom, moving it side to side and up as far as she can reach. She stares intently at the digital screen. After a few minutes she turns to me with an expression that could best be described as astonishment.

Edmund had seen Frida, then Josef, join Addie at De Quentin Matsijs. So far no sign of the Czech who had been sent to interfere. He sits under an awning outside a cafe down the street. He is not reading the book that is open before him. The hat and jacket protect from the cooler temperature, as the sun is going down, and hopefully from any recognition. Patrons, equally bundled, sit at a few other tables.

"Hello, Josef," he says, answering the buzzing phone. "You have been in there awhile. Anything interesting?"

"Amazingly, yes." Josef does not hide the excitement in his voice. "There is definitely a void in the wall of the stairwell to the Ruien. And there is something in the void. What we cannot yet tell."

"What does Frida say about that?"

"She thinks we need to take a look, of course, but it will require a permit. She thinks maybe she can expedite it. Rank has its privileges, you know. A crew would have to be available, though, so it could take up to several weeks."

"How much longer will you be at the tavern?"

"Oh, not much longer. I promised Frida an evening out, and Addie seems to be in a bit of pain. I should think that we will be packed up and gone within fifteen or twenty minutes. I will drop Addie off at the hotel while Frida takes the equipment back to the office."

"Good. I'll watch until you leave. Enjoy your evening out."

"I will. It is good to know you are watching."

Edmund waits for Josef to leave with Addie and Frida. He stretches and walks around the corner to his rental car. Probably no need to be so vigilant, as Addie will surely not leave the hotel the rest of the evening. But it might be a good idea to spend some time in the lobby, just to be sure.

Josef drops me off at the hotel. I'd never admit it, but I'm tired and my leg throbs. I take a long soaking bath, and nap for an hour. When I wake, my stomach is faintly growling. My hair needs attention, but I decide on a quick braid. It turns out rather frizzy, but serviceable. I tuck one crutch under my arm. My bicep twitches and almost audibly groans. I wish I had one of those little scooter things that you put the knee of your injured leg on and push yourself around. I must be out of genie wishes, as no scooter appears. Darn. I decide it is a two-crutch evening, and slowly make my way down to the lobby, heading for the restaurant.

I'm surprised to see Mikiel enter from the side street. He waves and comes over.

"Good evening, Addie." He extends his hand. "It is good to see you are able to use a boot. You must be progressing nicely. I was going to dine at the restaurant. Are you just coming down or have you already dined?"

"Actually, I was going to have dinner at the restaurant here too. The weather seems a bit cool for wandering around this evening."

"Just what I was thinking," he replies. "Would you join me? I so often dine alone and would enjoy your company. Or perhaps you are meeting someone?"

"I'm not meeting anyone, and I'd be happy to have your company."

Mikiel takes my arm. “Please, let me take this crutch and you can lean on me. Your arms must be so sore by now.”

Yep, they are rebelling at the misuse. I welcome the firm hand on my arm. He smells faintly of citrus and the blue eyes behind designer glasses have a depth I had not noticed before. His sweater feels amazingly soft against my skin. Cashmere certainly, in a shade of rose that highlights his eyes better than even the dark blue suit did. Following the hostess to our table by the fireplace is an enjoyable experience.

He pulls out my chair and leans the crutches against the wall. I'm acutely conscious of how little attention I paid to my appearance before coming down. Oh well, too late now. I'm glad I at least brushed my teeth.

“Would you care for a glass of wine or are you still on pain medication?” he asks. “They have a very nice red blend, produced locally, if you would care to try it. Also an excellent selection of whites if you prefer.”

“I was intending to order a glass of red with dinner. I haven't needed the pain meds today. Just an over-the-counter. One glass shouldn't be a problem. Since you know the wines here, please order for us.”

Mikiel orders a bottle of a red blend, as he suggested. When it has been poured and approved, we place dinner orders and sit back to enjoy the wine.

“How was your seminar today?” I ask.

“We are in a period that I quite enjoy,” he responds. “The students have started on their projects, and it is at this point that they really begin to learn. Did you go to a museum today?”

I'm relaxing more with every sip of the wine. It is a dark red color, smooth, with very little tannin. "I approve of your choice of wine, Mikiel," I say, taking in the aroma of oak and berries. "I didn't go to a museum today. I didn't feel up to walking around that much. Instead, I visited that historic tavern we talked about, De Quinten Matsijs."

"Indeed. Did you learn anything interesting? Some more about its history perhaps?"

That little red flag is back. I notice, but maybe it's overly cautious. Maybe it should be just a yellow flag. No, I understand why it's red. He seems a bit too interested. Our meetings seem to be a bit too coincidental. Edmund's warnings come to mind. Things are getting stranger by the minute.

"It's really a great old place. The owner showed me around upstairs. She told me as much of the history as she knew. Some of the history has, no doubt, been lost over the four centuries it's been in operation. The current owners have done quite a bit of restoration, which was likely difficult because it's so historic."

"Since it is in Old Town I wonder if it is on one of the canals. Many of the businesses in this area are."

"It is, which is how they got supplies in the past. Now, of course, supplies come by truck rather than by boat. The canal entrance isn't used."

"I have taken a tour of the Ruien. It is intriguing. So important to the development of Antwerp as a busy port city. I once saw a plan for development of the Ruien, but it just seemed improbable. Did you go down to the water level?" Mikiel leans toward me a bit. He seems to be genuinely interested.

"I did. The door to the canal is still useable, so we stepped out onto the dock platform. The steps down to the canal are rather slick, though, so it was challenging."

"I can imagine it would be. I suppose the steps are worn, but perhaps they have been restored?"

"I think they're original. They're stone. Uneven, but quite sound."

"Have they found anything of historical significance in the renovations there?" Mikiel picks up the wine bottle, reaches over and pours until my almost empty glass is full again.

"We think we discovered a void in the canal stairway wall." Oh my gosh. Did that just come out of my mouth? Somehow that warning flag, which had turned yellow as my wine glass emptied, seems to have disappeared entirely. It should have been waving frantically in front of my face! Mikiel's eyes widen, almost imperceptibly.

"It's probably nothing but a few loose stones, really. Nothing to get excited about," I stammer. I had not realized the wine and pleasant company had allowed my guard to go down. A potential historic find is not something to be discussed casually.

"Old buildings are so much fun. You can never tell what you might find, right? Of course, this building has been so completely renovated that I doubt there is anything at all left to find. I'm quite sure we only found a couple of stones that need more mortar." The warning flag is back up and I'm careful not to seem overly enthusiastic.

Mikiel leans back. "Of course, probably nothing to be found there. I expect that the local historic excavation policies would assure that it will take months to find out." He cocks his head, lost in thought for just a few seconds. He is quickly back in the conversation. "Are you planning a museum visit or two tomorrow?"

"If my leg is doing well, I think I might. After all, that's why I came to Antwerp. I heard that it's supposed to be rainy, so exploring museums might be a good way to spend the day."

The conversation is light as we finish dinner. We discuss places we've visited in Antwerp and England, as well as places we would like to see. By the time dessert and coffee are polished off, I'm full and totally relaxed. Mikiel again refuses my offer to split the check.

As we start to leave, I feel a little dizzy. I don't remember finishing off the bottle of wine, but it sits on the table, empty. That may account for the problem with balance, for sure. Noticing my slight wobble, Mikiel quickly supports me. It feels every bit as nice as it did on the way in. Maybe better. He tucks the crutches under my arms. He keeps a supportive hand on my back on the way to the elevator.

"Addie, please allow me to walk you to your room. You are tired, and I would not forgive myself if you had a fall," he says as the elevator doors open.

I'm thought I was going to decline. Somehow I find myself accepting his offer. "OK, Mikiel, thanks. I hate for you to feel that you need to take care of me, though I would appreciate the help."

The elevator doors quietly glide open at my floor. I have no problem making it to the door of the room with just a bit of assistance. The dizziness has dissipated, and my balance seems as sure as it can be with a crutch and walking boot. I fish the room key out of my pocket and open the door. Mikiel leans in to hold the door. He steps toward me as the door opens and puts his arm around my waist. The dizziness returns as he pulls me forward and kisses me.

"I should not have done that, Addie. Please accept my apology. But Addie, may I please have another kiss?"

No need to ask, I'm already leaning into him, close enough to whisper "Sure," into his lips. The second kiss is even better than the first. "Mikiel, I really need to go in now," I say, reluctantly. Even the wine and a couple of kisses from this attractive man cannot erase the pain from my leg.

"I could stay awhile if you would like." His hand is still on my back.

"Under other circumstances I might accept, but not tonight. Let's say goodnight here."

"All right. Goodnight, Addie." He kisses me again, with more heat. "I hope you have sweet dreams."

I'm pretty sure I'll have sweet dreams. It's likely he will figure prominently in them. I close the door behind him. I double lock it.

Mikiel finds a stool at the far end of the softly lit lobby bar. He dials his cell phone.

"Hi, Roger. I spent the evening with Dr. Simmond. She was fitted with a walking boot this morning and is getting around rather well. She spent the afternoon at De Quentin Matsijs. They may have found something there. She was evasive when I pressed her, so I think it could be significant. It may well have something to do with the art." He paused to listen. "No, no sign of the motorcycle rider. And yes, I am close enough to Dr. Simmond now that I may have opportunity to distract her from her research here. Or at least learn what she is finding. I expect she will tell me exactly what is going on very soon."

Edmund quickly ducks behind the newspaper he'd been pretending to read, watching as Addie leaves the restaurant with a man he does not recognize. As they enter the elevator he feels a pang of anxiety regarding her safety, and something else, jealousy. He is about to call her when the man comes back down, makes a call, and leaves the hotel. Addie would be safe in her room this evening. He could sleep tonight without worry.

CHAPTER 21
1596
Ely, England

My dearest Mary, I write to you with my love and devotion remembering well how indebted I am to you for your modest and kind nature. When first brought to Ely I was in great fear for my life. The quarters allotted to me are the barest possible sheltered from neither cold nor heat. Food is meted out with a spare measure. The smell is loathsome though not so terrible as Hull, that place of torture. It is well known that recusants who are to be executed are often brought to Ely. My cell much indicates that my life is considered as nothing. In the months here I have seen neither lawyer nor magistrate. My treatment is not unkind only tis with little thought or consideration for my comfort or well being. The lung disorder with which I was plagued during the incarceration at Broughton has returned. The coughing and poor diet are rendering me weak. I expected that I would be executed shortly after arrival. When one of my cellmates was taken to the gallows on Tuesday last I was resigned to my immediate death. As that has not yet occurred perhaps it is not so imminent. Mayhap you could send to me some clean clothing and funds for my care. I have heard that the jailers are amenable to bribes. Such funds could result in some better portions of food and attention to my cough.

Though I miss you sorely I most seriously advise that you do not attempt the journey to Ely. The road is arduous and long and would surely be perilous. The town is set within a noxious marsh which must be traversed by boat to reach its gates though I hear that the town itself is prosperous and pleasant. Moreover the children and estate are in need of your daily devoted care.

Hold each dear child in a tight embrace for me. Call each by name and tell each one that I love and miss him or her. They come to me at night in my dreams holding hands and smiling. Sometimes singing psalms and aires and dancing. Richard has of late appeared astride a fine horse watching over all. None can match you in ability to raise such a family. They are all remarkably responsible, happy and healthy in spite of the frequent absences of their unlucky father.

Know that you have my admiration for the strength you have shown in all things. Your management of the estate and Hall is without fault and is surely the reason that I am allowed to live. I feel you with me during every moment of these tedious days. I imagine you going about the routine business of your day. It is a great comfort to me to think of you in the kitchen or garden, sewing in the day room or kissing the children goodnight. It is even more a comfort to imagine you beside me, warm and safe in our bed.

I humbly take my leave and rest for now and remain truly your dutiful and loving husband John

Towneley Hall

To my loving and long suffering husband John. My beloved today I received your very welcome letter. We have been most anxious to hear of your condition. We all miss you terribly. I have dispatched with the messenger bearing this letter a number of items that may ease your lot. Clothing, food, potions for your cough, books, funds and gifts for the jailers are packed in numbered bags with my seal attached. There should arrive for you five bags. The messenger has orders to hand the bags personally to you once the jailers have inspected them. Well I know that not all items I send arrive but do let me know if any bags are missing. Even if not all are delivered into your hands I rest assured that any missing will provide for the jailers and may ease your plight thereby.

You indeed have ample cause to be proud of our sons. They make every effort to ease my burden on the estates in your absence often checking on the sheep and cattle and conversing with the managers and even fieldhands to resolve any issues which may be evolving. We continue to seek out local markets for our wool though as you noted when you were released last the number of sheep in our folds is less than in years past. Queen Elizabeth's restrictions on who may participate in foreign trade companies has hobbled our exports to Europe. Richard has just recently been investigating the possibility of trade with the Americas though it may be difficult for the estates to produce sufficient wool to make such a venture profitable. Our daughters remain my succor. They wait upon me with great care and at least one accompanies me wherever I go whether on the estates or in town.

We look for your next missive and soon return. You are in our prayers morning and night. May God give you comfort and may you continue to have fond dreams of us as we do of you Your devoted wife Mary.

CHAPTER 22
Antwerp, Belgium
Wednesday

Frida was at her desk early. She had completed the tedious forms necessary for excavation of historic buildings in Antwerp. When the director arrives, she is at his door, forms in hand.

"Evan, please approve this. It is only a small space that needs to be investigated. We will not need to remove more than a few stones. It will hardly take any time at all. Could we expedite this?"

"I don't see how, Frida. The approvals will take at least two weeks, even expedited. Then we have to schedule the crews for the demolition. Heaven forbid if you actually find anything of significance. Then the conservationists will have to be brought in. How do you see this happening so quickly?"

"This is a slow week for me. They are not ready for me at the port site. I can fit in a quick job if we can start right away. I will walk the forms through the approvals myself. That can be completed today. It is a simple excavation, with evidence that there may be something of historical significance behind the wall. Why wait? Besides, a storm is coming in, and is due to last at least two more days. The crews will not be able to work outside most of tomorrow in any case. We could use their time effectively on this project."

"Alright, if you can get all of the approvals today, I will authorize a crew for tomorrow afternoon. If you are sure that there is something there, you should also schedule another conservationist to work with you to secure whatever is found."

"Excellent. The area is quite small, so we will need three people at most to remove the stones. They can start tomorrow afternoon. I doubt that it will take more than a few hours. I'll keep you informed about our progress. Thank you so much for your help."

Evan signs the forms and Frida rushes off to get the numerous other signatures.

Frida calls with the great news that she can expedite the excavation. She says it will take all day to get the signatures and the actual excavation cannot start until tomorrow at the earliest. I have a free day to do whatever I want. My leg hardly hurts at all. I can almost put my full weight on the boot, but not quite. Guess I'll be using the crutches again today. Getting dressed isn't so much of a struggle as it has been the last few days. The improved mobility is a relief.

I open the curtains to an other-worldly view of the square shrouded in fog, the cathedral spire jutting up as though attached to nothing more than mist. The windows are covered by the mist, with small rivulets running down them. A raincoat is a definite must today. A warm sweater and scarf are a good idea, too.

Taking into consideration my gimpy leg and the dreary weather, I decide to visit some art museums. Unfortunately, the Royal Museum of Fine Arts is undergoing renovation, and will be closed for several years. The collections are largely in storage or scattered among other museums, even some outside of Antwerp. So, it's the Rockox House this morning, then the Rubens House, and back to the Mayer van den Burgh this afternoon. Maybe Josef will be there to share a cup of tea and give me more detail on their Jan van Eyck exhibit from the Royal Museum. So nice to know someone in the art world here.

I tuck my small folding umbrella into my shoulder bag, don the raincoat and head for the lobby. The doorman hails a taxi, which pulls under the portico. The blanket of fog muffles sound and makes the few people on the street look ghostly. Everyone is wearing raincoats and head coverings. Many shelter under umbrellas. The dampness clings to everything, especially my hair, which I'm sure is once again totally unruly. Antwerp's humidity is even worse than Houston's, which is the worst, to this point. The problem with Houston is that it is hot, hot, hot. At least the heat is not an issue in Antwerp this time of year.

From the cover of a doorway, she watches Addie come out of the hotel and hail a cab. With the raincoat and umbrella covering her, it is unlikely that Addie could recognize her. She signals for another taxi. “Please follow that cab.”

From the taxi she watches as Addie enters Rockox House. She pays the driver and walks to a coffeehouse across the street. Too damp to sit outside. That would risk recognition in any case. She takes a table by a window where she has a view of the Rockox House entry, orders a coffee, and settles in for what could be a long wait.

She wishes she could have slipped into the museum unnoticed, but that did not seem likely. She would have loved to know what Addie was there to see. Might have made her job easier. The fog had cleared, but it was now raining. Addie stays two hours and is under an umbrella as she steps into a taxi. Again, she follows.

From his rental car parked down the block, Edmund watches Addie as she goes into Rockox, then later comes out and gets into the cab. He notices the woman who hails a taxi from the cafe. He recognizes her immediately. His level of anxiety dramatically increases as he realizes the second taxi is following Addie.

I am lucky at Rockox. Being mid-week and rainy the visitors are few. The curator, an expert on Flemish art, is kind to take time to help me learn more about the Jan van Eyck and Corneille de Lyon paintings that are on exhibit. At each painting he shows me, in detail, how the artist used color, light, texture and composed his subjects. He describes where each artist lived and the primary patrons of his works. I leave knowing so much more about both artists, but even more confused about how Corneille de Lyon could have been involved with Willem Broecher, and especially with the Towneley family in England.

I stop for a quick lunch, then on to the Rubens House. Who doesn't love Rubens? I've always appreciated that he paints women as they really are. An extra roll around the waist, big thighs, even cellulite, though I doubt that the term was common during his time. Rather common in my time. Rubens lived in Antwerp, and he is clearly a community celebrity. “House” is an inaccurate term. It is a small Italian Renaissance palace. The home and studio are worth a day's study, not even considering the art. The collection of his works is amazing. My leg is beginning to ache, and I frequently pause to rest. I will not make it to the Mayer van den Bergh today. I spend the entire afternoon communing with Rubens.

My phone buzzes while I'm gazing at his early masterpiece *Adam and Eve*. Eve is portrayed as a young, lithe woman, much different from Ruben's later style. I snap back to the present immediately.

“I got the permit!” Frida exclaims, rather breathlessly. “We can start tomorrow, late afternoon. I was able to free up a crew since the weather is expected to be bad. I'll pick you up at 4:00.”

“Oh wow.” I'm glad I'm sitting already.

CHAPTER 23
1597
Ely, England

To my gentle and devoted Mary. A remarkable and most favorable thing has happened. I can scarce believe it. I have been moved from the Bishops Prison in Ely to imprisonment at the Bishops Palace, there also in Ely. It seems that an old friend and fellow recusant, Sir Thomas Tresham of Northamptonshire has intervened on my behalf to lessen the burden of this continual incarceration. Sir Thomas is also held here as a risk to our beloved Queen Elizabeth's crown. The bishop has decided that some few of us who are of the gentry may be deemed to be useful provided we have some skills of which he may be in need. Sir Thomas being of exceptional talent as both architect and artist has been working on the design of the gardens and new buildings at the palace and cathedral. He is now painting the most beautiful window surround for a gallery window at the Palace celebrating the Trinity and the Passion. Having lately heard of my arrest and poor plight and ill health here in Ely Sir Thomas deigned to place my case before the bishop saying much of my skill with horses. In his gracious mercy the bishop agreed to my transfer to the Palace. Being now here I am much amazed. I have been allotted a private chamber with an antechamber. Medical care has been most solicitous and my health is gradually improving.

The Bishop being of a generous nature has suggested that I might benefit by the attention of a personal servant and would be amenable should I have one brought from Towneley Hall. Although I am loathe to remove a man from family and service at the Hall if my old and dear servant Samuel can be spared and is of sufficient vigor mayhap he would be of a mind to come to me in Ely.

Should Samuel or another be sent I would dearly love to see your beloved face. It has been a year since our last parting and I miss you more than words in such a poor missive as this can convey. It is now going into the dry season here and the passage is not so difficult as when the rivers are running high. If the children and estate can spare you for a time and if you feel strong enough for the long trip the bishop has expressed his welcome and will arrange for suitable accommodations. Do bring the sturdiest carriage as the roads are not so well maintained and may prove to be rutted in places but all passable. A small group of armed guards is most advisable as well. I beseech you do not leave without them.

I also hope that you may bring the black foal now a yearling you wrote of last year the one from our prized carriage horse. I would gift it to the bishop and train it for his carriage team as one of his four is aging and soon will not be up to the task. Also a few bottles of good wine would most certainly be most appropriate for my benefactor Sir Thomas.

Do not delay over much as the weather is changeable and the road conditions would be poor if heavy rains came to the area. I dream nightly of your sweet face and of our wonderful children around you. Do come to me should it be at all possible. Thus do I commit you to the protection of the Almighty and bid you farewell for now your loving husband John

London, England

To the most honorable and loyal friend Willem and in much remembrance of my humble duty owed unto you I am much distressed to find that you must leave Antwerp even if it should be for a short period. It is good to know that you have a trusted friend who is managing the tavern until your return. I doubt not that you will be a true solace to your family in Amsterdam. We had hoped to be able to arrange shipment of the merchandise you are so kindly holding for us but understand that it must wait until a later time. I beseech the Almighty on my knees that you may enjoy safe passage and good health. Your assured friend and servant Alexander

To my dear and much esteemed cousin Mary my humble greetings. It was with thanks to a merciful God that I heard from you that John is now in comfort within Bishops Palace. It is my belief that Richards plea for the life of his beloved father had some effect upon Lord Burghley, and therefore upon Her Majesty. No doubt his improved station is also due to Sir Thomas Treshams very kind intervention. I count the bishop as a friend though not close and also did I send to him my hope that Johns treatment would be tempered with Christian mercy as both John and Sir Thomas continue to be loyal supporters of our Queen even while suffering in sad imprisonment. I have ordered a box of choice figs and fine wine to be sent to the bishop as a small expression of gratitude for his care of my dear brother.

In the matter of your shipment from Belgium I am of no more knowledge than when we last corresponded. The agent has been called away and may be absent his duties for some time. I am assured that the goods are stored safely until such time as the situation in both Belgium and England is resolved to favor the shipment. As always most humbly at your service Alexander

CHAPTER 24
Antwerp, Belgium
Thursday

The morning is overcast and gray once again. It's not yet raining, but the air weighs down on me as I hobble from the hotel to a cafe a block down the street for breakfast. I'm not exactly avoiding Mikiel. I'm too attracted to him, and he's just a bit too available. Given my history with men, I might keep him at arm's length even under normal circumstances. I've learned to distrust men who come on too strong. But dang, he is so attractive!

I shake the drops from my umbrella before I go into the cafe. Tucking it into the stand by the door, I hang my raincoat on a peg above it. I'm walking rather well today, but try to be cautious, as the boot is still cumbersome. I bypass the tables near the door to avoid the chill drafts each time the door is opened. Luckily, a fireplace on the side wall is blazing warmly, and a table has just been vacated right beside it. I sit with my back to the fire to absorb as much warmth as possible.

I should call Jeanette. She's probably wondering what's happening, and I haven't given her an update recently. I have mostly thought about calling her in the mornings, like now, but the seven-hour difference between Fort Worth and Belgium trips me up. Matching her time zone and class schedule with my current time zone and activities just hasn't worked well. I'll call her when I get back to the hotel tonight.

The rain starts full force as I head back to the hotel. A small river is growing along the curb on both sides of the street. I carefully wade through it. As I walk up the drive, head down to watch my footing, a car door suddenly opens right in front of me. It almost hits me. I wobble on the crutch and wet boot, barely avoiding a fall. The driver hurriedly shuts the door and drives off. By the time I reach the hotel portico my slacks are soaked, as is my walking boot. The doorman is already hurrying toward me.

"Madam," he says, "you almost had another accident. I was afraid you might be injured again."

"Yes, being hit by that car door would have been a problem." I start to laugh it off, but don't. "Did you happen to see who was driving that car?"

"No, Madam. It had just pulled to the drive, and the driver did not leave the car. It was still running when you almost walked into its door. You did very well to side-step with that boot on. Then she pulled out without ever coming in."

I stood rooted to the floor. "She. A woman was driving?"

"Yes, Madam. A blonde woman, though the auto window was fogged and I did not get a good look at the lady, or even the car, as it left so quickly."

I take a deep breath, trying to compose my thoughts. As much as I want to dismiss this as a simple misstep, I find that I can't. Shivering, I walk slowly to the elevator. Once inside my room I double lock the door. I trade the cold, wet clothes for a pair of jeans and warm sweater. The message light is flashing on the house phone. I dial the message number and Mikiel's voice steadies my frayed nerves.

"Addie, this is Mikiel. I do not know if you have plans for dinner tonight, but if not, would you be so kind as to let me take you out? I know some nice restaurants in the area and hope to share the evening with you. Please call me. This is the cell phone I use when in Antwerp. I have a lecture this morning, but have office hours on campus this afternoon, and would love to hear from you."

Dinner with Mikiel might be just the thing, but it is unlikely that I'll be finished at Matsijs in time. I'll call him later this afternoon and decline his invitation, though I confess to some regret in having to do that. Maybe he'll be available tomorrow.

London, England
Thursday

Roger is reluctant to answer the phone. Seems as though lately it was never good news. He sighs and answers anyway.

"Yes, Mikiel. What do you have for me? Wait, slow down. This just happened? Why weren't you close enough to prevent that problem? Yes, I see. Of course she would be suspicious if you were supposed to be at the university. Well, at least the accident would have been minor. Really, are you sure? If she could have been knocked down and run over that is totally different. I was afraid there would still be problems, but not this serious. I have a call to make. Ah, good. Thank you for reporting this to me, and I hope she accepts your invitation to dinner. I will at least have some confidence that she will be safe with you. Call me if anything else develops. Yes, good bye."

Roger dials the number for the Saudi. His call goes to voicemail. He does not leave a message.

Antwerp, Belgium

The rain does not let up, and I spend the early afternoon reading and doing a bit of research on the paintings on the Towneley Hall list. Not that I learn much. That list really seems to be a dead end. The paintings were purchased in the 1400s and early 1500s and somehow, they are now mostly in the collection at the British Museum. That is all. I set my alarm for 3:30 so I can get a short nap before Frida picks me up. The storm has intensified since this morning, and thunder frequently rattles the windows. I sleep fitfully, waking before the alarm rings. Between the thunder and my excitement about what we may find at Quentin Matsijs, I'm getting little rest this afternoon.

I call Mikiel and explain that I have plans that will take most of the evening, and we make an appointment for dinner tomorrow night. Or maybe it's a date. Yeah, I think it's a date. So, OK.

I'm already in the lobby, unable to patiently sit still, when Frida pulls up under the portico just before 4:00. She hops out of the car, gives me a hug, and helps me settle into the passenger seat.

"Oh, Addie. This is so exciting. I can't believe I was able to get a crew for this evening. They had to finish up a quick project this afternoon, but the director gave permission for them to flex their schedules so they could work late today. The majority of their work is outside, so there isn't that much they can do with this rain, in any case."

She puts her little green car in gear, hits the accelerator, and slides sideways out of the drive.

"Oops, maybe I'm a bit too excited. Sorry. We're only going a couple of blocks, don't know why I'm in such a hurry!"

She drives at a more sedate pace the rest of the way. The streets are almost too flooded for the little car to pass, and the rain continues to be very nearly blinding, but she doesn't seem to be the least concerned. I'm relieved when she pulls up to De Quentin Matsijs. As there are few customers braving the storm, she is able to park close to the tavern. She opens a large umbrella, and we huddle together for the short walk to the door. A gust of chill air and rain enters with us.

Frida's crew has unloaded the equipment and is waiting for her in the storage room. Stephen unlocks the stairway door and shows the crew to the spot he had marked. The GPR system is used to mark the exact outline of the cavity behind the wall. Frida marks the excavation area, and we go back upstairs to wait until the heavy work is done.

The small crew sets to work carefully chiseling the mortar, stone by stone. They start at the top of the cavity, working slowly, making sure that a minimum of dust and debris falls into the opening. Once a few top rows of stone are removed, they attach a heavy plastic sheet inside the opening to keep dust away from the contents, and carefully and methodically remove each individual stone. The process is tedious and time consuming. The stones are carried up to the storage room where Frida numbers and stacks them. Although we are all anxious to see what is behind the wall, Frida will not lift the protective sheet of plastic. It is crucial that the contents are protected from the dust that is now in the stairway, so we all wait impatiently. It takes several hours for the bricks to be removed. A special vacuum is taken down the stairway to clean up the chipped mortar and dust. The crew finally finishes their task and hauls out the equipment around eight. Frida will not let us even peek into the excavated space yet, as she wants to make sure all the dust has settled out of the air.

She laughs when I beg.

"Not yet. In archeology, patience is a requirement. Whatever is in there will not be going anywhere, and we do not want to chance contaminating anything. We could have dinner and see how well the dust has settled in an hour or so."

"My intention is to stay right here until I can see what is behind that plastic," I reply. "How about you?"

"I'm with you. Maybe Stephen and Rachel wouldn't mind having another couple of customers for dinner."

We shut the stairwell door, as well as the storeroom door, and go to the main dining room. Very few customers remain. Those who are finishing up their meals seem to be discussing the awful weather and checking the road reports for closures. Storms are not unusual for Antwerp, but they are still respected. Living so near a major river, flooding is always potentially a problem.

Frida calls to give Josef a report of the progress. He is still at the museum, dealing with a small leak. She suggests that he not try to come over to the tavern, given the bad weather. She calls the conservationist she had scheduled to work with us to let him know our progress. He says that the roads are flooded, and he does not believe he will be able to make it to the cafe. He suggests that if there is in fact anything in the wall, she should not remove it until he can come in tomorrow. We relax and visit over dinner as Stephen and Rachel finish their responsibilities for the evening and see the last of the customers out.

"What do you think about closing now? It is early, but I really don't expect anyone to come by with this storm," Rachel calls over to Stephen, who is restocking the bar.

"Well, it is ten already, so I think it would not be a problem. I've already sent most of the staff home. I'll tell the last two to go on home. Frida and Addie, you are welcome to stay as late as you would like. I know you would hate to leave before you see what is in the hole in the wall downstairs. If the roads are treacherous, please stay overnight. We have two vacant bedrooms and would be honored to be your host."

"I really do want to see behind the plastic before leaving," Frida says. "Thanks for letting us stay so late, and the invitation to stay overnight. I think we can check pretty soon. It will depend on how much dust is still in the air. We won't move anything, though, until tomorrow when the conservationist can come around. I'll fetch you both if things are clear."

Rachel goes up to the office to close out the day's business, and Stephen goes into the kitchen to shut down the equipment. Frida and I wait about half an hour and head down the stairs.

CHAPTER 25
Antwerp, Belgium
Thursday

She has dinner at De Quentin Matsijs, at a table in a dark corner. She is wearing a short dark wig and bulky clothing. With the very different appearance from the last few days, she is sure that she would not be noticed, even if Addie had gotten a good look at her before. It was obvious from Addie's trips around Antwerp that she had narrowed her search for the paintings to the cafe. It had been easy to watch her this evening without raising any suspicion.

She saw the crew leave, but Addie did not go, and nothing other than equipment left with the crew. It looked like Addie and the woman with her were staying late. She paid out and slipped into the storage room after the crew left, but while there was still plenty of activity in the tavern. She quietly opened the stairwell door and made her way down to the hole in the wall, covered in plastic. So, Addie had found the paintings, as she had suspected. The protective shipping crates were old and deteriorating. A board easily fell off when she touched the first crate, revealing a painting, also suffering from the poor storage conditions, but still recognizable.

She had taken care of the door to the Ruien yesterday, just in case. A bribe had given her access through a doorway near the cafe that was generally considered to be inoperable. It was short work to compromise the seal on the cafe door. That should solve the problem of the paintings, if they were in the staircase, as the water level in the Ruien was expected to reach near record levels before morning.

She was pleased with herself for having the foresight to damage the seal. Flooding would not generally be a problem at the Quentin, but with the door seal damaged, water should easily reach the alcove where the paintings are. She goes back up the stairs and conceals herself behind a stack of boxes in a corner. She waits for a chance to take the key and slip out. But when Addie and her companion come into the storage room and go down the stairs, she realizes that she might have an opportunity to solve the problem of Addie as well.

She quietly follows Addie and Frida down the dimly lit stairs. Given her training, it is elementary to avoid casting shadows and walk silently. Frida and Addie bend to peer into the alcove, talking excitedly about what they might find. She is just a few steps behind. It takes only seconds for her to knock the women unconscious with only one blow each. She checks their pulse. Not dead. She had not intended for them to be. But if they did not regain consciousness, their death would look like an accident. The water was rising quickly. They had simply slipped on the damp stairs in a desperate attempt to escape the rising water, knocking themselves out. They would not be found until morning. Then it would be too late. So sad, accidental drowning. In any case the paintings were sure to be destroyed.

Too bad she couldn't take the paintings with her. That would have been best, but it would be impossible to smuggle them out of the tavern. Best to just get moving. She hurries back up the stairs, quietly shuts the stairwell door, locks it, and pockets the key. It would look like a staff member had made a routine check before leaving and locked the door without realizing anyone was below. Even if foul play was suspected, she would be on a plane home by then, totally untraceable. Now to be sure that the proprietors weren't a problem tonight.

She completes her business and leaves the tavern, turning off the downstairs lights and pretending to lock the door. The keys had been on the man's belt, but she would not risk fumbling at the door to find the right one. No one would be out and about to try the door in this storm. If anyone was watching, which was doubtful, they would just assume that she was the custodian finishing up for the night. She puts her umbrella up before turning toward the sidewalk and walks quickly around the corner. She is out of sight of the tavern within seconds, and in her car two blocks away in only a minute more. No one is around to notice the dark car speeding down the deserted streets in the driving rain.

Josef is worried. It is almost midnight. He had expected to hear from Frida by now. Edmund answers his call immediately.

"Edmund, it's late. Frida isn't answering my calls. I'm worried. I'm on my way to the tavern. Are you near there?"

"I'm just down the street. I haven't seen anything unusual. The last staff person left about thirty minutes ago. There are still lights on in the top two floors. I'm not sure if I should go on over or not.

Addie doesn't know I'm in town and I don't know what she would think about my spying on her. Maybe I could go in with you and say that I just got into town and we had decided to meet here. The tavern usually stays open till one, so maybe that would not be unreasonable. She will probably see right through that, given that it is so late and raining buckets, but it's the best I can do for now."

"Well, give me fifteen minutes. Should be less, but the streets are flooded. I imagine they are all just in the office upstairs, having a beer and waiting for the storm to clear." Josef concentrates on getting through the deepening puddles without hydroplaning.

Edmund pulls to the front of the tavern, parks by Frida's car, and waits. Josef arrives and parks beside him. They make a quick dash to the door. Since the lights were off, they expected the door to be locked. Josef rings the bell. No answer. Edmund tries the door, and finds it unlocked. They step into the darkened tavern.

"I saw the last person who left turn off the downstairs lights and lock the door. I saw her do it. Now I'm worried. I'm calling the police before we go any farther."

Edmund reviews in his mind exactly what he had seen. Lights off, stocky woman opened the door and closed it without turning to the street. Appeared to lock the door and unfurled an umbrella. Quickly walked down the sidewalk and disappeared around the corner.

While Edmund calls the police, Josef turns on the lights in the dining room and looks around. Glancing in the direction of the bar, Josef realizes that the cash register is open, and the bar area is in disarray. He motions for Edmund to come over.

Edmund hangs up the phone and the two look around the main restaurant area.

"I'm not waiting for the police. They'll be here any minute, but something is very wrong. Come on, Josef. Let's check this out."

Josef nods, and leads the way through the dining room to the kitchen. Everything neatly in place for opening tomorrow. Then they hear a muffled sound coming from the back of the kitchen. As they walk farther in, they hear it again. It seems to be coming from the walk-in refrigerator. Josef opens the door. It makes a slight hiss as the seal loosens. A moan comes from the back corner. Stephen lays on his stomach, arms taped behind his back, feet bound at the ankles. His head is bleeding from a gash at the back of his skull. He is barely conscious. They rush to cut the tape from his hands and feet and get him out of the frigid air. He is shivering but beginning to be more aware as he warms up and circulation returns to his limbs.

"Damn, my head hurts. What the hell happened? I think someone hit me. Where's Rachel?" Stephen tries to stand but his legs are wobbly.

Sirens herald the arrival of the Antwerp police. Josef goes to meet them, and Edmund stays with Stephen. The officers check Edmund and Josef's identification while Josef brings them up to date on what they had found. An officer radios for an ambulance, which arrives while the police are still searching the first two floors. They find Rachel in her office on the second floor, also bound and gagged and semi-conscious. The office had been ransacked. Every drawer had been opened and the contents dumped on the floor. The desk, usually so perfectly organized, is a mess of tousled paper.

The ambulance crew bring Stephen and Rachel to the main dining room to assess the extent of their injuries. Josef sits beside Rachel, holding her hand while the medics work on her head wound as well as Stephen's.

Rachel begins to recover and looks around in alarm. "Where are Frida and Addie? Where are they? They were in the dining room when I went up to the office. We had locked the doors early. No one was here. Where are they?"

Josef puts his arm around her. "The police have instructed us to stay here with you. If Frida and Addie are still here, they will find them. I think they must be, because Frida's car is still out front."

"Josef," Stephen turns, his face even more pale than before. "They had gone into the Ruien stairway. I think it was just a few minutes before someone attacked me. Have the police checked there?"

Josef motions for a nearby officer and asks about checking the stairway from the storeroom.

"We have checked the storeroom," the officer said. "There is a doorway, but it is locked."

"No," insists Stephen, "it could not be locked. The key is in the lock. I remember distinctly that I left it there."

Edmund and Josef look at each other and rush to the storeroom. The key is not in the lock.

Josef runs back to Stephen. "Stephen, is there another key?"

"No, we kept that one in the office, or in the door when we were using the stairway. We didn't want anyone other than us to be going down there so we never made a duplicate key."

The police had finished their search of the building. Nothing was left to be searched except for the entrance to the Ruien. Stephen stands, though with some difficulty and starts toward the storeroom.

"They must be there. We must get that door open immediately! Officer, you must see to that door. Now. There is nowhere else they could be!"

The officer calls for the others to meet him in the storeroom and to bring tools. Stephen points out where his tools were stored as well. They set to work dismantling the door handle and lock. The progress is slow, as the old door had been replaced and this new one had an impressive locking system. They use a crowbar to jimmy the frame, finally freeing the door to swing on its hinges after a few minutes of work, though it seemed to be an hour to the anxious friends.

The officers stop Stephen and Josef from rushing down the stairs. Two proceed down, the others waiting impatiently at the top of the stairs.

"They are here!" an officer exclaims from the gloom. "They are unconscious. Bring the medics down here. Quickly. The water is only four steps away, and it is rising. We need to get them out, now!"

Two of the ambulance crew rush down the slick stairs to join the officers. They do a quick check and call up the stairs, "They have both taken a hard hit to the head and have lost quite a bit of blood. Pulse OK, breathing shallow, temperature below normal. We are bringing they up now."

With some effort the two women are carefully carried up the stairs and into the storeroom. They regain consciousness within a few minutes but are disoriented from the blow to the head and the loss of blood.

"Officer, did I hear someone say that there is water in the stairwell?" Stephen asks.

"Yes, and it is rising. Not unusual with the high tide tonight and the flooding from this storm."

Stephen turns toward the officer who spoke. "It is unusual here. The door to the Ruien landing has been replaced. It has a waterproof seal. It does not leak. Ever."

I'm beginning to follow the conversation floating around me.

"Water? Are you saying there is water in the stairs to the Ruien?" My head is pounding, and I'm not really sure whether I heard that correctly.

"I'm sure the paintings are there. They're in the alcove that Frida's crew excavated. We saw crates but didn't have time to really look at them. I think someone hit me. I blacked out. Where's Frida?" I'm panicking, not able to control my emotions. "Is Frida OK?"

Edmund is beside me. "She's still pretty addled, but the medics say she will be fine."

What is Edmund doing here? He's in New York. Maybe London. Not Antwerp. Or maybe I forgot something he told me. No, he did not say anything about coming to Antwerp. I probably look really confused, but the plight of the paintings takes over. I'll figure out the Edmund thing later.

"We have to get the paintings up here. We can't let them be destroyed!"

Edmund and Josef head toward the stairs but are stopped by the police.

"Sir, you cannot go there. It is a crime scene."

Josef stops, but does not turn back to the dining room.

"Well, it will be the scene of another tragedy if we don't get those paintings out. They may be centuries old and of immense value."

The officers confer and decide they will go down for the paintings.

"They could be of great historic value, and perhaps are fragile. May I at least go with you? I can assure they are not damaged as they are retrieved," Josef begs.

"Yes, that will be acceptable. Please let us go quickly, as the water is rising," one of the officers replies.

I'm too impatient to wait in the dining room. In spite of the pounding headache from the blow, I stumble to the stairway door and peer down.

As the first officer arrives at the alcove, the water is lapping at the next step below.

"We will form a chain. Please, Mister Bruding, come to hand the pieces out to us."

Josef steps around the officer and pulls the plastic away from the opening. The crates are all facing toward the back wall of the alcove. He gently lifts the first crate and hands it to the officer behind him. As he hands it off, boards come loose, and he catches a glimpse of a painting but does not take even a moment to register its content. One by one the six crates are carefully lifted to the safety of the storeroom. The procedure takes less than ten minutes, but the water is lapping at the step by the alcove when the last crate emerges.

As the crates come into view, one by one, I would be jumping up and down, except that, between my pounding head and heavy boot, jumping is totally out of the question. It hurts to even consider the prospect. I settle for simply dazedly watching as the paintings emerge.

The small rescue crew makes its way out of the stairwell. The crates are carried to the dining room. I slowly follow and sit beside Frida. “Frida, Frida, are you OK? Look, you can just barely see the paintings. Maybe they're the paintings on the Towneley Hall list!”

Frida slowly makes her way over to the wall where the crates are leaning side by side. She kneels for a closer look. Josef and Edmund join her as she carefully removes a few boards from each crate to provide at least a glimpse of the contents.

“At first glance I would say these are authentic.” She looks over to Josef. “What do you think, Josef?”

Josef nods. “I am inclined to agree with you. Unfortunate that they are in such bad shape. Perhaps they were not supposed to be stored for any length of time in the Ruien stairwell. They were afforded little protection from the damp or insects other than what the crates and sealed alcove provided.”

It's true. I lean on Edmund's arm and stagger over to the pile of paintings. Some are on wood, and the wood is showing rot. Those on linen are suffering from mold. Insect activity is evident from the holes in the fabric. Paint is peeling, though not faded. The colors, still vibrant, shine out from the deteriorating surfaces between the boards.

“Josef,” I ask, “do you think there is any hope that they can be restored?”

“Perhaps,” he replies. “Not to their original quality, of course, but the deterioration can certainly be stopped.”

The arrival of a forensic van reminds us that De Quentin Matsijs is now a crime scene. Someone went to great lengths to disable all four of us.

To add to the problems, it is still the middle of the night. The rain is beginning to lighten, but everyone is concerned about rising water from the runoff into the Ruien. While the police are investigating, Edmund and Josef start work on a temporary repair to the Ruien staircase door. It is unlikely that the water would rise that high, but there should at least be a seal against the moisture and any small creatures that are escaping up the stairs. The door itself is in good shape. They soon nail the damaged door frame back together and seal it with caulk.

It is determined that Stephen, Rachel, Frida, and I all have concussions. No surprise there. The ambulance crew insists all four of us must be transported to the hospital for a complete check. Frida refuses to leave the Matsijs until she is assured that the paintings will be well guarded. The police promise that there will be an officer assigned to watch them at all times, and that no one will be allowed entrance to the cafe. We load into the ambulance for a ride to the emergency room.

The headaches we all have are treated with medication and we're told to rest for the day. Not a chance, of course. The doctor also checks the progress of my sprained foot and tells me that I can leave off the boot unless I begin to experience pain. Not too much chance of that either, what with the happy pill they gave me for the headache, I'm feeling no pain.

As dawn slowly morphs into a gray morning, the rain abates, and the clouds begin to clear. The storm created near record flooding in Antwerp, especially in the Old Town area. However, the damage was surprisingly minimal, and as the tide turned, the flood waters receded with it.

Josef had met us at the hospital, staying to care for Frida. Frida refuses to go home until the paintings are secured. I agree with that, so all four of us pile into his car and head back to the tavern. None of us has had any sleep, unless being unconscious counts, which, believe me it does not. I have too many questions to be interested in sleep.

A staff member, who arrived early to ready the cafe, puts a sign on the door, "Closed for Repairs." Under the watchful eye of an officer, she makes coffee and calls the staff manager, who would call the rest of the staff to let them know what had happen. She insists that she will not leave until she sees to the needs of Rachel and Stephen, and firmly plants herself at a table, assuring the officers that they would have to carry her out. As they were glad of the coffee and possible breakfast, she is permitted to stay.

After determining it is safe to investigate the Ruien stairway, the police tell us the flooding had indeed come to within a few steps of the storeroom and had inundated the alcove completely. Even more concerning, they confirm that the seal on the door to the Ruien had been tampered with. It did not take long for it to occur to me, and of course to the police, that had Frida and I still been unconscious as the waters rose, we could have drowned. Even if we regained consciousness, the paintings would have been destroyed, as it would have been impossible to get them above the water level without access to the storeroom. Josef and Edmund may well have saved our lives. They definitely saved the paintings.

Which reminds me, how is it that Edmund happened to be here at just the right time? I understand how Josef might come over when he didn't hear from Frida, but how does that explain Edmund's presence?

CHAPTER 26
Antwerp and London
Friday morning

The police were gathering evidence at the tavern. Edmund was asked not to leave. He would much rather have been at the hospital. He dozes for awhile, but it is impossible to sleep with the investigation going on around him.

From a quiet corner, Edmund places a call to the British Museum. He recounts what transpired last night, assuring the director that everyone seemed OK, and that the paintings are secure.

"What have you learned about the paintings?" the director asks.

"There are six. They have not been totally uncrated, but the crates are in poor condition, and it is obvious that these are the paintings that Addie was researching. Two are included in the pending sale. The other two that are part of the sale are not in the Antwerp group."

"I'm distressed to learn that Addie and the others were injured. It could have been a tragedy. That it was not, I am thankful. I'm glad to hear it is only two of the paintings involved in the sale. I think we are both certain that Roger has been involved in this somehow. Keep me informed about the investigation there in Antwerp."

The director calls Roger, telling him to stop by his office. Roger arrives within a few minutes. The director motions him to a chair but remains seated at his desk.

"As you know, we have been negotiating for the sale of several works of art on loan to the museum from a private source. We are assisting with this sale only because the owner wishes to have the paintings sold, and also wishes to offer a commission to the museum for our assistance. The buyer has assured that the collection, though private, will always be accessible to the public, so we have been comfortable in providing our assistance. Our buyer has not authorized name disclosure, nor of the intent to purchase these works. The seller has not offered the paintings on the public market.

We received, however, a significantly higher offer for the same works from the representative of another potential buyer. Such an offer was unexpected. It appears that there has been a breach of confidentiality, most likely within the museum. We have thoroughly researched how such a breach might have occurred, and who may be responsible.

"Roger, you were the only person who had access to this information and had experience with the agent for the competing offer. At this point I can only surmise that you may have an arrangement with the agent that would bring you significant personal gain. Such an arrangement would be directly contrary to your contract with the museum, and a serious breach of professional ethics."

Roger's hands begin to tremble, and he clasps them tightly in his lap. What he might have thought would be a conversation about acceptance of the higher offer had taken a decidedly different path. His breathing is shallow. A flush creeping up his neck reveals his anxiety.

Roger takes a deep breath. He now has a light sheen of sweat on his forehead. “I did not know of the new offer. Surely a higher price would be an advantage. I have no idea why you might suspect me of anything unethical. I have been a faithful member of this staff for many, many years. This is baseless conjecture, and I am truly offended by this allegation.”

The director watches Roger's reaction carefully. It is very clear that Roger is lying. His bravado and denial did not convince him that Roger was uninvolved. He had hoped it would. With the assaults in Antwerp, the charges could in fact be much more serious than fraud, perhaps even conspiracy to commit murder.

“This is a serious situation. If proven, it will result in your termination from employment here and could result in filing of fraud charges. You are being placed on suspension until such time as we have completed a full investigation.”

He picks up his desk phone and calls for security to come to his office.

“Give me your badge and keys. A no-trespass order has been filed. You are not to enter any museum property, starting now. Security will escort you from the building.”

The director did not mention the paintings found in Antwerp. Roger did not need any information on that front at this point. He was not sure whether Roger had any involvement with the near tragedy at De Quentin Matsijs, though it was possible. Best to leave that path of questioning to the police.

Roger sat, stunned. He had been concerned that Dr. Simmond's activities in Antwerp would jeopardize the sale, but he never anticipated that their scheme would come so totally unraveled. His hands shake as he gives the requested items to the Director, and his legs are unsteady as he rises and turns to leave with the security officer.

He walks down the street to a coffee shop and places a call on his cell phone. Mikiel answers immediately.

"Good morning, Roger. Hope things are going well. It has been flooding here. Thankfully, it looks like a drier day today. I will be having dinner tonight with Dr. Simmond."

"No, Mikiel, things are decidedly not going well. You need to leave Antwerp. Now. My interest in the transaction involving the paintings has somehow been discovered. I cannot risk your continued involvement with Dr. Simmond. Someone may become suspicious. Take down the cover website immediately. Get rid of the phone. I think right now there is very little evidence of my involvement, but I have been put on suspension. I expect that the person we have been working with will withdraw from the deal or the museum may not consider the offer. My contact will send your final payment to the account."

"Understood, Roger. I will be on my way now. Good luck to you." He makes a reservation on the first flight home, quickly packs, and checks out of the hotel.

Roger makes another call. It is only three A.M. in New York and he is going to be waking the Saudi with very bad news. This was going to be unpleasant. He is surprised when the Saudi answers on the second ring and does not sound at all like he had just been aroused from slumber.

"Good morning, A.D. I have a bit of bad news. I have been suspended from my employ at the museum. The Director suspects my involvement with you. I have sent my man in Antwerp home. I would not want him to be connected to this in any way."

"I see no problem, Roger. We will of course deny any collusion. I have hope that the sale may be completed by tomorrow. The offer is totally legitimate, so there should be no issue there. I will certainly say that my buyer learned of the possible sale of the paintings from gossip at a party. You and I have had a few conversations about the paintings my buyer is interested in, that is all."

"I hope that can be the case. It would be a great relief to me. I confess that I am quite worried."

"I think you can relax. We should not talk again until the transaction is complete. I will wire your commission to your safe account when the sale is made. Go home and have a brandy. I will let you know when all is done."

The Saudi smiles as he hangs up. Roger had no idea how well things might turn out. The Czech had reported to him on her success in Antwerp. She assured him that the paintings would be destroyed in the flood. Her untraceable phone would be destroyed right after the call, and she was on her way out of Antwerp. The problem there should be resolved. Even if it was suspected that there was more intent than a simple robbery of the tavern, there would be no proof. Serious harm had never been part of the plan, and the women should be OK. And if they were not, well, that would not be desirable, as it would lead to a more serious investigation. The Czech was quite skilled at leaving no tracks. He was sure that there would be no way to trace the incident to him. In any case, if the paintings in Antwerp were destroyed there would not be any evidence to challenge the authenticity of the paintings in the British Museum. He did not anticipate any barriers to closing the deal for his buyer, perhaps even today.

The police keep Edmund at the tavern, questioning him closely about why he was there at the apparent time of the assaults, and what he had seen. They are polite and thorough, but it is obvious that he is on the suspect list. Hopefully low on it. Although at this point it looks like a very short list. A list of one. They advise him to be available for further questioning. He could see how they might be suspicious. After all, he had opportunity, and since he is involved in the art world, perhaps motive, though they were hard pressed to say what that might be. Josef's call to him that evening raised more questions. The detective suggested that would have alerted him to finish up and get back to his car before Josef arrived at the tavern. They had not been able to verify his statement about the woman he saw leaving the tavern.

By the time the police finish his interview it is almost noon. Shortly after that, the group from the hospital return. He checks to see how they are feeling, gives them an update on what had been happening at the tavern, and excuses himself to make some calls.

He walks down the street to a nearby coffee shop and calls the director to give him an update.

"The paintings are being removed from the Quentin. The police are still investigating. I imagine they will give you a call to confirm that I was in Antwerp with your knowledge."

"I can confirm that. What of the paintings? Does it seem that they are legitimate? Is this going to be a problem with the sale? We might need to postpone for awhile."

Edmund was afraid that finding the paintings in Antwerp was indeed going to throw the sale schedule off. It was sounding like the director might already be considering delaying. Damn.

"I shouldn't think they will be a problem, though right now it is hard to tell. It could be months, even years, before they are fully analyzed." Edmund pauses to consider what might be the next steps. "The buyer is aware that the provenance of the paintings is vague. The price reflects that but is still excellent. The question is, do we contact the agent with this information? Closing the sale today or tomorrow as we anticipated might look bad if this find is made public. On the other hand, the paintings here might have little or no relevance. They do seem to be the same as those in the museum, but could prove to be poor quality copies, with the originals being the ones in the museum. Your call on what to tell the buyer, of course." Best not to seem too eager.

"Well, I will have to make a decision soon. We have two offers, one from our original buyer and one from the buyer being represented by the Saudi. Of course, the latter may be tainted by Roger's personal involvement. We are looking into that now. The evidence is rather strong that Roger has been using his influence and taking kickbacks for aiding the Saudi dealer in making successful bids for pieces from public museums for years. I've placed Roger on suspension. So, what is the status of the works in Antwerp?"

"They're going to the vault in Antwerp City Hall at this point. Josef and Frida expect they will be transferred to Brussels for thorough analysis at the university." Edmund's voice does not betray his anxiety.

"I expect that they will also want to analyze our paintings. I would, in their place. What has Dr. Simmond to say about all this?"

Edmund thinks for a moment before replying. "I don't believe she has connected all of the dots. She has done some excellent detective work to link Towneley Hall with the old owner of De Quentin Matsijs. It was pure luck that the alcove was found. Well, to give credit, also some good instincts and powers of observation on her part. We have discussed that her work could challenge the provenance of the paintings at the Museum. We have not discussed the pending sales."

"I must say, Edmund, that you have given me something to think about. The timing of all this could not be worse. This would be an important transaction for the museum. I anticipated that the funds would enhance the Egyptian exhibit. I do wish that the sales contract had been negotiated and the paintings in the buyer's hands weeks ago. I think I must put the sale off, at least until Monday. I'll let you know what I decide. When do you expect to come to London?"

"The detective told me to plan on being in Antwerp for a few days. I'm hoping they let me leave by Monday."

"In that case I am going to call the two agents and let them know we will not make a decision until at least Tuesday. I would like for you to be here when we talk with them in more detail. Give me a call if anything more develops there in Antwerp. Take care, then."

"I will do that."

Maybe a short delay will not be a problem, but it would be so much better if they could close the deal sooner, rather than later.

Chapter 27
Antwerp, Belgium
Friday

Frida, Josef, Rachel and I sit at a table at Matsijs. We are a rather morose little group. Edmund left shortly after we got back to the tavern, saying he needed to make some calls. I'm still wondering what he's doing here. Although the tavern is closed, a couple of the staff have come in anyway. They and Josef are providing us with a good amount of pampering. Right now, it is hot tea and appetizers. None of us is quite up to a full lunch. My stomach is rather queasy. The tea is helping, though. Frida is nibbling, without much enthusiasm, on a croissant with strawberry jam. I wish she had chosen something else, like marmalade. I look down at my blood-stained shirt. The stains are now mostly brown. No chance they will come out. It is destined for the trash. Good reason to go shopping before I leave Antwerp. That lifts my spirits somewhat. I really like European sizes because I wear a zero. That somehow makes it more fun to buy clothes.

The conversation naturally revolves around the events of last night. The police are still here, and we are being interviewed individually. It's taking some time. They're talking with Stephen now, in the side dining room.

I ask Rachel for a notepad and pen, which she has one of the staff retrieve from the upstairs office.

I need to get my disorganized thoughts into some coherent form. Things are happening so quickly that I haven't taken the time to replace my missing notes.

"Frida and Josef, help me out here." On the paper I write "Towneley art purchases."

"The Towneleys bought these six paintings in the late 1400s, early 1500s – a Campin, a Sandro Botticelli, a Durer, two by Hieronymus Bosch and a Jan van Eyck." I write them on the note pad under number 1.

"Secondly, mid or late 1500s they start disappearing from the Hall inventories. No record of sales. Third, during that period payments listed as 'for art' are being made to Willem Broecher of Antwerp, who turns out to be the owner of a tavern, which is now called De Quentin Matsijs. There is no record of his being an artist. He could have been an art dealer on the side, of course. Also no record of what art was purchased from Broecher.

"However, fourth, Broecher's records during this period show payment to only one artist, Corneille de Lyon. No titles of any artwork are mentioned. De Lyon is not the painter of any of the six works in question." I stop to think a minute.

"And then, fifth, these six paintings on the original Towneley Hall inventory show up hidden in the Matsijs. What are they doing here?" I look around the table and see only questions on the other three faces.

"Sixth, adding to the mystery, during this period in the late 1500s, John Towneley is imprisoned for sedition and being a recusant, eight times if I remember correctly. Why would the family be making art purchases through Willem Broecher when they were paying heavy fines to Queen Elizabeth?

"And seventh, the paintings missing from Towneley Hall are all now in the British Museum and National Gallery, and they are the same ones we just found at Matsijs. It seems clear to me that all of this must be connected."

Josef stares at me with what might be a look of surprise. Since he is the only one in our little group who has not been knocked senseless, literally, maybe he is seeing something the rest of us are not.

"Addie, how long have these six paintings been in the possession of the British Crown?" he asks.

"That's not such a simple question, Josef. For a long time. But the museum is not certain when they arrived, or how. There is basically no provenance."

"Corneille de Lyon kept a residence in Antwerp, as his family home in the Hague was a bit far for casual travel. He was known as a talented portrait painter in France, England, the Netherlands, and Germany, as well as Belgium. He would have been quite old in the very late 1500s, though I do not remember his date of death." He pauses for a moment, seeming to be sorting things out in his head.

"It seems obvious that the paintings in the museums and those here are the same. We do not know at this point which are older, those here or those in the museums."

I'm beginning to pick up his thread of thought. "Is it possible that de Lyon actually painted duplicates?"

"Well, it is possible. The Flemish artists were known to be masterful copyists. At one point, artists considered it a compliment to have their works reproduced. Those new works would be signed as 'in the style of' the original artist or with the original artist's signature with the addition of the initials or signature of the artist who copied the painting. However, Corneille de Lyon is not known to have ever copied another artist's works."

I'm much more awake now. "How soon do you think the paintings can be analyzed? That would tell us if the ones here are authentic, right?"

"I don't know," Josef replies. "Several months, maybe longer. We can always ask for an expedited analysis."

I turn to Rachel. "Rachel, what is missing from the tavern from the robbery last night?"

"We had sent the evening's receipts to the bank, so there was not much to steal. The intruder rifled through things. I haven't had time to do an inventory, but I don't think anything is missing, except the key to the Ruien door."

"I wonder. Edmund warned me to be careful because things seemed to be happening to me. When we were in London, he mentioned that an associate of his seemed to react strangely when he saw my list of paintings from Towneley Hall. What if all the problems I've had since arriving in Antwerp are an effort to keep me off the track, in case the paintings were actually here? What if last night's attacks were to assure that the paintings were destroyed? Am I making any sense?"

Josef nodded. "Yes, when all of this is laid out, what you are saying does seem to be a possibility. But what would make it worth injuring you and the others, or possibly even committing murder?"

"Well, I don't have a logical answer to that question. Edmund is here in Antwerp. He must have some reason to be here. I think we need to have a serious conversation with him when he gets back." I lean back in my chair, arms crossed. My head is pounding, and I pop another pill with a sip of tea.

Josef turns his head slightly to the side, looks down, and picks randomly at an antipasto platter. He is obviously distracted, maybe avoiding looking at me even. My public health training on recognizing deception kicks in.

"Josef? You know something you aren't telling us. What?" I demand. He shakes his head no, but is still not looking at me. "Something you didn't tell the police?"

He bites his lower lip. "I don't know. It does seem as though he has been involved from the start. He knew from you what paintings you were tracking, and that you were going to Antwerp. He connected you with me. You say he warned you to be careful. I called him when you had the motorcycle accident. I knew he had come to Antwerp. He has been here several days, but seems he never made any attempt to contact you. I found that rather strange, I admit." He looks at me now. "He has been keeping an eye on you, Addie. I assumed he did not want to alarm you or make you feel that you couldn't look after your own interests. I did not mention all this to the police. I have known Edmund for a long time and would not want to involve him in this anymore than he already is."

"Josef, Frida and I could have died! Someone really, really doesn't want these paintings to come to light. From what you said, it could be Edmund!"

Edmund steps back into the room from his phone call just in time to hear my last comments. He walks slowly over to the table and sits down beside me. He takes my hand and looks at me, his gaze never flinching. My heart beats double time and I have a fleeting vision of how I must look with my hair pulled back from the bandage over the head wound, and my blouse filthy and blood-stained.

Then I realize that I'm holding the hand of a man who may well have tried to kill me. I jerk my hand back and drop it into my lap. Edmund's gaze still does not waver, though I think I detect a look of pain in his eyes.

"Oh, Addie. I would never, never harm you. I can understand, though, how you could suspect that I tried to do exactly that. I didn't, but I do believe I know who did, and why. I told everything I know to the police. I'm still the only true suspect on their list, but they will be investigating the names I gave them. They asked me to stay in Antwerp until at least Monday while Interpol investigates the case. I am not under arrest, but I guess I might be, if they are not able to trace the leads I have given them.

"Addie, I came to Antwerp to try to protect you. Which I have clearly failed miserably at. The person I believe is responsible for your assaults is well known to me. She has been linked with a somewhat shady international art dealer. She works alone and specializes in the seedier side of the art world. She has been sent to interfere with other art deals and is implicated in a number of thefts of valuable pieces. Interpol is tracing her now. I doubt they will find her, but they may be able to verify her presence, especially since she was seen, however briefly, and they might find video from the airport. No one has ever been able to find enough evidence to press criminal charges against her.

"She would have been sent to assure that the paintings you were looking for were either never found or that they were conveyed into other hands. Her problem last night was that the paintings could not be removed through the Ruien, which would have been her best route, because of the flooding. She might have been able to carry them out through the tavern's front door after Stephen and Rachel were out of the way, but it was raining too hard to do that without ruining the paintings, and she would have had to make several trips, each risking detection. The best solution would have been to let the paintings be destroyed in the flooding.

"I doubt that her mission was to kill you. But I imagine she would not have cared if her actions resulted in your death. I believe that the person I saw leave the Matsijs last night was her. The tavern's security tapes are being reviewed by Interpol's facial recognition computer program. She is in the Interpol database from previous occasions. I am certain they will find a match, even though she was using a disguise. They use a very sophisticated algorithm that measures facial features incredibly accurately."

I must admit that Edmund's explanation is intriguing. But there's a missing part. "Edmund, I don't understand why these paintings would be so important. Why are old, poorly preserved paintings worth someone's life?"

Josef spoke up. He is staring at Edmund. His hands are in his lap, but I can tell that his fists are clenched, as well as his jaw. "Because there must be a lot of money involved. So, Edmund, where is that money trail? I hate to suspect a friend, but maybe your pockets were destined for new green lining. Maybe the shady one working with the mystery woman is you."

Edmund flushed, but remained calm. "Josef, you should know better than that. I've told you what I know. I'm leaving. I'm not going to sit here and have my integrity insulted." Edmund rose to leave but found his way to the door blocked by Josef.

"My wife was damn near killed. You are in this up to your neck. You are not leaving until I'm sure you had nothing to do with what happened last night."

"You're right, Josef. Money is involved. Maybe tens of millions. But none of it will be lining my pockets." He sat back down. Josef remained standing.

"I can't give you all the details right now, but the museum is negotiating the sale of several works. Some are either the originals, or perhaps copies, of ones Addie and Frida have found. There are two offers on the table. Until both groups of paintings are analyzed we will have many questions about who painted the works that are at the British Museum and the National Gallery, and when. This find may jeopardize all or part of the sale. To complicate matters, the Museum is currently conducting an investigation into possible fraud, separate from, but also linked to the sale. Not on my part, I assure you. Charges are likely to be filed." He looked from Josef to Frida and to me.

"This is an ongoing investigation," he continued, somewhat defensively. "I have told you more than I am authorized to say. I know that you likely still have some suspicion that I am involved on the wrong side of all of this. All I can say is that I understand that, and everything will be clear in a few weeks when the investigations are complete."

Stephen comes into the room, along with two of the investigating officers. He sits at the table beside Rachel and looks around with an expression of confusion on his face. The tension is obvious. Josef has relaxed very little and is still standing.

"All I ask of you, Addie, is that you trust me," Edmund again takes my hand. I again pull it back.

"Not that I deserve it, goodness knows. Perhaps the officers can relieve your suspicions a bit. Captain, my friends need some reassurance there are leads you are following. Have you talked with the director of the British Museum? Maybe Interpol has made some progress on the facial recognition of the woman from last night?"

The Captain, having escorted Stephen back, stands beside Josef. He nods. "Indeed, Doctor Petersen. The director has explained the investigation being conducted in London and your part in it. I can confirm that you are not a suspect in that issue. Interpol has run the security tapes from inside the tavern, and they have identified a probable suspect for the assaults last night. We must still require that you remain in Antwerp until Monday, while we tie up the loose ends, but you are not under arrest, and we do expect to be able to clear you of involvement. I was just going to let you know we are through for the day. You may all go whenever you desire, so long as we know where you will be and have a number at which we can reach you. We will need to meet with each of you again in the next few days, so please don't leave the area. We have collected the necessary evidence here, and the tavern may be reopened tomorrow. We look forward to one of your ales tomorrow evening perhaps, Stephan. Good evening to you." He tips his hat and pats Josef's shoulder as he leaves.

Something the captain said clicks in my brain. What is it? Evening, evening, oh right! I'm supposed to have dinner with Mikiel. I surely do not feel like going out for dinner. What I feel like is going to the hotel, spending an hour in the spa, getting a massage and whirlpool bath, and having dinner delivered by room service.

I excuse myself to call Mikiel to cancel, though I'm not sure I ever actually called to accept his invitation. Things got a little hectic yesterday. I dial, but the phone is not answered. I receive a recorded message, "This number is no longer in service." Really? Oh well. Maybe his seminar is over, and he left without remembering about our dinner, which is rather hard on my self-image. Easy come, easy go. But strange timing.

Oh. Oh! I think my suspicions were right to begin with. I catch the captain while he is gathering his notes and tell him about my interactions with Mikiel since arriving in Antwerp, and my suspicion that he has been following me. The Captain says he will put an investigator on that right away. Things just keep getting stranger.

Josef and Frida offer to drop me off at the hotel, which I gratefully accept. Edmund offered, but I just can't say I trust him. I want to, but I don't. I stop at the desk and make an appointment for the spa. I slowly trudge to the elevator and down the hallway to my room. I open the door with caution, half expecting someone to jump out at me. I confess, I'm a bit paranoid right now. Of course, it is not paranoia if someone really is out to get you. Justifiable caution. Whoever she is, she is still out there. Mikiel is still out there. Someone, or maybe more than one, is still wanting to close a big deal. I'll think about that later.

I take a quick shower, stretch out on the bed, and call the front desk to get a wakeup at six. I'll get in a good nap before my spa appointment. I'm asleep almost as soon as I gently settle my aching head on the pillow.

When the wakeup call comes, I'm dreaming of artworks floating down the Ruien and into the river. I'm sitting atop the van Eyck, trying to both protect and steer it down the flooding waterway.

I dress without much attention to my appearance, and head to the Spa. Fortunately, I don't have to go through the lobby. I'm quite a sight with my bandaged head and slight limp and very dark circles under my eyes.

The spa is heaven. I change into a soft robe and slip-on cloth sandals. In the women's lounge new-age music is playing softly, barely louder than the sound of the fountain in the center of the room. Rose petals and lemon slices float in the pitcher of ice water. I reluctantly skip the champagne resting in a hammered aluminum ice bucket. Not a good idea with the pain meds, lack of sleep and warm whirlpool. I've escaped drowning once and would like to keep it at that. I settle into the gently heated lounge chair, with cucumber slices over my eyes, until an attendant comes to lead me to the whirlpool bath. I choose a lavender scent, for relaxation. The attendant recommends I also use sea salt to help with the bruises on my leg. Twenty minutes in the fragrant bath has me totally relaxed.

When asked whether I would like a male or female to do my massage I choose male. Might as well feed my prurient fantasies. The hour-long massage assures that every muscle feels like it has been paid special attention. I shower and wash my hair with their upscale products.

I assess myself in the dressing room mirror. The dark circles under my eyes have been banished. My cheeks are rosy. Even the bruises on my leg are disappearing. My head is still bandaged, but I think I can probably cover that with my freshly clean hair.

I actually feel pretty good, considering how much trauma I've been through in the past week. Yep, all in all, not too bad. I finish dressing and head back to my room to order a wonderful meal, including a huge slice of decadently smooth cheesecake, delivered by room service.

As I'm finishing the coffee and savoring the last of the cheesecake my cell phone rings. Caller ID says Jeanette. Good. There's no one I would rather talk to.

"Why didn't you call me!?" Jeanette doesn't even give me a chance to say hello. "Edmund just called and told me what happened. You might have died! I had no idea things over there were so serious! When are you coming home? Now is not too soon, but I'll settle for tomorrow."

"I can't come home tomorrow. I need to buy a new blouse. I just might buy a new suitcase and fill it with a whole new wardrobe. Including shoes and a couple of purses. And since Antwerp is the diamond capital of the world, maybe some jewelry. I'd better check my credit card limits. Oh, and the police insist that I stay another day or two. Which is a good idea, as my head hurts, and my vision is none too sharp right now."

"Honestly, Addie, I'm worried. Edmund says they haven't caught the person who locked you in the tavern stairs. You could still be in danger."

"I don't think so. She's probably left town thinking that the paintings have been destroyed or that Frida and I are dead, or both. I doubt she stuck around to find out for sure. But I do intend to come home as soon as the police will let me leave. I don't think they'll need me much longer."

"So, what's happening with the cute blonde guy?"

"The cute blonde guy disappeared. Phone disconnected. Seems he may be connected to all of this somehow."

"Darn. That's disappointing, but not a problem since Edmund is there to distract you."

"Well, that could be a problem. He's a major player in this too. He seems to be one of the guys in the white hat, but I could be wrong. And I'm not willing to take any chances on that. Too many things have been happening."

"Roger that. I hate not being there for you. Who's left that you can trust?"

"Frida, since she almost died with me, and maybe Josef. Not sure about Josef. The sooner the police let me leave the better. I'm going to amuse myself with shopping till then. Short trips, taking a taxi everywhere. I'll let you know as soon as I book my flight."

"If you're going shopping, I want diamond ear studs for Christmas. What did you say your credit card limits are?"

I laugh, and don't tell her that I've already bought them for her.

"J, I've had a whirlpool bath, a massage and a nice meal. I'm dog tired. I really need to get some sleep. I'm OK and intend to stay that way. Don't worry about me. I'll be home in a few days. 'Nite."

"Goodnight, Addie. I'm truly sorry you are hurt. Get better really quick. And don't forget those diamonds. Maybe matching ones for both of us."

New York, USA
Friday

The Saudi calls his client and informs him that they would not be able to complete the deal. He failed his buyers rarely, but an occasional deal gone bad was to be expected in this high-stakes art world. It would not affect his business, as his connections were worldwide. He boarded the plane and settled into his first-class seat for the very long journey back to Saudi Arabia. If the problems in Antwerp were traced to him, he would be home, and home had no extradition treaty with the Brits or Belgians. And the Czech was totally untraceable, as always. When the aircraft reaches cruising altitude, he orders a glass of wine from the attendant.

CHAPTER 28
London, England
Saturday

The director sits at a table in his office in the British Museum with Roger, and two police detectives. Roger fidgets. He was hoping that he had been called to the museum to be told there was not sufficient evidence to accuse him of criminal behavior. He had accumulated quite a bit of wealth over the past fifteen years, all in accounts in the Bahamas. As soon as he left the office, he intended to head straight for the airport for a flight to the Dominican Republic. No extradition treaty with Britain. He had already purchased property there. He would lead a very good life away from the cold weather in England. He would have left yesterday but could not book a flight. In any case, that would certainly have confirmed that he was doing something under the table. Best not to add to the director's suspicion until he could get out of the country.

The director starts the conversation. “Roger, the police obtained a warrant yesterday for your bank and phone records. Detective Harmon will explain what they found.” He nods at one of the officers.

“Dr. Jimeson, we compared your bank deposit records with records of sales made by several museums. We found a correlation between those sales and deposits made to your account from an account in Saudi Arabia. They were not especially large deposits individually, though they were large enough to raise suspicions when taken as a group. In reviewing your cell phone records, we found numerous calls to the same foreign phone number, most of which also corresponded to dates around the sales by public museums. That number is known to the museum staff as belonging to an art dealer, Anton Dawoud, who has arranged sales for several important buyers. It is especially problematic that you have been in regular contact with this dealer, as many of the sales had nothing at all to do with your areas of expertise.

"It appears that you have been accessing internal confidential information regarding pending sales in order for the agent to assure his buyers of having the high bid. Your actions may have in fact been driving up the sales price, which would have resulted in a significantly higher commission for the dealer, and a significant cut for yourself. The information is sufficient for the museum to press charges against you for fraud.

"In addition, we found that you have made or received a number of calls to a temporary cell phone number traced to Antwerp. A number of these calls correspond with your calls to the art dealer. On Thursday there was a serious assault in Antwerp which appears to be related to the sale of several pieces of art at the museum.

"I must inform you that you are being arrested for conspiracy to commit assault as well as conspiracy to commit fraud. You will be transported to the police station for detention and further questioning. Depending upon the decision of the justice, you may remain incarcerated pending further investigation. If you are released after questioning, you are prohibited from travel outside of London until such time as this case is totally resolved.

"You do not have to say anything, but it may harm your defense if you do not mention, when questioned, something which you later rely on in court. You have the right to say nothing. Anything you do say may be given in evidence. Is this perfectly clear, Dr. Jimeson?"

Roger nods, "Yes, I do understand. If this is related to Antwerp, I assume you are referring to the research Dr. Simmond is conducting there. I talked with her and Edmund about it. I was not involved in an assault at all. The calls to Antwerp were to a person who was to distract Dr. Simmond from her search, or at least delay it until the sale was complete. When he reported to me that she had been injured, I was surprised. As far as my contact with Mr. Dawoud, I do know him, and he frequently asks me about art that his buyers are interested in. He has occasionally paid me for my time. As you can see, the payments to me were very small, and I doubt that my help to him was a factor in any sales."

"Thank you for that information, Dr. Jimeson. We will check it out. In the meantime, you must come with us." He motions for Roger to stand and cuffs his hands behind his back.

Roger holds his head high as they leave the building. He had not really been concerned that his arrangement with Dawoud would be found, but he is pleased that he had made the decision to take small amounts directly from Dawoud into his local account. It may have paid off. He is sure that his major dealings could not be traced. It was highly unlikely that any charges could be filed. He certainly would not be held in custody. His ticket to the Dominican Republic is for late this evening. The house in the Dominican Republic is fully furnished. He has already packed all he needs in a small carry-on. He will head out of the country tonight.

The director places a call to Edmund.

"Roger was just arrested. Undoubtedly, we will learn more about his activities, but I doubt he was involved in Dr. Simmond's injuries. It is looking like that was probably orchestrated by Anton Dawoud. Roger did admit that he had worked with him, but insisted it was not related to kickbacks, only to helping him with research. It may be difficult to make the fraud charge stick, though what he did is certainly grounds for termination. You said you had spent some time with Dawoud. Is he still in New York?"

"I don't know. If he has been involved in this, I would bet that he has already left the country."

"I would not be surprised. I already informed him that I expect to disqualify his buyer. I think that I should let our primary buyer know about the status of the paintings as soon as possible. Of course, we will be withdrawing them from the sale. I would not like for her to learn about the problems from the rumor mill. Since you need to stay in Antwerp till at least Monday, I'll call her myself."

"That's a good idea, but I'd like to call her agent before you talk with her. He's a good friend and deserves that courtesy. I had a rather terse conversation with him when I started to hear the rumors, and I need to apologize. I don't know what his buyer will think about all this, but he may be able to convince her to complete the sale for at least the paintings not in the Antwerp group. I'll let him know you will be calling her personally."

"Hello, my friend." Edmund's call is answered with a cheerful greeting.

"Hi, Frederick. I'm afraid I'm going to disappoint you this time. There is a problem with the sale. I apologize for being so rude to you when we spoke last. We were just beginning to figure out what was going on, and I had to be sure of the source of the problem. As you know, the provenance of some of the paintings, specifically the two by Hieronymus Bosch, have been unclear. We now have new information which must be researched. As a result, we must withdraw them from the sale. The other two that your buyer is interested in are not part of the group in question, and we can still proceed if she is willing. There is another bid for them, but we have chosen to disqualify the buyer."

"Some good news, some bad," Frederick responded. "Isn't that the way these things work? We knew the provenance was questionable, though if you still have questions about their authenticity, I appreciate that you are letting us know. I believe she will still want the other paintings, though she will be sorry to lose these two."

"We are hoping for that. Would you be so kind as to delay your call to her for a few hours? The director will be calling her personally today to express our regrets that we must withdraw two of the paintings she wants. She has been a good patron of the arts in London, always offers an excellent price, and keeps her collection open to the public. We appreciate our relationship with both of you."

"I will of course wait to call her. We enjoy working with you as well, you know."

"Thank you for your understanding, Frederick. I will be back in touch with you in a few days."

"So, until then, my friend. Good day."

CHAPTER 29
Antwerp, Belgium
Saturday

I buy a small carry-on suitcase. Then I go shopping and buy enough clothes to fill it. Short trips, by taxi, over a couple of days, as I promised Jeanette. I stop at two blouses, three pairs of slacks, a soft celery-green sweater, two pairs of designer booties, comfy walking shoes, and one purse. I also indulge in a pair of emerald and gold filigree earrings, at which point my wallet clamped down on the credit cards and refused to let me spend another penny. The new clothes made my leg and head feel much better. Well, at least the comfy walking shoes make my leg feel better, for sure. The head, it's gonna take a bit more time.

Edmund calls and asks if he can take me to dinner. Says he has some information for me. I accept the invitation, but with some hesitation. I suggest we stay at the hotel, as I'm totally tired after all the shopping. Really, I'm still not sure about his role in the problems here in Antwerp. As much as I would enjoy dinner, I don't want to go off in a car with him. We agree on eight, and he says he'll make reservations.

I slip on the new silk blouse and wide-legged slacks. I opt to stick with the comfortable walking shoes. Maybe not the perfect match, but at least I can walk. I have managed to get my hair to cover the bandage. All in all, I'm pleased when I look in the mirror.

At 7:45 I go down to meet Edmund in the lobby. I thought I would probably beat him there, but he's obviously early. The hug that goes with his greeting is nice, even if I am still suspicious of him. He puts his hand on my waist as we walk over to the restaurant. The host greets him by name and shows us to a table set for two. Wine glasses are already filled with red wine, the open bottle resting beside a bouquet of roses. I look around at the other tables. None has a bouquet of roses. Edmund has obviously gone to some trouble to make me feel special.

"Edmund, how nice of you," I say as he pulls my chair out for me. I take a sip of the wine, glad that I did not take a pain pill today. It's an excellent vintage, much more effective than any pill.

He sits across the table from me, and picks his glass up too, holding it over the table. "How about a toast? To the Towneleys!"

"I can certainly agree to that." I tap my glass to his, the excellent crystal ringing softly.

"Thank you for agreeing to have dinner with me. You must still have so many questions. I may not be able to answer them all, but I can answer most. So, shall we order first?" His gaze looks sincere, I think. No alarm bells or red flags. He has a very slight flush as he cradles his wine glass.

"Absolutely. I spent the day shopping and I'm starving. Then I want to hear what you have to say. You're right about my having lots of questions." I'm determined to keep my distance.

Over our meal, Edmund explains in detail what has happened since I left London.

"You need to know that Roger was upset about your research on the Towneley paintings because there was a large sale pending that included two of those paintings. It looks like he has been taking kickbacks from an art dealer to assure that the dealer's clients are able to purchase the art that they are wanting. Both Roger and the dealer most likely had very large commissions at stake. Roger sent someone to divert your research until the sale closed. We believe that person was the man who you know as Mikiel. That name and his employment story are a cover. At this point we do not know exactly who he is. Roger has provided another surname and contact information, but he seems to have disappeared, or at least is staying out of contact. Of course, that makes it difficult to verify Roger's story, but it does fit with what you have reported."

He finishes his salad and continues. "The art dealer Roger was working with is well known to us. He is somewhat disreputable but has some very wealthy clients. He has tried to cause problems for sales before. If he cannot arrange the purchase through a simple high bid, it is not beyond him to cast doubt on the provenance of the piece, try to discredit the other potential buyer, or to divert others involved until he can close the sale for his client.

"The woman responsible for your injuries was undoubtedly sent by him. It appears that both she and Mikiel were following you to discourage you from your search for the history of the paintings, just in case you were right about their provenance. No one expected that there would be copies, of course. They just did not want any complications related to ownership. We were only a few days away from closing the sale, so they did not have to divert your efforts for very long. A couple of times in the past, I have had confrontations with the woman who was following you. She is quite expert at manipulating situations to encourage the competition to drop out. I have never known her to go so far as to cause an injury, but she has been identified as the person who attacked you in the Ruien stairs and is assuredly the motorcycle driver as well as the woman in the car who tried to knock you down at the hotel. It is alarming that she went so far to assure that the information about the paintings would not be found. Of course, she too has disappeared."

I have been listening intently, paying little attention to the excellent meal, though I am making my way through it quite efficiently. Edmund continues.

"Josef and I were thinking this through yesterday. It seems reasonable that Corneille de Lyon made copies of the works in the Towneley collection. That makes the link between payments to Broecher by the Towneley family and payments made to de Lyon by Broecher. It appeared to Frida that the paintings were rather hastily hidden in the stairwell, not intending that they be left there for centuries. I expect that the testing will tell us which are the originals. Since the paintings have been in the possession of the Queen for so long, it seems likely that they were provided as part of John Towneley's fines during his imprisonments. Does all that sound about right?"

"I think that is quite plausible. What happens to the paintings now?"

"I talked with the director earlier. Two paintings were part of the potential sale. Those have been withdrawn from the sell offer. There are two other pieces offered for sale that are not in question, and they can still be sold if the buyer is willing. All of the paintings you found will be evaluated, as will those in the museum, to ascertain which are the originals."

"Edmund, I've been wondering, who owns them? If they were basically stolen from the Towneleys, which is what fines for recusancy were, in my opinion, is there a possibility they are still Towneley property?"

Edmund raises his eyebrows and shrugs. "That is going to be a difficult question to answer. Some things from that era have been restored to the original owners, so that is a possibility, if there are direct heirs. Since Towneley Hall is part of the National Historic Register and owned by Burnley, the paintings may go there. Or, of course, it may be ruled that they stay at the British Museum, especially since Charles Townley willed the Hall's collection to the Museum. The current private owner of two of them would certainly have a claim, but would likely leave the paintings at the museum. It may also be that Antwerp will claim ownership of those you found. It may take awhile to work all that out, especially since it is yet to be determined which are the originals."

"Not mine, huh?"

"Well, probably not, though it may be worthwhile to file a claim. Stephen and Rachel could do that as well, since the paintings were found on their property."

"I thought it would be a complex question." I swish my wine around and think for a moment. "Will it go to a court for settlement?"

"It could be decided by a judge, it could be decided through mediation, or even an agreement by all parties, without needing mediation."

"Going to take awhile, I guess."

"I would expect so." He leans ever so slightly toward me. "What are your plans? Are you going back to Burnley now?"

"Ya know, I think I'll head home. I need a rest from all this excitement! And Jeanette made me promise to come home as soon as the police here say it's OK. They say I can go home tomorrow, and I've already booked my flight."

"I must say I'm disappointed, but I understand why you might want to go home."

"You're disappointed? I would think you are well rid of me and all the accompanying chaos." I laugh for the first time in days. Feels great.

Edmund smiles. "My job is rarely this exciting. Interesting yes, exciting, not usually. But the disappointment is personal."

He has a great smile. I realize I'm staring. The blush I felt when he kissed me in London is creeping back. He reaches over the table and takes my hand. This time I have no objection.

"Addie, I intend to make plenty of opportunities to see you again, if that's OK with you. My job often takes me to the States, and maybe you will find reasons to come to England."

It's easy to stare at him. Now I'm smiling too.

"I bet I can find a few reasons, just let me know if you need any help solving an epidemic. You guys pretty much took care of the mad cow thing, and the COVID 19 pandemic is abating, but no telling what may pop up next. And I will be the one who's disappointed if you don't call when you're in the States."

"I've been hearing rumors of a mad chicken disease in Wales. Very mysterious."

I laugh. "You can do better than that."

"Mad squirrels in Oxfordshire. Attacking everyone. Throwing walnuts. Very dangerous."

"Not sure if I should call the Centers for Disease Control or the Forest Service."

"Whichever will send you the quickest," he replies. "Maybe you should just come over and do some preliminary research."

"Maybe I will. Right now, I'm afraid I need to claim temporary disability. I'm really needing to prop my leg up and get some rest. Dinner was wonderful and thank you for the flowers. May I take them upstairs with me?"

"Of course. I'll walk you to your room. I do not expect anyone is lurking in the hallway, but I'd like to be positive. Here, lean on my arm and take some strain off that leg." He picks up the flower vase and offers his arm as I push the chair back.

The arm makes its way securely around my back. Yea, the 'poor me' ploy worked! Not that I had a ploy, but if I did it would certainly have resulted in something like his arm around me.

We stand close together in the elevator. His arm does not leave my waist until we are at the room. As I open the door, he steps inside, drawing me with him, and shuts the door with his foot. The kiss is a big improvement over the one in London, which was pretty darn good itself. He runs a finger around my cheek, lifting my chin to stare into my eyes. He gently strokes the back of my neck and down my shoulder.

"I know you are in pain, and you are clearly worn out. But, bandaged head, gimpy leg and all, you are beautiful. When you are recovered and have your energy back, I want to explore this feeling I have for you some more."

I lean against the wall as he steps back to put the vase on the desk. "I'm a pretty good explorer myself," I say languidly. "Maybe we'll find something interesting. Our record is excellent so far. But could we please leave out the almost getting killed parts?"

"Oh, most certainly. Only emotional danger from this source."

"I'll risk that."

"Glad to hear it." He pulls me even closer, arm around my shoulder, other hand on my hip. "It could be a pretty big risk."

I'm not sure if he kissed me or I kissed him, but oh my, it is absolutely the best kiss ever. And I'm no amateur when it comes to kisses.

"Good night, Addie. I'm going to take you to the airport tomorrow. What time do you want me to pick you up?"

"That would be wonderful. I need to leave here around two."

"I'm scheduled for an interview with the detectives tomorrow morning. Two will work perfectly. See you then."

He kisses me more gently this time, and I lock the door behind him. Just the hotel room door. Because there seems to be some lock inside me that just opened another door, to a place I think I want to go. I take a long warm bath, slip into bed, and dream of a man with green eyes.

CHAPTER 30
Antwerp, Belgium
Sunday

I pack slowly, not in any hurry to leave Antwerp. The new bag is my carry-on, and Wheeler gets checked through to Dallas/Fort Worth. I'm glad that Edmund offered to give me a ride to the airport. It will be nice to have some help with Wheeler. It was difficult enough maneuvering him through crowds when I was walking just fine. The smaller bag is more sophisticated. The handle has three positions, the wheels turn 360, and it is red. It clearly has a bit of an attitude sitting there beside the clunky and worn Wheeler.

I had stopped in the hotel's gift shop to buy an Antwerp coffee mug. It will be added to my already extensive collection. One for each special trip. I have way too many mugs but wouldn't part with even one of them. My morning coffee is always accompanied by memories. I wrap it carefully and tuck it into the carry-on with the one from Towneley Hall, along with souvenirs for the family and the diamond earrings.

This has been some trip. I was certainly not imagining so much adventure when I sent that email to Towneley Hall. I called James at the Hall yesterday, and he sounded as excited as I am. I know he thought I was on a bit of a wild goose chase, tracing the Towneley paintings. Honestly, I thought so myself. The outcome is a lot better than either of us anticipated.

I take a taxi to meet Frida and Josef at De Quinten Matsijs for lunch and to say goodbye to them, Stephen, and Rachel. We discuss the future of the paintings. They agree with Edmund that the future of the artworks is not at all certain, but we are all truly proud that they have been found. Frida and Josef drive me back to the hotel. Hugs all around. I hate to leave them.

A porter brings my bags to the portico. Edmund is already there. He opens the door to the rental car for me and easily tosses the bags into the "boot." His biceps ripple under the Kelly-green sweater. I bet he knows how great he looks in green. Couldn't he have been nice and worn something gray maybe?

At the airport Edmund takes Wheeler to the bag check and pulls the new bag to the security line. I'm not about to let him leave me without another of those great kisses. I hold his free hand until we get to the security area, then pull him to the side. No need for encouragement. Our kiss is full of longing and perhaps promise. As I lift my bag onto the conveyor belt to go through the x-ray machine, I look back. He is standing exactly where I left him. Somehow, I expected that. I wave, blow a kiss, turn quickly and walk through the inspection station. I'm hoping he didn't notice the tear in my eye. I never get that emotional. Never. At least not until now.

CHAPTER 31
1601
Burnley, England

The carriage was of poor construction and rocked precipitously side to side with each rut traversed. It was not barred, as the one that had brought him to Ely had been. Likely because he was too old and blind now to consider an escape. John had been surprised when told to gather his meager possessions and board the carriage. No explanation offered. They had been traveling for six days now. North, he believed. With failing eyesight, he was unable to pick out the landmarks as he would otherwise have done. He had not been told to where he was being transported. He thought, with some trepidation, that if headed north, it may be that he was being taken to York. If he were not going for execution, the transfer might be beneficial, as it was so much closer to his dear Mary than had Ely been. Her visits had been rare, as the journey was long and she had many responsibilities at the Hall. How he missed his sweet wife and large, noisy group of children. He missed his horses. He missed the village church on the banks of the River Brun, with its Towneley chapel and crypts, even though for many years it had been Anglican rather than Catholic.

The driver turned the carriage slightly to the west. They were passing through a village. Perhaps another stop, to rest the horses and take some refreshment. He leaned toward the window of the carriage. Oh, how cruel. They were traveling through Burnley. There - the church. There - the commons. Mayhap he was being granted one last look at his village before execution. But the carriage took a turn that he well knew. This lane led to Towneley Hall. A rider pulled his horse beside the carriage, and the driver reigned the horses to a stop. The carriage door opened, and John recognized the Sheriff of Lancashire.

"John Towneley. I have come to escort you to Towneley Hall. Your loyalty to Her Majesty while you were at residence in Ely has been noted. You are being released and will be bothered no longer with arrest. You are hereby ordered to remain within five miles of the Hall, and to take part in no meetings of any group, nor plot sedition with any. Do you swear to abide by these restrictions?"

"Gladly will I do so. You bring news of joy to my ears. I pledge my loyalty to Her Majesty Queen Elizabeth, as have I always."

The sheriff nodded and spurred his horse to lead the carriage. The carriage horses, although tired, picked up their pace behind the faster lead. The carriage bounced dreadfully, but John cared not.

"Home. I'm going home." He moved as close to the window as possible. Though his eyesight was dimmed, he could still see that the pastures were as green as he remembered. He could just make out the sheep, cattle, and horses grazing on the hillsides, distinguishable to him now only by color and size.

As they pulled into the courtyard, the butler came down the steps to greet them. Realizing that it was John himself, he let up a cheer, which brought dozens of others running from the house and stables, spilling out from every door. Mary rushed to the window, quickly taking in the carriage, the horses, the wide expanse of lawn, the rolling green hills, the confusion of staff. She ran down the corridor.

Arms reached in to support John as he stepped from the carriage. He was surrounded by a cacophony of voices, some cheering, some weeping, some calling his name. The crowd parted and Mary froze, mid-step, not breathing. Yes, it was John. She picked up her long skirt and rushed to his arms. Never again would she be without him.

CHAPTER 32
April
Fort Worth, Texas

I confess, I've been happy just to be home for the past few months. I sit on my porch, sipping coffee, wrapped in a blanket to ward off the cool spring air. The river willows are putting out tiny light green leaves. The lake is full. With amusement, I watch Henry the Heron chase off another pesky great egret. It leaves with a loud, offended-sounding squawk. A flock of fat mallard ducks has no trouble at all getting to the corn my neighbor scatters for them. Nanny goose is still hanging with the mallards. She seems pretty content, though I do still occasionally hear her honking. Surely some nice male goose is going to see how beautiful she is and decide to stick around.

The director of the British Museum called. We've been negotiating the future of the paintings for months. Turns out the Antwerp paintings are the originals, and those at the British Museum and the National Gallery had all been painted at approximately the same time, most probably by the same person, though the forgeries were quite excellent. Due in large part to my research, it is now presumed that Corneille de Lyon was the forger. Supporting this theory, when the paintings at the museums were closely examined, an almost invisible "L" was found cleverly disguised in each painting.

The mediator had signed off on the final agreement between all interested parties. The agreement is to be announced at Towneley Hall, and it is hoped that I would be in attendance. Hoped that I would be in attendance? Ha. Just try to keep me away! Luckily, it's scheduled in late May, after school is out, so maybe Jeanette will be able to join me for the trip.

When I call Jeanette her usual full-on enthusiasm blasts through the phone.

"Of course I can go to Burnley with you! Of course! I can't wait! Will it be like a formal event? Very artsy and British? We have to go shopping! When do we leave? Bet you can't wait to see Edmund. Me too. This is going to be great!"

"If you're imagining ball gowns and wigs, I would say no. We'll be getting invitations, but the director said the suggested dress is "evening dress." In England I think that means not quite formal. So, no ball gowns, but long dresses or something like our cocktail dresses would be about right. Come to think of it, I need to go shopping too. And yes, I have to admit that seeing Edmund again would be worth the trip by itself."

"Well, then we will have ourselves a day of shopping. How about Saturday? We'll go over to the Galleria in Dallas. I'll pick you up at nine."

"Sure. I'm in. See you then." I suffer a quick pang of trepidation at the thought of shopping with Jeanette. I prefer shopping in Fort Worth, but I know I'll lose that battle. I'd better check my credit card balance, again.

The trip is weeks away, but I start packing mentally. Not Wheeler. I have given the intrepid rolling suitcase to Goodwill. The smaller, sleeker, red bag will be going along on this trip.

May
Burnley, England

The chestnut trees are in glorious bloom, long stalks bright with multicolor flowers. Otto picked us up at the airport last night for the trip to the Oaks Hotel, and these amazing trees were only large shapes in the dark. When I was last here, the chestnuts surrounding the hotel were sadly losing their leaves, covering the lawn in a yellow carpet until the groundskeeper arrived to tidy up. Today they are one of the most beautiful sights I have seen. There is no tree more beautiful than a chestnut in bloom.

Most of the group are staying here at The Oaks. Jeanette and I visited with Frida and Josef over breakfast and met Stephen and Rachel at the historic Boot Inn in Burnley town center for lunch. James had stopped by last night for a beer and quick visit. Edmund called to say that he would be arriving late, just before the event. The commission from the sale of the two legitimate paintings provided the much-needed financial infusion for the Egyptian exhibit. It's moving along quickly, and he has been busy preparing for the opening.

Early evening Jeanette and I dress for the event at Towneley Hall. Jeanette has chosen an ankle-length form-fitting dress in gold and silver. She wears the diamond ear studs I brought her from Antwerp.

"I'm glad you agreed to that green dress," she says. "It's exactly the right color for your eyes and hair. And the draping complements your figure perfectly."

She has styled my hair in soft, loose waves that tumble below my shoulder and shimmer whenever I move my head. I put on the emerald and gold earrings from Antwerp and stand beside her, looking into the mirror. She's right about the dress. I'd been concerned that it was cut lower than I'm usually comfortable with. The soft fabric almost brushes the floor in the back and rises in a front slit to just above my knee.

"Well then, shall we go down?" I suggest. "Let's take the long way, by that beautiful staircase and stained-glass window. When I stayed here before, I imagined coming down those stairs in an elegant dress. Never imagined that would really happen, though."

We descend the staircase and turn at the landing by the stained-glass windows to take the next level to the lobby. Edmund stands at the bottom of the stairs. I take a quick breath, then can barely breathe. He looks amazing in a tux. Totally amazing. He comes up the stairs and takes me on his right arm and Jeanette on his left.

"I am honored to be the escort this evening for two such stunningly beautiful women. Towneley Hall has sent a limousine for us. It is waiting in the portico."

I can barely move. It's fortunate that he has my arm and is moving down the stairs. Jeanette's full-throated laugh fills the lobby.

"We are delighted, Edmund." She gives him a kiss on the cheek. "Hope they have champagne at the Hall!"

At the bottom of the stairs Edmund releases Jeanette's arm and turns to me. He takes a box from his tuxedo pocket and opens it. I am staring down at a lovely emerald and gold necklace. And, oh my, it matches my earrings!

"Oh, Edmund. It is marvelous. But how...?" I stop mid-sentence. The dress, the hair. She knew all along!

"I consulted with your designer, Jeanette, of course, who sent me a photo of the earrings and suggested that you had no necklace fit to complement them. Seeing you at the top of these stairs makes me think that there is nothing fit to grace you, but I hope you will find this satisfactory."

He leans over me and hooks the necklace. It settles in as though it should have been around my neck all along. He gives me a long, perfect kiss, to applause from Jeanette and our friends, who are gathered in the lobby.

As we all pile into the limo, the talk is animated. Lots of compliments all around, hypotheses on the outcome of the mediation, talk about how beautiful Burnley is. The conversation becomes muted as we make the last curve toward the Hall. It is beautiful and imposing, softly lit all around. The stone glows. It is easy to see myself in a carriage, arriving for a grand ball. James greets us in the drive. He leads us through the guest entrance and to the Great Hall.

James has taken Jeanette's arm. Edmund and I are a step behind, closely followed by Frida and Josef, Rachel and Stephen. As we step into the Hall those waiting break into applause. A distinguished man steps forward. Edmund introduces him as the Director of the British Museum and beside him, the Director of the National Heritage List. The Director of the National Heritage List leads us around to introduce us to the large group gathered in the Great Hall. He makes a point of introducing the members of the Burnley Town Council, the curators of Towneley Hall, members of the Towneley Hall Society, and dignitaries from Antwerp. The remaining members of the Towneley family, who still own a portion of the original property, are especially honored guests. The Antwerp group has brought with them our marvelous researcher from the Archives, Gretel.

Champagne is indeed passed through the gathering. The British Museum director steps onto a podium when each of the gathering holds a glass.

"Let us toast to the historic finds of artwork, and to the person who so doggedly followed her intuition, resulting in their discovery. To the Towneleys and to Dr. Addison Simmond."

All raise their glasses with shouts of "Hear, hear!" and "To Addie." I blush, of course. Can't help it.

"I know you are all anxious to learn of the final mediation results," he continues. He reads from notes on the podium. "It has been determined that all six of the paintings in the British Museum and the National Gallery, on the list found by Dr. Simmond in the Towneley archives, are copies. It has been further determined that the six paintings found at De Quinten Matsijs in Antwerp are the originals of those same six paintings in the British Museum and the National Gallery.

"All parties have agreed to the following disposition of the twelve paintings. The British Museum will retain three of the copies, which currently hang in the museum. These will be exhibited beside their originals, with a history of the works and how they came to be in possession of the Crown, as best we can surmise. Two of the copies, with their originals, will go to the Royal Museum in

Antwerp, and will, as well, be exhibited with the history.

"The ownership of all the works could have been in dispute for years. The issues are very complex. The Towneley estates were part of the Duchy of Lancaster, and its possessions could be considered to be property of the Crown. By transferring copies of the paintings, rather than the originals, from Towneley to Queen Elizabeth, it is clear that the family had the intent of retaining the originals, perhaps for exhibit at the Hall should the Tudor rule fall or sold quietly to private collectors in Europe to raise funds for John's fines. Some property taken from Catholics by the Tudors has, in fact, been returned, so the Towneley heirs may have a claim. As the originals were found in Antwerp, Belgium has some claim to them. As the person responsible for finding the originals, Dr. Simmond may also have some claim. And as they were found on the privately owned property of De Quentin Matsijs, the owners may have a claim.

"Although the originals are in very poor condition, they, especially along with the copies, are still quite valuable. All potential claimants have agreed to the results of the mediation. This says a great deal about their ability to set aside individual interests in favor of the greater historical significance.

"You may have noticed that I have only mentioned the disposition of five of the works. I am most pleased to announce that one set of paintings will be exhibited at Towneley Hall, in recognition of the sacrifices of the Towneley family, and of the outstanding detective work of Dr. Simmond in bringing these home."

The director stepped forward and removed a black cloth from two easels at the front of the podium, revealing the Jan Van Eyck, the original, which had been restored, and the copy from the British Museum.

I manage not to burst into tears, but a few escape anyway. Glad I had the foresight to use waterproof mascara. I had no idea any of the paintings would be coming to the Hall. I am surprised and delighted. And to think that my very favorite has been sent here is rather overwhelming.

"Dr. Simmond, I know that everyone here would like to hear from yourself how you came to be in Burnley, and what led you to finding these historic works of art. Please do us the favor of coming to the microphone."

Edmund still has an arm around my waist, and he urges me toward the podium. He walks me up the few steps, bows, and kisses my hand. He turns to the microphone and announces, "It is my pleasure to introduce to you Dr. Addison Simmond."

I look out over the gathering and smile broadly. I look at my new friends, who I can no longer imagine not being in my life. I look over at the paintings, waiting to be mounted on these ancient walls. The sense of history permeates the atmosphere. How very wonderful this all is.

"Well," I start, "don't ever let anyone tell you that genealogy is boring!" Everyone laughs and I relax. I try to be mindful of the time. Genealogy might not be boring, but I certainly could be. I try to keep to just the facts.

I did family research at home. I came to Towneley Hall to work with James and found a list of paintings in the Archives at Preston, though they disappeared from the inventories in the late 1500s.

Notations related to art purchases from Willem Broecher in Antwerp around that time piqued my curiosity. I went to London to see the listed paintings, and met Edmund, who introduced me to Josef and Frida in Antwerp. We found that De Quentin Matsijs had been owned by Willem Broecher. Frida and I, with the help of the owners, Rachel and Stephen explored the cafe. We had not anticipated that there might be copies of the paintings in the British Museum. Clues and luck lead to the location of hidden paintings, which were rescued from a flood by Edmund and Josef. I leave out the more personal parts of the adventure, like being tracked by nefarious characters and almost getting killed.

"Those are the simple details. More complex are the issues which created this mystery. Religious persecution has resulted in irreparable damage to societies the world over, and it continues to this day. How much more advanced would the human race be if the energy and wealth that has gone into fighting each other, over what amounts to nothing, had instead gone into the education, health, and well-being of our world.

"We are linked not only to our immediate ancestors, but to billions of ancestors. Our family history is not written in centuries. It is written in millennia. We are, quite literally, all cousins.

"Our world can be a better place if we understand that we are all related, and must spend our lives together, on this small orb, circling a small star, in a small galaxy, in a vast universe. Although we have made amazing scientific advances, in many ways we are still in social adolescence. We can do better for ourselves by doing better for our worldwide family."

The evening passes in a blur of handshakes and hugs, delicious canapes, champagne, dancing, and talk. At midnight the limos and cars begin queuing in the drive, and the party goers gradually disperse. Our little group piles back into our limo. I'm not a bit tired. I feel fresh and animated, floating on a cloud of adrenalin.

At the Oaks we part with hugs, to gratefully head to our rooms. Edmund walks with me, an arm around my shoulder. I unlock the door and he holds it as I step inside. I look up into those green eyes and nod. He steps in, closing the door behind him. He leans against the wall and pulls me to him for a kiss. I knew I liked him but had no idea how much I was hoping for this. I kiss him back with as much intensity as he had given me. He picks me up as though I weigh nothing at all and carries me to the bed, where he gently removes my shoes and takes off his jacket. He sits down beside me and kisses me again, his hands running through my hair and down my back. He slips the dress from my shoulders and kisses along my collarbone and down to the rise of my breast.

"Oh, Addie," he says, with a breathiness in his deep voice. He rubs his hand along the necklace. "What a pleasure to see this beautiful emerald against your skin. It's the perfect jewel for you."

I think that might seem a bit hokey sometime later, but it sounds sublimely romantic right now. At some point earlier this evening he had shed his tie and undone the top buttons of his shirt. I finish the job. I had imagined him bare-chested the first moment I saw him at the museum. This moment feels every bit as dream like.

I hear the clink of his belt being loosened. I laugh. He looks a bit confused.

"Oh, don't you know? The two nicest sounds for a woman are of a man undoing his belt and taking his wallet out of his pocket."

He laughs too. A deep, amused belly laugh. "I intend that you shall hear plenty of both sounds."

I lay back and pull him on top of me. "Make that a promise," I whisper as I nibble his ear.

"Do that some more and I will promise you absolutely anything."

"It's a deal."

I wake at first light. Edmund's leg and arm are flung over me. I snuggle closer, memories of the night with him floating around my mind. He stirs and rolls over on me. Well, OK. With him I'm ready for anything. Breakfast can darn well wait. We shower together and dress. He puts his dress shirt and tux back on. I leave the necklace on, tucking it under my sweater. I head down for breakfast, and he goes to his room to change, promising to meet me in the restaurant.

Jeanette is sitting at a table by the window, holding hands with a very attractive man. I vaguely remember him from the party last night. She smiles at me and gives me a knowing nod. I roll my eyes. "Good?" she mouths silently.

"Great." I whisper back as the waitress ushers me to a table. I order coffee, and Edmund joins me in a few minutes.

Jeanette and her companion walk past us as they leave. She leans over behind Edmund's chair and gives him a hug and a kiss on the back of his neck. “Take care of my girl,” she says with a laugh.

“I think I have. You can ask her yourself.”

“I'll get full details from her later. Better be good! Addie, I'll meet you here at two to go to the airport.” She waves and walks off with her date, a bit of extra spring in her step.

“Edmund,” I say as we finish our meal, “Otto is picking me up in a few minutes to go to Towneley Hall. Would you like to come along?”

“Wish I could, but my flight is at noon. I'm afraid I need to leave soon for the airport myself. I'll be in New York next month. Would you come spend some time with me there? If you can't do that I will absolutely make time to come to Fort Worth.”

“New York it is. That will be great. Let me know when.”

We walk together to the portico, where Otto is already waiting for me.

“Addie, this whole adventure with you has been wonderful, except for the part where you got hurt, of course. I will make sure our paths cross frequently. With my job that will be easy, even if you are on assignment in some remote African village. I can find a reason to be there if you want me to be.”

“Right now, I can't think of anything more romantic than cuddling with you in a grass hut in Mozambique in the middle of an Ebola outbreak,” I reply.

Edmund laughs at that. “Well, I would prefer to skip the Ebola part. Grass hut sounds like fun, though.”

He kisses me, holding me a few extra seconds. “Have a good trip. Please call me when you get home. I know that is immature, but you seem to attract trouble.”

"Oh, I'm lots of trouble, believe you me! And I would have called without even being asked. You have a good trip too."

Edmund closes the car door, smiles and blows a kiss.

CHAPTER 33
May
Burnley, England

Otto drops me off at the Towneley estates gate and I walk the mile up the hill. So many Towneleys have walked this very route to the Hall. I really didn't think I would feel this much kinship to a family so very distantly related.

As I walk through the courtyard, kicking up dust, I can almost hear the horses stomping, impatiently waiting for their riders. I enter by the main doorway under the Towneley crest, lightly tapping the ancient knocker as I swing open the heavy wood door. It's not the public entrance but is not locked in order to accommodate access for tours. The knock echoes in the Great Hall, and the door shuts behind me with a deep thump. The staff know I'm there, as cameras monitor each room and the exterior of the Hall. A docent looks in, recognizes me, and waves. She is dressed like Mary Towneley, which adds to the feeling of being in another century.

The podium is gone, but the Jan Van Eyck paintings sit on their easels side by side. On the wall above them is a portrait of Mary and John Towneley and their fourteen children. It was completed sometime after 1601, when John came home from his last imprisonment. It has no artist signature or date. It does have a list of the prisons John was in, and the amount of fines they paid to the Queen, a record of unjust and unnecessary persecution.

I gaze out the windows at the rolling hills, bright green with new grass, dotted with sheep in one pasture, cattle in another. Horses are being put through jumps in the exercise yard. For some reason a psalm comes to mind.

The Lord is my Shepard. I shall not want. He maketh me to lie down in green pastures, he leadeth me beside quiet waters, he restoreth my soul. He guideth me in paths of righteousness for his name's sake. Yea, though I walk through the valley of the shadow of death I will fear no evil, for thou art with me. Thy rod and thy staff they comfort me. Thou preparest a table before me in the presence of mine enemies. Thou anointest my head with oil. Verily my cup overfloweth. Surely goodness and mercy shall follow me all the days of my life and I shall dwell in the house of the Lord forever.

A soft “Amen,” comes from beside me. The ghosts of John and Mary stand, holding hands, gazing out at their green pastures.

NOTES REGARDING CHARACTERS, SITES, AND PLOT IN *SECRETS OF THE HALL*

HISTORICAL CHARACTERS

Mary Towneley, heiress of Towneley Hall

John Towneley, husband, and cousin, of Mary

Alexander Nowell, Dean of St. Paul's Cathedral in London, John's half-brother

Queen Elizabeth (I), daughter of King Henry VIII and Anne Boleyn

Willem Broecher, owner of tavern in Antwerp, now De Quinten Matsijs

Corneille de Lyon, well-known artist in Europe

Lord Burghley, (Sir William Cecil), chief advisor to Queen Elizabeth

Richard Towneley, Mary and John's oldest son

Samuel, the Towneley butler, and Jane, head of household

CONTEMPORARY CHARACTERS

Dr. Addison Simmond, lives in Ft. Worth, Texas, and is a consultant in epidemiology

Dr. Jeanette Tyler, Addison's friend, professor at university in North Texas area

Dr. Edmund Petersen, Egyptologist at the British Museum

James Norton, historian at Towneley Hall

Dr. Roger Jimeson, curator of Medieval Art at the British Museum

Josef Bruding, Director of the Museum Mayer van den Bergh in Antwerp

Frida Bruding, wife of Josef, expert in Antwerp history, employee of City of Antwerp historical preservation and research department

Stephen and Rachel, owners of De Quentin Matsijs

Otto, Burnley chauffeur

Gretel, Antwerp Archives Researcher

NOTES

The Towneley family, British, and Antwerp history are portrayed as accurately as possible. All of the historical characters are authentic, including names and positions. The sole exceptions being Captain Farrow, though a character similar to his must surely have been part of the scenario at the Hall; and the name for the original owner of the tavern in Antwerp. I apologize if I have represented the culture or conversation of this period inaccurately in any way. It may be a bit of a stretch to believe that the Towneleys in the 1400s and 1500s were art patrons, as collecting art would likely not have been common at that time. Please keep in mind that this is a work of fiction and should not be considered a fully accurate picture of Elizabethan England.

You can learn more about the Towneley family and Towneley Hall on the Towneley Hall and the Burnley, England websites.

The Tavern De Quinten Matsijs is actually a block from the Ruien, though I put it on the Ruien for plot development. The current fictional owners are based on the actual current owners. They own the restaurant, though do not own the property itself. I am grateful for their hospitality and answers to my questions when I visited Antwerp.

If you visit Burnley, Towneley Hall, London, the British Museum, Antwerp or Fort Worth, Texas, you will find them to be very much as described in the book. The sites used in this novel are all authentic in both the historical and contemporary narratives.

The contemporary characters are fictional. The paintings and mystery surrounding them are fiction. I intentionally did not identify names of the paintings to avoid casting any doubt on the excellent collections of the British Museum and the National Gallery.

My main source of information on the Towneley family is "Tracing the Towneleys," by Tony Kitto. A link to the document can be found on the Towneley Hall website.

Information regarding the prison at Ely is from *Ely Prisons* by Dame Pamela Blakeman, published by the Ely Society. My thanks to Dame Blakeman for sending me a copy.

ACKNOWLEDGMENTS

I would like to express my thanks to the following people, who provided input and ideas for this novel:

Tony Kitto, without whom the Towneley series of books would not have been possible. Tony has donated his time and expertise to Towneley Hall and is the expert on all things Towneley. I am grateful for the time he spent with me when I visited Burnley, and his enthusiasm to help me learn more about the Towneley family. He has been both gracious and gentle in his critique of this novel. It is tricky to incorporate history and present into one story, and I have no doubt that I have made many errors in my attempt to bring historical characters to life and create an interesting mystery and characters in the present. I hope that he is not disappointed with the finished product.

Sir Simon Towneley, and daughter Cosima Towneley, who opened their home, which was part of the original estate, to me and offered ideas and information about the family.

Colin Sanderson, who was a member of the Towneley Hall Society and the Rotary Club in Burnley. Colin provided critical introductions and encouragement. Regretfully, Colin passed away before the book was complete. I am honored to have known him.

Librarians at the Burnley Library who provided suggestions for my research and access to the Towneley archive.

Staff at the Oaks Hotel who were helpful and informative during my month-long stay.

Publishing preparation and cover creation by Larry Morris, who also provided education, suggestions and encouragement during pre-publication.

And a special "thank you" to my editor, Elizabeth Lyon, for patiently helping this novice author learn to craft fiction through many drafts of this novel.

CONTACT

PO Box 1232, Kyle, TX 78640

Laural@lauralharris.com

LauralHarris.com

Made in the USA
Columbia, SC
21 March 2021

34364103R00166